REYoung

THE IRONSMITH

A Tale of Obsession, Compulsion and Delusion

THE IRONSMITH

By REYoung

This book is available in print and electronic format at most online retailers.

ISBN 978-1-7334461-1-2

TageTage Press

REYoung-author.com

BOOKS BY REYOUNG

UNBABBLING
MARGARITO AND THE SNOWMAN
INFLATION

For Adria Forever

out of stone, iron

out of iron, ink

inka dinka doo

I

WIZARD, WISE MAN, *OLD FOOL?*

THE IRON IS NOT DEAD. Never think that, never say that, never allow yourself to believe that. Raise it over your head and hold it there long enough for God and man to see that it can be done, that you have done it. And then you will be forgotten, no one will care or remember anymore that you were the first or even that there was a first. First atom, first stone, chisel, wheel, wing, someone had to conceive of it, lift it, shape it in his hands. In her hands. Why not a she? The iron takes everyone. And now that person is gone, forgotten. Dust to dust and iron to rust. Just as you will disappear and be forgotten in the dust that blows across the plains, in the dark earth where your remains will disintegrate into nothing even as iron oxidizes into rust and then nothing. But you don't believe me, you shake your head no, impossible, life is yours now, everything is yours. You can't see the truth anymore. You've forgotten all that you already knew when you first opened your eyes on this world. All is illusion, none of it real. But how do you tell that to a fourteen-year-old boy convinced that youth is his forever, that an iron bar is a cold and unyielding thing that must be overcome with brute strength and possibly even that a woman is the same thing? How do you say to a fourteen-year-old boy, you will grow old, your body will wear out and become useless and you will die?

But you don't want to hear that. You look away with contempt. You think to yourself, no, it's not true, I'll never be like that, an old man with sagging breasts and withered arms.

I'm young, the world is mine, get out of my way you old fool.
Yes, now, now the world is yours, when you have nothing to do
all day but lie in the green grass and watch the clouds drift
across the blue sky and dream of all the great things you're
going to do when you become a man. Remember well that sky
and those dreams when you go down into that forge and begin
to work with the iron, when every time you raise the iron bar
over your head is both a surrender to and a refutation of death.
The iron is not dead, I am not dead. Say it to me, boy. Say it
aloud. Say it in your head, in your sleep, in your dreams. Make
a mantra of it, a prayer, the beads you tell. The iron is not dead,
I am not dead. Because if you don't believe that, if you don't
say that, if you don't remind yourself over and over again, if
you don't put up that resistance, demonstrate that will, you let
in the cold and the damp and the despair, the sickness and smell
of death and you are defeated before you begin, before you even
touch the iron or attempt to lift the weight, a weight so
impossibly heavy it cannot even be thought of as such, like a
flat iron or a block of cement with a weight and a heft you can
conceive of and move in your mind before you actually pick it
up and set it on the ironing board or place it in the foundation.
Not a weight like that, but one you must raise up out of nothing,
a quantity of gravity that has never before been lifted up or
presented in such a way that it could be measured or defined.

But what do you know about that? Why do I waste my
time on you, you inconsequential spot of bacteria, you feckless
germ! You've never done any real work, never felt the weight
of the yoke on your shoulders, never come home after a long
day of labor so worn out and exhausted you can't even sit down
at the supper table without falling asleep in your soup, and then,
only *then*, say to yourself, now I must go down into that pit, that
forge, now I must go back to work again on the real thing, the
only thing that matters. Ehhh, you wretched boy. You sit there
sullen and brooding. Are you afraid to speak? Afraid I'll laugh
at the stupidity that comes out of that hole in your face? Worm.
Did you shit in your pants? Or is it only the time of year for

your bath?

But it wasn't fear. Even when his mood changed, when he mocked and taunted me, when he got drunk and raged against the night, against the world, against the only audience or should I say victim within his range. Even then it was not fear, or not only fear. Fascination, maybe, bewilderment, sometimes my own anger in return, although I never showed him that, never allowed that, because even then I knew it was better not to say anything, not to reveal anything, to force myself to sit and take it while he went on with his diatribe, his face half in darkness, half in the firelight, a light that in itself had no substance until it found an object, a surface, and then it gleamed like molten glass, a humid orange or amber or red light depending on whether it touched the polished wooden floorboards or the bottle of liquor sitting half empty on the wooden table in front of him or his face, that part of his face that I could see, shadowed and dented like the copper pots and kettles hanging from hooks in the ceiling. How could I not listen? How not stare at that face, at those hands, thick, heavy things capable of crushing stone into gravel and gravel into dust, of bending iron rails as if they were made of rubber. That monstrous trick of architecture and engineering that made those shoulders appear broad and erect like the columns and entablature of an ancient temple even though the man that owned them had long ago collapsed into ruin and a rubble of despair that I could not begin to fathom, even when that voice extruded itself from the rusty slag heap of his body, from the wheezing bellows of his lungs to berate me yet again for *his* failings.

What are you staring at, boy? You think I don't see? Fourteen years, isn't that what it is? And you still haven't learned any manners? Maybe there's a girl, is that it? Some little strumpet you met in town, or a blushing dairy maid out in the country? Don't tell me you don't lie awake at night with that ache and yearning between your legs, that you don't feel that stirring when every pretty face you pass in the street adds another flower to the necklace, the chain of your accumulated desires, when you aren't even old enough or experienced enough in worldly matters to imagine what she must look like naked, to picture the soft swelling of her breasts with their promise of sweet nourishing milk, the smooth softness of her belly like a religious icon carved out of marble, the dark mystery between her legs, the fertile springs you would kiss and drink from in search of the healing waters, the grotto within where new life arises, even monsters like you. Does she ache with the same longing that makes you ache and yearn? Does she put her hands under her gown at night and explore those revitalizing waters? What do you think hands are for if not to touch, to feel, to seek pleasure? But you don't want to hear that either. It disturbs you that an old man has such thoughts. It horrifies you to think that one day you might feel the way you do now and find yourself locked inside a useless old body like the one you see before you. Oh God, whatever god that may be, what must it be like to lie down in a green meadow in the spring with a young maiden and breathe, smell, inhale the milk sweetness of her breath and touch, feel, bathe in the wetness and warmth between her thighs like summer rain. Is that how it is, boy? That innocence yet? Or do you say in your mind like a longshoreman leering at every pretty face you see in the street, Damn, I'd like to have me a piece'a that, not even *her* but *that?* When a piece of meat or your own hand or even a young ewe will substitute? No, not like that. Not yet. That time will come later, after you've gotten past all the garbage, the proscriptions and injunctions of church and state, *greed and hate*, of your own censorial mind. And then it will be too late because a forty or fifty or even sixty-year-old convert to life isn't any good to anyone, least of all himself.

So many years, and for what? That pile of junk, scrap metal, stinking of rust and sweat and machine oil? Everything I have given my life to gone because my body can no longer accomplish that which my mind still demands of it. The will. The terrible will. If only I had known when I began. But there was no one to tell me. No father, no teacher, no wise old man. Listen to me, boy. Better if you find something else, a practical career. Accounting, for example, your mind, your soul buried in columns of numbers all day. Or the law or business, something that you can still pursue after you've become a crippled old man with aches and pains all over your body. If only I had chosen to become a cobbler, a mender of pots. But it's a lie. There was no choice. I didn't decide. I didn't choose this madness. It chose me. When I should have pulled on my traveling coat and my walking boots and gone out the door and down the lane and gone on walking for the rest of my life, I went down instead into the damp and cold and gray smell of death and did as much work in two or three hours as any grown man does in an entire day's labor in the filth and sweat of a coal mine or a steel mill where you would be now, boy, if you lived in another time and place, if the laws were different and you had to work for, *earn* your daily hunk of bread and your cup of milk.

And now you say you want to go down into that mine with me, into that forge. You come to me saying, help me, teach me how. Teach you what, boy? More lies and hypocrisy? More old man's delusions, dreams and memories of what was and never was? How can I teach you something that you must already know, that aches and burns inside of you when you lie awake at night unable to sleep because of the terrible urgency you feel because you've already begun to grasp in the still inchoate forge of your mind, in your still growing bones and in the marrow of those bones that there isn't enough time, that there will never be enough time to do all that you want, all that you must, all that God has apportioned and demanded of you? Because all this time you are also giving your life to that which means nothing to you, that which you must submit yourself to, the job, occupation, that lifelong stint of indentured servitude, slavery, because you have to eat, you have to work to buy food, to keep a roof over your head. And, irony of ironies, only after you have exhausted yourself, expended your strength and energy working all day at that meaningless job, in that mine, forge, office, in that necessity driven forfeiture of life, only then can you approach that which means the most to you, but even then you must force yourself, you must find some additional reserve of energy, of will, you must make time out of time you don't have, time your body and mind should be resting, or, who knows, pursuing some leisure activity like reading a book, yes, *reading*, or, almost as inconceivable, making love to a woman. And you go on telling yourself until it becomes a litany, when things change, when I don't have to work at this stupid job anymore, when I finally have the time, when I've found another way. And all day long while you are away from the iron you think, if only I could touch it, caress it, squeeze it in my hands, mold and shape it as it molds and shapes me. Yes, like that, boy, as if it were a lover, another warm body lying in your embrace, and not some inert object, cold, rigid and unyielding. The iron is not dead. Never allow yourself to think that, say that, believe that. It lives and breathes with the life you invest in it. At night you can feel it aching and sweating in the dark as you ache and sweat for it in your bed, it hungers for you even as you hunger for it at the supper table. Even with a woman, if you can find a woman, if there is a woman who will go down into that mine with you or tolerate your long absences when you do. Because no matter what you are doing now it is always the wrong thing if it is not the iron. Whether you are on the job or traveling home from the job or making love or even taking a shit, you worry over it and gnaw at it, you imagine what it will be like the next time you approach it. Until that time of day, of night, and that moment arrives when you will actually go down and put your hands on the iron. And then, greater irony still, the thing you ached and yearned and longed for when you were away from it suddenly terrifies you and fills you with panic. You feel like you're going to shit yourself, your hands shake, your mind races ahead, past all the previous successes, past what you may accomplish today, to failure, all you can foresee is failure. Do you know what it's like to be so afraid, boy? Can you imagine such terror? No, you've never known as your fathers before you knew the taste of blood, of rust and defeat. You look away with disgust, you aren't afraid, you don't fear. Who knows, maybe you will succeed. Maybe the iron has chosen you. At least it will be easier for you. You have someone to teach you. You have me.

Although there was never any question that I was his or in any way bound by living flesh to him, an old man who sometimes called himself my grandfather in the company of strangers, even though anyone who met him had to know that he was too old to be a grandfather, too old to have sired any children still living on this earth. Although why I say old man, why I make him out to be such an impossibly old man, whether I have aged him in my own mind as I have aged, whether I have aged him beyond all possibility and reason and into the realm of myth. Maybe it's just that in the mind of a one or two-year-old larva crawling across the cold stone floor on chubby knees or standing for the first time on uncertain feet, he seemed so old, to an imperious and howling three or four-year-old brat impossibly old, especially in comparison to the village girl who came to assist him with my care, or even the well-seasoned wet nurse who first fed and nourished me. But even with their help still somehow he must have learned those duties he had never known or known so long ago he had to learn them all over again, how to diaper and feed, wash and bathe and look after a screaming dollop of flesh. And still somehow in those first weeks and months of nurturing me, of handling me, chafing and prying at my soft unformed flesh with those rough heavy hands, somehow he must have learned love, taught love, enough that when I began to make sense of the things of the world around me I was not terrified by the prospect of existence.

How I came to live with him I have no idea. Was there someone before? A mother and father who did not love me, who cast me out upon my first breath, who denied me from the moment of my conception, or, who knows, a mother and father who loved me dearly but because of too little money, too many mouths to feed, too much hunger, out of necessity relinquished me, flesh of flesh, blood of blood, cast upon the waters in a reed basket, in a dinghy barely larger than a child's coffin, a cardboard box packed with old newsprint for swaddling? Or a mother who lost her husband in the war or a father whose beloved wife died at childbirth or who lost her to the tyranny of men with power, with money and guns, or any of a hundred, a thousand other possibilities, but who nevertheless abandoned me on the doorsteps of the first house he, she, they came across, unable to bear that burden farther lest the sorrow be too great, the stone walls they had erected in their minds, in their hearts and souls against that sorrow, crumbling beneath the prospect of that unhappy parting, the mother, father, progenitors of that child crying out no! against that purposed crime, clutching tighter in their arms that treasure and forfeit of life and go into the wilderness to die all but together? Or perhaps, pure speculation, a word let slip to a sister, neighbor, a *known gossip*, they, whoever *they* were, knew in advance that that house of all the others was the right house, that within its stone walls lived one kind enough and well off enough (both premises questionable) to care for this child. Me. Perhaps there was even an omen, a prophecy, the message to them, take your beloved child to this place and leave him to him, the man within those stone walls, and to him, that man who dwelt there, a similar message, a child will come to you, receive him.

And so they left him in a reed basket or wrapped in swaddling blankets or utterly naked on the cold stone with a letter they had painstakingly composed themselves or with the help of the one barely literate person in their village, or else bearing a scrap of parchment with the signs printed long ago in an indelible ink in a language they themselves did not understand, please, whoever you are, take this child and raise it as if it were your own and maybe even give it love. And hope and pray and try to believe every day afterward that it was so when they knew it was just as likely and even probable that the new father, parent, *owner* of this child they had surrendered may just as well be a tyrant, monster, abusive and cruel, who would beat it, mistreat it, raise it with all the pain and injustices of the world, perhaps even, while raining down blows of the fist and lashes of the whip with a perverse savagery and even glee, telling the child it was for his own good so that he may be prepared to face the cruel vicissitudes of life.

But somehow this child, the I to be, arrived outside that stone wall, at that heavy wooden door bound and braced with iron, with only a hollow knock for a greeting and goodbye before they, the putative, the must have been parents, fled, maybe in tears, in utter desolation, gasping for breath through their sobs. The door opened, a craggy face appeared in the shadows like a stone promontory, a strong brown hand with the power to crush crude ore into molten iron reached down for the bundle of soft unformed clay, took it inside and placed it on the table before the fire, with thick, clumsy fingers fumbled open the blanket and looked with, what, shock? surprise? dismay? upon that tiny infant face, *mine*, stitched with lines of pain and hunger and blind impotent outrage at this betrayal, that horrible shrieking yowl that wanted to come out, that would come out later, but for now the only noise those strange little birdlike *awk awk* sounds, the whisperings and crepitations of parchment when he, the to be father god master took up the letter, broke the seal, unfolded the paper, his dry and crevassed lips moved, mouthing the words on the page in a voice that was not just a human voice vibrating with the familiar tonalities of human emotion, but the sound of the forge rumbling in the earth, casting molten iron into solid and permanent shapes, things, *words*, with a weight and a meaning that inculcated themselves in my infant brain long before I could even begin to understand them, that voice I have always heard and carried inside me, instructing me, chastising and directing me, the voice that first gave name to the things of the earth.

But whether I was left on his doorstep or he tore me from the embrace of some terrified and weeping woman of the streets or even from her womb with the same rusty straight razor he used to cut her throat, or, who knows, possibly more unbelievable, somehow managed to father me with the exhausted seed of those withered loins planted in the womb of some prematurely aged wreck of female humanity, or even more impossibly still, myth again, just as justifiable in the cosmic chaos, maybe a beautiful, nymph-like creature, the succubus, siren, of an old man's dream and fantasy, got him wine drunk, seduced him, impaled herself on him wet and dripping when he could barely get it up, a half-masted erection, which may have explained why, when I was older, I saw him constantly searching my eyes, my face, my features as if he were looking for something in particular, perhaps signs of the iron, perhaps something of his own features. But somehow I came to be there, in that house, in that part of the republic and the world, perhaps once a thriving town or village situated in the bend of a river with lush agricultural fields, grain mills and animal husbandry in a pastoral idyll of yore, but now a scattering of dwellings arisen out of the rubble and ruins of some past conflagration and inhabited anew by a race and a people who survived, who picked and foraged among the vestiges of past civilizations and somehow learned again to live, to grow what was needed for food, for sustenance, for visions of God, I don't know what god, a god when only to survive for another day seemed impossible, a god to ponder and perhaps even to offer thanks to when there was reason to give thanks, when things finally improved enough that life seemed worth living, that de facto fathergod who sat before me, my infant eyes, on a stone bench in this retreat, hermitage, this house he built out of timber and stone and this garden he planted and constructed out of some inspiration or design he managed to keep alive over how many years of struggle, a house more like a primitive temple, a garden created for meditation, contemplation, neither of which you would expect from a monster like him, too calm, too tranquil to have been built out of such a simmering tempest. Water trickling over stone, quiet pools with hyacinths and lilies and golden fish that moved beneath the smooth still surface. Bright sunlight shining through the green canopy of trees. The sculpted trunks of bush and shrub. Gravel and stone paths that found their way according to an order and design established long ago in his brooding, in his ponderings and musings, and reestablished now in mine as I try to remember, to reconstruct it as it was or I have made it or want it to be. But all those things I saw first through an old man's rheumy eyes with their light hidden behind a gray curtain, the rain of a thousand years. One thousand and fourteen he said, because those extra fourteen years he raised, mentored, *imprisoned* me were my gift, recompense to him, for taking me in and nurturing me and allowing me life. That in keeping me alive he found life or reason for life again himself, even, briefly, Merlin-like, grew younger thanks to my youth.

When I was older, when my mind began to awaken out of the primordial slough and become aware of itself, when I walked and ran and jumped with the confidence of a sentient being first discovering its ability to think, to walk, to propel itself on its own two feet, sometimes I woke early in the morning, pulled myself up out of the black lethean waters of childish sleep and went out into the first golden sunlight and the sound of birdsong in the trees and found him already seated on that stone bench, not a raging mass of energy barely contained in a battered, rusty block of iron, but a serene, ethereal old man with soft white spun cotton hair wearing a soft white cotton robe. Maybe he heard the door creak behind him, the soft susurrations of my bare feet on the iron gray flagstones, but he never turned, never acknowledged my presence with a smile or a wave or the words good morning or even a growl of disdain for my disturbing him, and all I could do was stand at his back like a factotum awaiting command from a wise old vizier or mandarin. Despite this sense of timelessness and age beyond aging, each morning re-amazed to find him still alive and still so unlifelike in the way he sat motionless and lost in contemplation, staring at a rounded gray stone with crystalline interstices that may have made him think of ancient waterways on Mars, or a cleft in a tree trunk that reminded him of the juncture between a woman's thighs, or a bird with crimson patches on its wings that led his thoughts to a different kind of flying machine, one still in the future for those in the past, in the past for those in the future, a flying machine capable of carrying in its belly the wrath of God or, more prosaically, pacifically, several hundred *living, breathing* human beings, all mindlessly eating and drinking and totally absorbed in their electronic devices as they traveled through the ethereal medium several miles above the surface of the planet earth at, for all intents and purposes, an impossible speed. Or something else altogether that lay beyond my youthful ken. For all I knew and at times suspected with sudden heart-pounding alarm something catastrophic, that he was not lost in thought but catatonic, transfixed by a stroke, an aneurysm.

I don't remember now if there was a precise daily ritual. Maybe I set the table. Prepared the food for our morning meal, one of many simple chores I might have performed. Heat water for tea and coffee, toast bread, make porridge, set out milk, yogurt, cheese, fruit. If I had to go to school I went, sat at my desk, an obedient drudge, yes, teacher, no, teacher, I don't know, teacher. If I had a day off I wandered around town or out in the country or hiked up into the mountains, trying to identify unseen birds by their song, resolve chirp and tweet and whistle into beak and bill, feather and wing, or the berries clinging to branch and vine or the flowers growing wild among meadow grass and fieldstone, all those things he knew intimately while I, I was left guessing at the properties of a leaf, a berry, a flower, whether deadly poison or beneficial for stomach distress. At the end of the day we joined together again for the evening meal, the food he had grown and gathered himself, coarse food but good, the cheese and yogurt he made from the milk he squeezed from the teats of the goat or cow he kept, the vegetables he grew in his garden, the nuts and fruit he picked in the wild. But maybe this is all my imagination too, false memory, maybe he just went into town and bought our food from the store, the loaves of bread from the baker, the sacks of beans and grain, the boxes of vegetables and fruits from the greengrocer, maybe a boy even came from the store once a week on bicycle or donkey or in a small truck with the food that provendered our table. All this good food I give you for free, boy, and what do you do to deserve it? Wretch, I should send you back out into the street to earn a living for yourself, then you'd know where food comes from.

Because he always started after the evening meal, taunting me, mocking me, pouring himself a glass of fire from the bottle as an introduction to that night's catechism in ill manners and perseverance. I think it was then that my life and my memory really began, when I first began to sit at his table at night, when he began to talk to me or rather at me, belittle me, harangue, abuse and challenge me, knowing that I listened closely, that I always listened, for the words he didn't mean to say, the truths he didn't mean to tell, waiting for the time when he would say at last, Tomorrow, then, we'll begin to train you, to teach you something you don't already know. Ha! Insolent pest! Don't think I don't see you watching me, hovering around, spying on me, prying into my things, trying to sneak up on me as if you wanted to steal something from me. *Secrets?* What do you think I have that you might need to know or even begin to comprehend? Stupid boy, do you believe everything I say despite the fact that you only have to look at this ruined old body to know it's all a lie? And still you listen, you wait, you think I have something of use to you, you think that if you manage to take it from me then one day you will succeed. And what kind of success will that be? After all the years of pain, after all the work and the sweat and the blood and yes even tears, and don't—don't ever forget—loneliness, yes, don't let us forget that, loneliness, the loneliness that will be your best, your only remaining friend when you finally emerge from the mine and the forge you have dug in the earth and gone down into like some mythical hero of old descending into the stygian depths to discover and carry unto safety his beloved, his patrimony, his soul. Oh failure, oh hubris—oh shit, what was I saying? What?

Yes, that's right, loneliness. And then, only then you look around to see what it is you have become in all that you have abandoned and left behind. Life, that is what I mean. The life in the streets of the cities, the life of the world, of the men and women who will have become strangers to you as you will become a stranger to them. They will be afraid of you, call you monster, lunatic, mad, and every day of your life you will believe you are mad. You will languish in your hopelessness and despair without anyone to comfort you, you will bow down your head beneath the burden and the weight and pray for— maybe not death, maybe not even an end to your suffering, because suffering is good, suffering is progress, suffering means you're alive, but something, perhaps a glimmer of meaning behind this madness and obsession. Because you can not endure forever, you can not retain the hopes and dreams of your youth forever, you can not pursue the way of the iron forever and not question, not doubt, not believe that you are wrong, that you are in fact insane. Your only reassurance those scattered, those rare moments of inspiration when you remember why you are doing this, when you look up at the sky at night and swear to God—I don't know what god, whatever god you choose to recognize, that's none of my business—that you understand, that you know why you are doing this even though you will never be able to explain to anybody else, even though the very next day you yourself will have forgotten what you realized, what you thought you understood and cried aloud in the silence and vastness of night so that you would know it was true. I exist! I am here now! I have a course, a purpose, a reason, and I will pursue it into the wilderness if I must and I will succeed even if success means death. And not remember or question for another six months or a year that purpose, that reason, nor experience again that inspiration, that certainty of God, of yourself and your success. And for that you live, you go on. For that you endure this madness that you desire to inherit from me now. Do you understand? Do you realize what I'm saying, boy? Oh, I know, I know. Right now, this very moment, you are saying to yourself inside that worthless little skull of yours, yes, yes, yes, I do know, I understand, I am not afraid, I will succeed. But you don't know. You have no idea. I had no idea. No one ever knows.

But even when he quit speaking, when the rumbling ceased from the volcano, when the return of silence only reinforced those words he spoke to the night, to himself, to a lesser extent, me, when he reached for the bottle, filled again his glass until it brimmed with the liquid firelight, when he leaned forward with the dented copper cup of his chin grasped in his hand and peered into the fire crackling and flaring on the hearth, returned his gaze to some place in the distance, a crashing cataract in the side of a mountain or a battlefield strewn with bodies, knowing that I should not disturb that silence with empty questions to meet the questions he had asked me earlier, each question leaving me with more questions than answers, each answer casting another iron rung out of molten ore, sliding home another iron bolt, locking another iron door as he led me further and further down the corridors of his peculiar catechism, as I penetrated deeper and deeper into the labyrinths of his mind, world, mythology, until neither he nor I knew if he led me with his questioning and interrogations, his challenges and demands, or if I led him with my willingness to listen and hear.

Finally he'd pull himself up from the table, changed again, no longer an old man or even a man at all but the shadow, the soot-covered casting of a man, uttering not a fond goodnight but his final growl, It's late now, boy. Go to sleep, leave me alone, I need to rest. Even though I knew he never slept, no more than I, that he stayed awake late into the night lost in his own musing, maybe knowing, *amusing* himself with the fact that I would not, could not sleep, even though I told myself again and again now I will sleep, my mind burning with excitement because of all that he had said that evening, performing my own catechisms, demanding answers to my own questions, knowing that if I did not find them, and even if I did, the very next morning when I woke because of course at some point I did sleep, deeply, profoundly, in the dark well of subconsciousness, that it would start again, he would start again, the interrogations, the questions. Eh, boy? Have you slept so long in the past that you no longer need sleep? Look at your eyes. Did you wander the countryside last night in search of a lighted window behind which you spotted a silhouette that you invested with a pretty face, a kind voice, the smell of a young girl's hair, the softness of her breasts? Better for you if you had. Better for all of us if she lies sleeping this moment in the rumpled luxury of her bed with the warmth and the wetness still seeping out of her springs and the message in her dream of a child already conceived in her belly. And why not? The world needs more drones and worker bees to dig iron and coal out of the ground, to build temples, to wage murderous wars, to father more fatherless sons and send them out into the streets, into the mines and factories and mills, above all onto the fields of battle. No, you don't know what I'm talking about, do you? You look at me as if I'm speaking in a foreign tongue. But the time will come when you do understand, when you will experience these things. And then it will be up to you to decide, the iron or la patria, the iron or a good job, a career, the iron or her. And you will have to make that decision not once or twice but every day of your life. The iron or this, the iron or that.

Of course it didn't occur to me then that he might be lying to me, trying to frighten, intimidate me, to discover if I really was a coward, deathly afraid of the monsters and phantasmagoria of my own imagination. Or if I was only fearful as a man who has fought in previous battles is rightfully fearful as he girds himself for yet another struggle with death, his or his opponent's but somebody's. If in fact I was wasting his time or, conversely, worth his time. That somehow I was the one, that I could carry that burden, believe in that which he had believed for so many years and professed no longer to believe. But how could he not believe? I asked myself with incredulity. After all those years of struggle, how could he not believe? And then I realized that was the trap again. Because I was no longer

struggling with my own conscience, my own will, but his, his
doubts, his fears, he was giving them to me, forcing them upon
me, making me assume his burden. But then, when his fear
infected me, when I needed him the most, when I whimpered
like a frightened little child in my bed at night because I could
find no answers when I desperately sought answers, he pushed
me away, turned his back on me, swore at me, Shut up in there!
You filthy bastard child! How dare you disrupt the silence, my
silence, the silence I need to finish my work?

His work. But what work was that if his work was with
the iron? Something to do with those glimpses I caught of him
through a crack in his door at night, bent over his desk in his
room, over his books and papers, in the dim pocket of
lamplight, *lucubrating*, illuminating esoteric things? Or perhaps
the reverse, peculiar alchemy, transforming simple things into
mysteries, code, cabala, those strange incantations I heard him
muttering to himself, *this is the transformation of dross into
gold, of iron into words, of sword into pen*, the primitive pen,
quill, he held in his hand, a brass inkpot nearby, the brownish
purple ink I watched him manufacture himself, grind and mix
out of the galls of the oak tree in the courtyard and the rust he
filed and sanded off the iron in the never ending battle against
the oxidation of iron and blood? The stacks of parchment paper,
onion skin, vellum, hand-beaten papyrus, the bark of birch he
covered with nearly indecipherable chicken scratches? Latin
backwards? Ancient Greek, Etruscan, *Martian?* An
untranslatable language spoken only by a seldom seen
indigenous tribe in the steamy tropics of the Amazon?
Something I was forbidden from knowing—the keys, as it were,
to the castle? A treatise or dissertation on the art of the iron?
Detailed instructions, diagrams, lengthy arguments, hypotheses,
speculation, the magic abracadabra that revealed, explained
everything? All kept secret, hidden from my sight, locked in
bound books in a locked and bound chest in the recesses of his
chambers? As if he didn't know how I yearned, dreamed of,
desired entrance to that citadel of iron, even as he led me on

with the promise of the iron, filled my nostrils with the smell of iron, erected in my brain that imagined structure of iron until it had grown out of all proportion and reason into a towering iron giant from waiting and anticipation, from listening to him talk, threaten, cajole, and when that failed, promising again, when you begin to train with the iron, when you put your hands on the bar, close your fingers around the rough knurling that enables you to grip the bar even tighter, when you feel that molecular exchange between iron and flesh. Not realizing that even then we were training, that from the moment I opened my eyes on his face and his world and my ears filled with his voice and I heard the words he spoke that he was already beginning to train me, preparing me to enter that world, creating within me the need and desire, the hunger, for that day when I would finally be allowed to touch, close my hands around the iron bar, to squeeze the months and years of ache and yearning out of my hands, out of my body, when just to stand next to it, to know that it was real would have been enough, I would have that much at least to take to bed with me at night and ponder after he said, That's all for now, I have other things to do than waste my time on a worthless wretch like you.

And each day after that for how many more days and weeks of his saying, all right then, tomorrow we will begin to train, tomorrow and tomorrow and tomorrow, compelling me to follow him, sit with him, listen to him, his steady attendant, acolyte, hand always out for the few crumbs of wisdom that might inadvertently fall from his plate, whether he sat facing me over the dinner table or he led me through the house, noticing without really noticing at the time, without attributing value to the way he brushed his hand over black lacquered wood and bamboo gleaming damply in the dim light, learning without realizing I was learning with my own hands and bare feet the qualities of the wooden railings and doorjambs, the splinters and polished spots of the heavy wooden floor boards worn smooth with so many years of bare feet it would have been sacrilegious to go shod, to have worn anything more than bare and callused soles. Even in winter when I stood shivering on the cold gray flagstones outside in my wooden clogs and oversized wool coat, formerly his, while he sat in the garden with the snow at his sandaled feet and his hair like snow and the snow on the dark hollies and evergreens and our breath hanging like cotton in the cold air, waiting for, hoping to hear the minute mechanisms, springs, levers and gears set in motion, that iron jaw cranking open and closed, forming the words, Today, then, you begin to train. Or in the spring when the welcome sunshine warmed the earth and the newly opened peach and cherry blossoms perfumed the breeze and the entire courtyard was lush and bursting with color, flowers everywhere, and I carried rocks, buckets of water, brought him tools he needed as he turned compost into the soil, planted vegetables and herbs. Or later still in the summer when the heat enveloped us and I, as always, followed behind him, trying to learn by example as he prowled the garden, picking injurious insects from plants, raking the gravel paths into a more orderly order, yanking invasive weeds out of the ground by their obstinate roots, as if by virtue of his physical labor he could force the resolution of the problem he was working on in his mind.

Because there was always some problem, some distraction that made him barely aware of my presence, and even when he remembered, when he paused to offer me some advice, to encourage me in my daily chores, to be more precise, when he roused himself from his thoughts to chastise, abuse, scold, castigate me, Go on, boy, get down on your hands and knees and scrub the floor. No! Not like that! Not like some sullen, recalcitrant scullery maid. Scrub as if you were a murderer washing away the telltale blood of your victim, as if you were washing the back of the elephant god, a humble offering and gift of piety to a divine being of strength and wisdom. I know it's hard, it hurts, my knees are older and more brittle than yours. But don't hesitate, get down on your knees, get to work, put all of your mind and body into the task at hand, rid yourself of all the bad thoughts, negativity, empty your worthless little skull of all the trash you've picked up in the street.

   And then, while I knelt on the hard wooden floor with the bucket of soapy water by my side, the stiff brush in one hand, my weight leaning on the other, my head bowed in the posture of the penitent, the novice, the chastened apprentice, the condemned awaiting the coup de grace, my body bent in the form of a tied knot, a clenched fist, trying to adapt itself to the rigors and demands of an old man's demented notion of piety, prayer, meditation (when did I begin to think of him only as an old man and not wizard, demi-god, at the very least, out of respect, *master*?), wherever he went in his mind when he lapsed into silence, when his gaze went beyond the garden, the stone wall, the trees rising into the blue sky in search of or abiding for that protracted moment in a place of no thought where hawks and eagles soared without concern for gravity or the weight of mountains, of iron, while I continued to kneel on the floor, grinding my knees into bone meal, my back stiff, neck aching, afraid to move, to disturb his silence, even if all that time he was laughing to himself at my folly, even if he had fallen asleep, a senile old fool who'd forgotten all about the world around him. What? Aren't your knees hurting, boy? Don't you have enough sense to get up on your feet? Ha, you can't even stand. You look like an old man trying to get out of bed in the morning. You look like *me*.

   Then he went on again as if there had been no interruption, pointing out things that had nothing to do with the iron, his words like brushstrokes on rice paper that seemed simple at first glance, the crude marks of childish hands, but with each successive examination revealed yet another layer of meaning, that sometimes *coincidence?* seemed to touch on or spring from the thoughts I myself was having at that very moment, maybe a word or a phrase that evoked the smell of machine oil and sweat, that sounded like the clang and bang of iron. But when I listened more closely he had already gone off in another direction about a bird he saw this morning or a new

flower bud in the garden, a flower that seemed to have been
blooming eternally the way he described and pointed out each
petal, the pistil and stamen, when all I saw was the flower
already made, a bed of flowers, a mass of color that either was
or wasn't but nothing in between. Or the shape of the clouds
that morning, like fish bones, mares' tails, feathers, angel
wings, and from that whether or not it was going to rain or snow
or turn hot again in a week or a month or a year. Or an entire
hour on the color and texture of a stone or an insect or a leaf he
pointed out to me on one of our rambling journeys through the
nearby woods where roots crept over the ground like snakes and
emerald green moss and ferns clung to rotting logs and crowded
burbling springs, or sometimes up into the mountains where he
went to gather the special herbs for his tea, a counter to his
drinking, he claimed, a cure for his aches and pains, he said,
puts iron in the blood, he actually believed, drank gallons, tons.
No wonder he had to pee all the time. (Yes, I know, irreverent,
learned from him, I guess.)

    And then the way he transported that very same log or
stone into his garden with the roots and moss and ferns and
smell of the woods intact without actually disturbing the stone
or the fallen log in the forest but recreating it with his hands, his
memory, until that stone or log actually appeared in front of my
eyes, highlighting a curve in the path or sitting on the edge of a
dark little pool for the frogs and salamanders to hide under. Or a
bee his eyes directed mine toward on a frosty fall morning as
the first yellow sunlight lit its tiny glassine wings and filled it
with radiant energy and it slowly began to revive itself, to move
and come alive again, watching with almost awe when he let a
drop of honey fall at its tiny feet and it pulled itself up and fed
on the thick amber light, product of its own labor, another irony,
and suddenly its wings buzzed experimentally and then it lifted
itself from the earth like a little alien flying machine and droned
away, free of gravity. To think I should ever associate that old
man of iron with such images of weightlessness and light. How
is it possible that same old man transmogrified himself into and

coalesced with the monster, thing, I also remember, not an old man but a groaning, creaking prehistoric dredging machine rousing itself from the slumber of rust, or a mountain moving through time, the evolution of shoulders, arms and legs, of stone become man, or man emerging out of stone. And then I would wake from my daydream to see him become again only an old man retreating into the private chambers and solitude of himself, eluding me once again.

Worst of all when he got drunk at night over the bottle bought in the village or, affecting an air of rustic refinement, the white ceramic cups into which he decanted the liquor he himself distilled out of the honey, the fruit, the flowers and bitter herbs from his garden like one of those silent ascetic monks who goes barefoot in the snow and consumes only bread and water and sleeps little and who sometimes sings and laughs and raves to himself inside the monasterial walls of his mind, while I tried to be patient, to endure, to play the part of the obedient young servant, squire, novice, apprentice, whatever my role was meant to be (*court jester?*). Even when he chided me and goaded me, I don't think you're right for this, boy. I think I've wasted these last fourteen years on a donkey, not a man. Maybe I should have kept you in a stall, fed you raw oats, hired you out for labor, just don't let this beast in your kitchen, he'll eat everything in sight and shit on the floor, ha! ha! ha! When he mocked me and laughed at me with that gape-mouthed idiot guffaw—a miracle he didn't crack his dry old ribcage, tear loose ligaments and tendons and burst over ripe organs inside. What if I had let loose my own anger and impatience in return? Finally unleashed all my years of torment and simmering impotent rage? You drunken old fool, you lying imposter, you never lifted the iron, you never lifted anything but that glass in your hand. What contests did you ever win? Where are your medals, trophies, awards? Even as I said it horrified at myself, at the words coming out of my mouth, fully expecting his anger and rage in return, So that's how it is you filthy little mutt! I knew it all along. Liar! Cheat! Thief! Now go! Get out of my house! Go back out in the streets where you belong and see how easy it is to find a bone with enough meat or marrow to chew and live on for another week! But it never happened that way, he always saw it coming first, warded off my anger, my frustration, like the perfect martial artist with a simple turn of the wrist, of a word. So, you're tired of an old man's talk, you don't want to hear it anymore, you ache to test yourself against the iron, to feel the weight of the iron in your hands as you lift it overhead in triumph. Despite everything I've told you, despite all the misery and loneliness and pain I've promised you, you want to build your own empire of ruin. Don't worry, wretch, your time will come.

Of course I didn't understand then, not even the next morning when the old man threw a broomstick at my feet. There, rodent, lift that. What, you don't think it's manly enough? Idiot, I don't want you to sweep the floor with it. There's plenty of time for your chores later. You can carry all the water you want from the well, you can pile stones and chop firewood and make your little muscles grow. But this is for something else. I want you to practice with it. Take the bar in your hands, yes, the fucking broomstick, what else do you think I mean? Place your feet apart. Like that. Now bend down, squat, yes, like that, like you're taking a shit. Now lift your head up, push your shoulders back, take a deep breath. Now start your pull, shoulders over the bar, back still indented, rise on your toes, shrug your shoulders, elbows up! Now drop under the bar—the *broomstick!* Catch it on your deltoids, yes, there in front. Now stand erect, take a deep breath, bend your knees slightly and *drive* the bar overhead, drop beneath it, *lunge*, legs split front and back, exhale, *hard!* and take another deep breath. Now stand straight again, knees locked, bar held steady over your head. Good.

And so I began. Beneath his gaze I raised the broomstick over my head as if I were raising the arch of heaven, every repetition an offering to God, every breath I exhaled a prayer and mantra and a propitiation to God, *his* god, *his* prayer, the prayer I learned from him, the breath he expelled to say that prayer become my breath. The iron is not dead, I am not dead, because if the iron is dead, you are dead, if you treat the iron like a dead thing it will defeat you, you will defeat yourself. You must give the iron time to breathe and to rest as you must breathe and rest. You can not sneak up on the iron, you can not outsmart the iron. Sometimes when you approach the iron you will lift it as if it were no more than a feather, a trifle, an unimportant thing. Just as in a dream, suddenly you can lift more than you have ever lifted before, you feel as if you can lift the entire world. And sometimes when you say to yourself now I *must* lift this weight, today is the day I've determined that I *will* lift this weight, the iron will seem unbearably heavy and impossible to lift, and then it's better if you do nothing at all, if you turn out the light and go to bed. Because you cannot overpower the iron. You must penetrate the iron and allow it to penetrate you. You must breathe the iron into your lungs, absorb the iron into your veins, until your flesh is permeated with molecules of iron and the iron with molecules of your flesh, of your breathing and life and consciousness, until there is only one, not you and the iron but you who are the iron, the iron that is you.

But that's enough for today, it's getting late, now leave me alone, you're wasting my time, my precious time. Tomorrow, or the next day, I'll show you a few things, a few simple movements, nothing too much. We don't want you to strain yourself. And just be thankful you don't have another master. You'd already be nursing your broken bones and torn muscles. You'd be pushing coal carts up out of the ground, pounding iron into picks and shovels. Or else training to enter the arena with a dozen other overfed beef cattle to satisfy the bloodlust and fantasies of a thousand, ten thousand, cheering, leering and largely indifferent spectators. But maybe you desire that world, maybe that world will be yours. You'll find out soon enough, boy, soon enough. Insults, mockery, belittlement, that was his method, his manner of teaching. Who knows, maybe it was me, maybe I really was such a donkey and a dunce. Maybe some other student would have excelled under his tutelage, grasped in seconds what it took me weeks, months, to understand. Another student who remembered him as a wonderful teacher and a kind old man, a gentle, smiling grandfather with golden sunlight in the soft spun cotton of his hair and kindness in his crinkled eyes.

Odd that I can't remember now what I thought the first time he actually led me in front of the iron, whether it was something more or less than I expected. Maybe my first memory of the iron was only a dream, a memory falsified by sleep. Maybe what I really remember is the great iron wheels and axles glimpsed beneath a steam locomotive pulling into the station in the village, or the enormous iron cogs of some giant machine of industry. Or maybe it was that he only allowed me that one glimpse before closing the door and locking it behind him and leaving me to reformulate and cast that iron in my mind again and again with a frail wooden stick that itself weighed less than a loaf of bread, to impose upon that brittle stick a mass and weight that equaled some substantial part of the universe, to lift it as if it were loaded with heavy iron plates as big as those railroad wheels I remembered. I was lifting nothing at all and yet that nothing became so heavy that the muscles in my arms screamed as if all their nerve endings had been doused with gasoline and set on fire. Beneath the old man's gaze that dry stick forced me to my knees again and again and even that I did wrong. No! Not like that you stupid donkey! You're not carrying a load of firewood to the market. You're lifting an offering to the gods and the gods want beautiful young boys, not hobbled old beasts. Stretch! Bend! Float on the water and the wind! And then he made me stretch like a cat after a long nap, like a heron stalking the marsh for insects, frogs and small fish, like a snake squeezing the last joy of life and little oinky pleasures out of a suckling pig. And don't ask about, don't say anything about, don't think about the weight, about gravity, about an iron bar, because now, now it was only the strain and effort of stretching inside that drafty gymnasium of my own body. And how much longer would I sweat and slave inside that gymnasium, that furnace and forge of my own mortal coil until I became conscious of every movement every day, whether I was simply walking along a street in the village, when I was allowed that freedom, or doing my chores or sitting at a desk over my school work, and always with the weight and the iron in my mind, always the reminder even when I felt the lightest and freest that there was a weight, that it still had to be lifted. And so I went on as he instructed me, obeying him out of fear and out of faith that one day I would thank him with my own success.

And then something odd happened. A day came when we did not go in to train with the broomstick. When I looked to the old man for an explanation, he only said, I think now you are ready, I think it is time you begin to train in earnest. For the rest of the afternoon he sat out in the garden on his stone bench, his head tilted slightly as if listening to the wind or the faint burbling of the stream. He sat that way all day without speaking, without moving, without encouraging me to come closer or go away. When I brought him his tea he looked at the cup in my hands and then at me, a long look, maybe only reminding himself of what he saw, a cup of tea steaming in the cupped hands of a fourteen-year-old boy on a cool fall afternoon, the trees behind him stippled with spots of color, some limbs already bare.

The old man did not wake the following morning. I knew by the stillness of the house and the thin yellow light pervading the house that he had not awakened, that he would never wake again. If you want I can tell you what he looked like lying on his bed, and yet it will still be a deception, a lie, like every other memory or recollection sworn and professed to be the truth. Not an old man but a very old child, or not even that but the conception of a very old child, luminous, imbued with light, more accurately a beam or plank of light invested with ribcage, femur and glowing skull. It was if he had waited, held on until I was finally old enough to go on on my own, and then he went on, but even his dying was somehow slowed, protracted, negated, because he is always both alive and dying in my memory.

II

AND SO HE BEGAN

BUT MAYBE NONE OF THAT WAS TRUE. Maybe there never was
an old man. Just a boy who lay awake at night in restless, pre-
adolescent notsleep and notdream, his body and mind a torment
of yearning and awakening unto itself and the world around
him, a boy who because of his loneliness and confusion wanted
and needed there to be an old man, more than an old man, a
mentor, wizard, magician, sometimes stern, angry, but above all
good and wise and kind, a boy who out of that loneliness and
need, out of the witches' brew of his own imagination, of comic
books and cartoons, fairytales, movies, songs, embedded myths
and fantasies, created that old man. A boy who awoke one day
sitting in a classroom with the first fourteen years of his life
irreparably closed behind him and his mind burning with
questions the teacher never asked, only, Why aren't you paying
attention? Why didn't you do your homework? Why don't you
know the answer? And what could he say? That he was paying
too much attention? That at that very moment the whole tired
process had become immediately clear to him, that he and his
classmates were sitting at their desks like rows of obedient little
cornstalks expecting nothing more than to grow up and be
harvested. Listening and not listening as the teacher droned on
and on *in the year thirty-four forty-two, old King Toon took a
poo*, while outside the window the whole world was exploding,
the green flames of the trees and the white-hot solar furnace

roaring overhead in the vast blue sky and the birds singing their mindless joy to God, to whoever or whatever listens, and the kids on the playground shouting, screaming, laughing, and the honk and roar of cars, buses, trains and planes, and the clash of nations at war and the silent shriek of stars falling out of the sky, even then that impulse, inspiration, inchoate, inexpressible even to himself, if only he could take all of that in his hands and shape it, make something of it, express it, purge his soul of it with a pencil or paint brush or chisel but something solid and real that he could hold up to the world and say, this is mine, I did this, look at me, I'm alive, I exist. And then the teacher called him back again, demanded that he turn all of life and existence into a sentence or an equation to fit the formula stamped on the blackboard. You weren't paying attention again. You're disrupting the class. There'll be no currants in the porridge for you this week, young man.

But don't think I'm like that, not your math teacher, your writing instructor, the old hag, old bag, old saggy sad sack who nails you to your desk with terror, tortures you with rules and regulations. Oh sure, there are plenty of those if you want them. But that's not why you're here, that's not why you've come to me. You want a different story than that, you want a sad, desperate, tragic, heroic story. You want a story of oppression, of struggle and rebellion and finally triumph. You want your story.

A fourteen-year-old schoolboy who lived with a man and a woman who called themselves his parents to explain their existence in conjunction with his own, even though his knowledge of how much they were not and could never be his parents disavowed them and made them strangers for life, the life he lived, coexisted, perhaps better to say survived with or parallel to them. They were his unwilling keepers, nothing more. They fed and clothed him, at least to the minimal extent expected of sound parenting, exhibited him in public on those occasions when public display of patriotism or community spirit demanded it, then largely ignored him except to condemn him now and then for some perceived infraction of their rule of law no matter how big or small, a chip in a teacup, a shirttail untucked, a laugh too loud, a trail of mud tracked on the floor, sometimes even to yell at him, erratically, out of the blue, those thunderbolts from the heavens, the voice of the notfather, loud, shouting, You idiot! You moron! I'll kill you! break your neck! The notmother cooked food (not well), washed and mended clothes (sometimes), read cheap romances, talked to herself when she thought no one was listening, sipped white wine *discreetly*. The notfather went away to work each day, came home at night angry, sometimes drank, got drunk, raged against the world, shouted at, slapped and shoved around the notmother, terrorized, threatened with death, knocked across the room the notson. Maybe it wasn't quite like that, not exactly like that, maybe. Nevertheless, a man and a woman who by their shared anger and contempt, by their combined neglect and madness—oh, who knows what kind of madness, choose from any of the thousands of afflictions of the minds of the men and women who bear children into this madness—who, by all of that, condemned him to that dungeon, hell. Okay, yes, exaggeration, hyperbole. Not really a dark, fetid prison cell swarming with rats, not demons prodding him in the ass with pitchforks amid leaping flames. Maybe it was only a fruit cellar or spring house or, more likely, a basement, damp, gray, dispiriting, yes, but certainly not a forlorn prison cell in the Château d'If. But why quibble over details. It doesn't matter what it was, only that he forsook the sun and the blue sky and the birds singing in the trees and went down into that forge, furnace, okay, that basement stinking of mildew, of sewage and rotting cloth, the smell of graveyards, of bodies disintegrating into the earth, the smell he breathed and inhaled into his lungs every time he put his hands on the iron bar and raised it over his head, every repetition a surrender to and a refutation of death, *the iron is not dead, I am not dead*, that rancid, nauseating smell of death, decay, defeat he breathed into his nostrils, lungs, brain every time he lowered the bar back to the floor and sat back down on the wooden bench gasping for breath, his head bent in disgust at this pathetic effort and still knowing that tomorrow and the next day and the day after that he would go back down into that pit and repeat that effort, that he would come back up again out of that same pit two or three hours later, exhausted, filthy with sweat, rust, oxidized metal and machine oil and face again the contempt, the absolute hatred in the notmother's eyes. You stupid boy! You'll break your back! You'll ruin yourself for life! She said, and did not say, And then you'll be no good to us, a liability instead of a paycheck, years of wasted investment in food, shelter and clothing that could have been better spent. The anger and rage in the notfather's voice, shouting, red in the face, You blasted idiot! You moron! You worthless, good-for-nothing imbecile! I'll kill you! Throttle you! Strangle you within an inch of your life! The man who called himself father on the occasions he was required to call himself anything in relation to the notson. The coward, bully, buffoon who, when he was not raging at his own family, threatening, bullying, terrorizing them, when he was confronted by anyone, the boss or a grumpy co-worker or a slightly irate neighbor or even the most subordinate government agent, the fucking meter reader for Christ's sake, avoided conflict at all cost, bowed and scraped and apologized like a groveling stable boy, if at all possible abstained from any public comment or opinion, practiced mimeticism with wallpaper, matte cubicle dividers. No one say anything, maybe they won't know we're here, maybe they'll go away. As for this madness of the boy's, don't mention it, don't take it seriously. Except when you need a few chores done around the house, someone to uproot a tree stump, to haul the year's accumulation of garbage down the hill and dump it in the ravine, and then it's, Where's the boy? Get the boy to do it. Otherwise it's all nonsense, this business of the iron, put away that childish stuff, learn to do something useful with your life.

But their imprecations, their condemnation, their threats spoken or un- weren't enough, they couldn't stop him. Night after night he went back down into that dungeon, forge, pit, okay, basement, to create an order of his own making, to build an empire or if not actual empire, the foundation, prototype, the dream, vision of the empire supported upon the marble white columns of his soft, skinny arms and in absolute SILENCE, without disturbing anyone, without reminding the notparents *what he was up to down there*, he had to muffle the clanking and banging, not a single *cling* or *ding* could he allow to penetrate the strata of flooring above his head, joists, planks, tongue-in-groove and raspberry red acrylic carpet, slightly worn. Increasingly difficult as he grew older, stronger, taller, and the ceiling, the splintery, nail studded, cobweb clotted wooden beams of the rafters grew increasingly lower. Wrenching bones in their sockets, straining sinew, ligaments and tendons, trying to guide, control, move the iron along a perfect trajectory, avoid collision with the joists, mere inches, fractions, for error on either side. If, when, he failed, made a mistake in judgment, slammed the heavy cast-iron plates into the wooden beams over his head *BOOM* and the whole house shook as if struck by thunder and then the thunder resounded again *Boom Boom* when the notfather stomped on the floor above and shouted down at him through carpet, lathing and plank like a fire and brimstone preacher, like Jonathan Edwards himself exorcising the devil in the fiery pit below. You blasted idiot! You moron! If you don't stop that nonsense down there I'll kill you! I'll break your neck! You're ruining the house! And yes, despite the anger, the rage, the real threat and danger of infanticide in the notfather's voice, he, the blasted idiot, the moron, did picture for an instant the house knocked on its side, windows smashed, a big dent in the roof. But, oh no, don't laugh! That inside voice, that tyrannical internal censor learned, inculcated almost from birth, permitted no humor, no comedy, no room for laughter, *irony*. Then he, the boy, notson, the idiot, moron, donkey, sulked and skulked and felt even guiltier, not for this folly of his, this *nonsense* of the iron, but the mistake he made that revealed his folly, which made him that much more determined than ever to be quiet, unobserved, *stealthy*, determined above all to continue his pursuit of the iron. At the same time hating and despising them even more, the notmother and notfather, for their softness, their weakness, for their cowardice in the face of the world and even, for that matter, their own son, above all for their will to paralysis, failure, inaction, the will to believe that it, *something*, whatever must be done cannot be done.

But this is going too fast, we're skipping important details, you should probably know what brought him to the iron, when and how he got started and so forth. So let us begin.

Once upon a time …

No, wait, stop! You see, we're already off course, or rather too much on. Let's try again.

… there was a wise old wizard.

No! No, no, *no*! It doesn't work that way, not so simple.

Maybe one day he was at a friend's house, maybe not even a friend, just some kid in the neighborhood, his family newly arrived, the urbs swelling into the 'burbs, or maybe the opposite, his family one of the first, the early settlers, bringing TVs, toaster ovens and SUVs into the wilderness, and they, he and this new (or old, not in age, of course) kid were having a manly test of strength, the kind of thing young men do, twelve, thirteen, fourteen years old, almost adolescents, just beginning to get a sense of their approaching manliness with an old set of barbells this new-old kid's father had lying around in the garage gathering dust and flirting with rust, and, hmm, interesting, he discovered he could lift a few more pounds than the other kid, maybe he'd already developed little muscles from performing chores the notmother and notfather ordered him to do around the house, hauling rocks and dirt to build a wall and make a garden, carrying buckets of water from the spring to water the crops, turning the family's worthless plot of clay into a worthless garden in which they might dig up and harvest a few stunted tubers, a few wormy peppers and tomatoes. Pioneers in their own right, settlers of the already settled, struggling with the elements, the vicissitudes of a civilization in decline. But that's going too far back in time, that's a history before this history, or maybe a history yet to come. We were talking about his first experience with the iron. We were. There was maybe fifty, sixty pounds on the bar, about half his own weight. He bent down, gripped the rough, machined iron in his soft fists. A warm tingling *thrill* surged through his entire body, a residual telluric force emanating from the iron ore torn from the raw earth and forged, milled and machined into a relatively exact quantum of mass, this Iron Age relic called a *barbell* (see Webster's, Merriam-Webster, Cambridge and Oxford dictionary entries). Awkwardly, clumsily, like the first human being struggling to extract its her his newly minted self from the clay, he lifted, yanked this insignificant weight to his shoulders and jerked, pushed, raised it over his head, this brutish act, troglodytic, Neanderthal, simultaneously, counter intuitively, producing a blue electric flash in his brain, an *epiphany*, big screen, blockbuster, *coming this summer!* Himself, godlike, lifting great iron works, buildings, bridges, entire cities, the whole *fucking* world over his head.

But now, now we've turned the clock, the balance wheels and gears of the clock, a notch or two too far forward (always so difficult to locate a specific place in time, to say *this*, this is when). Because there was another time, a time before this time when the iron caught him by surprise, terrified, overwhelmed him. There, there he is, twelve years old, his first year in junior high school, a freshman, a soft little bread dough homunculus fresh out of the oven, confronted with a brave new world, a time of many changes. Why, for instance, should he take notice of the girl who sat next to him in home room? Because she *was* a girl? Because she was sitting right next to him at the same table? Because she had begun to show the slightest signs of change herself, yes, breasts, they were, he could see, didn't mean to stare, barely there, not bare, those very slight risings—unleavened?—discreetly discreet beneath frilly ruffles, a plain little schoolgirl from out on the plains, a little house on the prairie home companion who would one day grow up to be a plain old housewife, secretary, schoolmarm, nurse? But that's unkind, also unlikely, not a twelve-year-old boy's crystal ball intuition of the damsel's dismal future speaking, but an old man's cynicism, the old grouch up the street who yells at noisy kids, at people walking their dogs, even at the young parents pushing prams, cutting edge, aerodynamic, nothing's too good for their pwecious widdle bundles of joy screaming their heads off *waaaahhh*, even at doddering old fools like himself tottering all over the place on their hi-tech, ergonomic, cutting edge walkers, *Quit making all that goddamn racket! Get off my lawn you damned old fool!* An old man embittered by his own folly, the futility of life, who can't stand to see anybody else happy, laughing and carefree. But the hell with the old fart, this isn't his story, go fuck yourself, Abe, we're talking about a boy, just waking up to the opposite sex, the little twelve-year-old gamine, vixen, tart seated right next to him.

One day he noticed a small bright brown disk gleaming on the highly waxed and polished yellow linoleum floor approximately midway between his right foot, shod in black patent leather, and her left foot, shod in—freckle-faced Mary Janes? Penny loafers? Fringed Moccasins? Black-and-white saddle shoes? What boy notices things like that? Or her ankle length, lace trimmed, white bobby socks or her bare calves or … He perceived that this object was a button, most likely plastic. Quick as the dickens, the sly young devil, he bent down, picked it up from the floor, determined that, yes, indeed, empirically, it was a button, plastic, and—the novice sleuth, the young Sherlock Holmes, Inspector Clouseau, hot on the trail— began to search for its origin. The little calculator in his brain made a simple computation, his eyes went to the buttoned bodice of the young lady in question's brown cotton dress. What color of brown? A kind of mottled brown, with shades of mustard yellow, like a field overgrown with goldenrod, timothy and milkweed late in fall, or the thatched roof of a bucolic country cottage warm and cheerful inside with a bright red fire crackling merrily on the hearth. But all of that for a simple dress off the rack? Ah, romance. And sure enough, his sharp eyes, ferret-like, furtive, stealing peripheral sideways glances, detected a gap, a missing element in the vertical arrangement of similar buttons on the front of said dress. Hmm, dilemma. What to do next? The obvious solution would be to return this fastening device to its owner, which in itself would have been a nearly impossible act, um, I think this is yours? I think it came from there? nodding, pointing, indicating with his eyes, index finger, accusatory, that specific location on her dress, her chest, her barely burgeoning breasts—really, nothing there at all, a lifetime of flatchestedness ahead of her, oh the shame, the *envy*, who would guess that a time would come when she thanked God she hadn't turned into some hugely bosomed moocow bent beneath the weight of an enormous udder. Anyway, no way, ixnay, could he say, mention *that*. So what did he do? Ah, the scamp, the rascal, he put it, the button, in his pocket and for the next month he carried it around with him, every afternoon after school put it in a little wooden box in his sock drawer for safekeeping, every morning put it in his pocket, perhaps with the noble intention, waning with each day that passed, of returning it to her at some opportune moment, um, is this yours? I just found it on the floor (where it had lain untouched by the janitor's mop or broom or floor polisher for the last three weeks—how likely is that?), perhaps simply to have, to hold, to touch something of hers, a part of her, that simple button become a synecdoche for the whole, okay, not really a part of her, but a thing that represented her, a metonymy then, let's get our terms straight, inert plastic button equals living, breathing, warm-blooded *she*. Once he even took it out and pressed it to his lips, kissed it, *one might even say*. How in the world did such an audacious act ever occur to *him*? It must have been something he saw in a movie, read in a book, *her soft lips, his noble kiss*, something that stuck in his feeble brain like the stainless steel needle in the groove of a brittle black disk revolving on a 78 rpm hand cranked Victrola record player, the brain, in other words, of a stupid young dreamer, yes, *romantic*. And what happened to the button? Don't know, he must have lost it.

But that isn't it, not what we were searching for, the right time, yes, but not the right event, circumstances. The bell had rung *brrinnngg!* Chaos in the hallways *the cheerleader's got a gun!* kids changing class, lockers slamming. He was waiting for the beginning of gym, a bunch of kids standing around, soft, skinny arms and legs sticking insect appendage-like out of baggy black shorts and white T-shirt, when he heard the clang and bang of iron calling to him like a ship's bell, a dinner bell, maybe not a bell at all, maybe more like Vulcan's sledge crashing down on his anvil, Thor's hammer crashing into Loki's shield. Intrigued, he wandered into the *weight* room. A couple of kids were lifting a barbell, a simple iron bar with a couple of ten pound plates on each end. It didn't look particularly big. The kids were about his age, they were easily lifting it over their heads, he should be able to lift it easily too. That was his logic anyway, his reasoning. Although what on earth gave him that absurd sense of himself, the young strongman, junior Hercules? He'd never lifted anything like that in his life. He bent down, grabbed the bar and yanked. *Ouch*, that was really heavy, it *hurt*, it caused him *pain* in his arms, in his back, it was like a *dragon* had caught hold of him, clutched his arms in its lethal talons, clamped his entire body in its great fire-breathing jaws, he could barely wrestle the bar to his shoulders, he struggled, pushed, *ouch ouch ouch*, but no way could he lift it over his head. There was something not just heavy but oppressive, threatening, about this simple iron bar and these black iron disks, as if it had a will of its own and its only will was to crush him into the floor where he let it drop now, *crash, bang*. But that's not a happy memory at all. How does that explain his, um, *interest* in the iron? The viewing audience is asked to choose *interactive* from one of the following possible answers: when the going gets tough the tough get going; take up the gauntlet; meet the challenge; rise to the occasion; face adversity. You left one out. Oh? *Obsession.*

Back to gym class. There he is, lined up in the gymnasium with the other boys, oversized sneakers to fit oddly oversized feet squeaking on the polished wooden floorboards, all of them croaking, squawking and squeaking like a mismatched vivarium of frogs, chickens and mice, their voices betraying them every time they spoke, because they were not men yet, just turned twelve, turned thirteen, fourteen, their vocal chords suddenly stretched too long, too thin, their bodies equally challenged, knobby elbows, knees and gangly limbs uncoordinated, untested, except for those monsters of genetic mutation who were already so much bigger, faster, stronger than the rest, so much surer of themselves than the rest. He envied them, feared and resented them, even hated them for their strength, their self-assurance. They were good at all kinds of sports, football, baseball, basketball. He didn't know how to do any of that stuff, he'd never participated in any sports, he and the notfather had never thrown the old pigskin around, never tossed the old horsehide back and forth. Not just the jocks but the little thugs, tough city kids. They weren't necessarily strong, but they were tough, fast, cunning, they used language, harsh words he didn't understand, *fuck you skinny little pencil dick*, they knew how to fight, to catch you off guard, to sucker punch you, smack you in the nose or the mouth or land a fist in your stomach and you wouldn't even see it coming. Or the rawboned country kids who climbed trees and swam in farm ponds, who loaded hay bales and bushels of apples in the summer, who could *wrastle* you into submission as if you were a newborn lamb. There were kids like Stephen and George, Benjamin, Travis and Harold. They came from wealthy families, manicured genes, perfect diets served to them on clean white plates with tall glasses of fresh squeezed sunshine and a vitamin pill every day. They had tennis and swimming lessons, private instructors to teach them how to take a shit and even how to jerk off. They all seemed to share some secret, to possess some truth or knowledge that he wasn't even aware of. They looked at him with the same contempt he felt from the notmother and notfather when he tried to accomplish anything, they ridiculed his slightest attempt, and it was only an attempt because he could never, would never succeed at anything, whether it was fixing a broken spoke on his bike or throwing a ball through a hoop, he'd try and fail and they'd all laugh at him because they wanted and expected him to fail, and deep down inside he wanted to fail, to meet their expectations, to prove to his notparents and the other kids at school and everybody else in the whole damn world including God and Santa Claus that he really was a worthless insignificant little piece of shit to be ignored, excluded, forgotten, largely left alone in that prison, that institution of yearning, hormone colliding, aggressive young male bodies. A pact, let's be honest, he earnestly endeavored to honor and, in fact, largely succeeded at, having already had it modeled for him by the notfather: stay out of everyone's way, don't draw attention to yourself, don't stand out, avoid conflict with, shield your countenance from the menacing gaze, the evil eye of the principal, the teachers, the other students, the janitor and cafeteria ladies, the school crossing guard and any other putative authority including last but not least, that exemplar of *mens sana in corpore sano*, the gym coach.

Oh yeah, gym class, thought we'd gotten away from that, didn't you? Escaped maybe? He certainly did, wished, hoped he could. They lined up for roll call, a long disorderly line of skinny chicken legs sticking out of baggy shorts, soft matchstick arms sticking out of oversized t-shirts emblazoned with the school mascot *Go tigers!* Tennis shoes as big as coal barges on suddenly outlandishly large feet. Unseen, that bizarre undergarment, the object, butt of jokes, jocular jockstrap, aka athletic supporter with its little pouch for just beginning to develop genitalia and the stretchy straps around the hips and thighs that left the buttocks, the crack of the ass and the rectum itself exposed, vulnerable. Wait, exposed and vulnerable to what? you ask. A spring breeze? A pedophilic gym teacher who'd love nothing more than to caress those bare adolescent bums with his hairy paws and shove his erect sausage up one of those virgin bungholes? A smoldering time bomb, ex-Marine or Army DI, beer belly, red in the face, who considered it within his province to inflict pain on those soft virginal butts with a wooden paddle or twist of rope? Count off! One! Two! Three! Four! Five! … Thirty! All present and accounted for, sir! All right you maggots, get down and give me fifty! *Huh?* That's right, kids, you're in the Army now, almost in the Army, and like it or not you're gonna do these stupid jumping jacks and squat thrusts, leg lifts, arm rotations and a whole cadre of drills and calisthenics adapted from a vintage WWI Army training manual, along with whatever other innovations in physical education the school board and the administration and the athletic department could come up with in the way of torture and humiliation—er, lifelong health and physical fitness activities. Followed by wrestling or bouncing balls off walls or off each other's heads in a round of the dreaded murder ball. Get the nerd with the glasses! Wait, he wasn't wearing glasses, it was somebody else, he was safe. *Bomp!* Or slapstick attempts at gymnastics. Okay, everybody, handstands! Nobody in the room has ever successfully attempted a handstand, Coach (the gym teacher is always coach of something, football, basketball, badminton) has almost certainly never done a handstand in his life. Or the pommel horse! Or the rings! C'mon, men (*men?*), get up there, give a me a three-sixty! An iron cross! *What the fuck?* Not that he would have ever said that, never even thought that, certainly not then, but somebody else did, muttered under his breath (but loudly enough to be heard), expressed the general attitude. *Ha! Ha! Ha!* all the other kids laughed (except him). Uh-oh, that did it. Now Coach was really pissed. Who said that?! Silence. Which one of you little bastards used that word?! Silence. Okay, that does it! Now they're all gonna pay. A hundred laps around the track! Even though none of them have ever run farther than the corner candy store. Guys are bent over double, gasping for breath, barfing up lunch. *Who the fuck* (that same kid? an irate parent?) thought it was a good idea to schedule PE after lunch? Coach herding them along this assembly line, shouting at them, *threatening* them, Come on, men, let's go! let's hustle! let's get a move on! Wilberstein! I'm gonna stick your head in the toilet if you don't pick it up! Coach's got a paddleboard with holes in it for recalcitrant ephebes, a knotted rope he's aching to beat your ass raw with. Better yet, get the whole class involved, collective punishment, community ostracism (we've seen how well that works in you-know-who's *cultural revolution*), also known as the gauntlet, all the kids line up in two rows, the miscreant's gotta crawl down the middle on his hands and knees while his schoolmates, loyal buddies all, rain down perversely gleeful Lord of the Flies blows on his soft piggy waddle butt *boo hoo hoo.*

   After fifty minutes of such ~~tor~~ instruction in physical fitness, the young scholars crowd into the rancid sweat smell of the locker room, step out of and strip off tennis shoes, socks, damp t-shirts, black shorts and the bizarre jock straps and shove, elbow, goose *woooo!* their way into the showers in the industrial gray prison ambience of cement walls, hot steam and naked young male bodies, some more male than others, some with more pubic hair, hair under their arms, hair even starting on their chins and chests, hair sprouting all over their bodies like little fucking gorillas, some more developed in a frightening way. He looked at them and he looked at his own soft, naked, barely developing self and he wanted to disappear, not to be seen, not to have to look at these other male bodies anymore, not to be reminded of what he was supposed to be and was not and never would be. He wasn't going to ripen and mature and grow up in that riot and rumbling thunder of cocks and balls and bloody war clubs. He wasn't going to wrestle and fight and struggle to bash in other men's brains. He was going to grow up to be a—thinker! a philosopher! a lover of poetry! Wait, what? Are you crazy? Where the *fuck* did that sick idea come from? A thinker? Philosopher? *Poet?* What the hell are you talking about, young man! We want Spartans here, not girly Athenians. Oh yes, because it's not so simple as that, is it? You can not be that, you are not allowed by the laws of nature and society to be that. You are a boy, a male child. At some point you are going to have to defend yourself, defend your honor, defend the honor of your gender, of your friends, family, country, your *wife*, for God's sake (lawfully wedded, to love, honor and *obey*. Children! Grandchildren! You must!) In other words you're going to have to *fight!* After all, he couldn't run around scared all his life, he had to learn how to stand up and defend himself and be strong. Yes, but in secret, so nobody else would know what he was up to, so nobody else would laugh at his puny attempts. *Shh.*

One Saturday morning in early spring, the snow beginning to melt, sudden shocking patches of green bursting from the frozen whiteness, chocolate brown mud puddles here and there, he rode to the local shopping plaza with the notfather in the notfamily car. While the notfather was off getting a haircut, How's it going, Joe (or Fred or Ralph)? Can't complain, Ed (or Larry or Pete), he, the wayward notson, to all outward appearances a bashful, decidedly not athletic-looking fourteen-year-old boy, entered the nearby combination hardware and sporting goods shop (fly rods and hedge shears thirty percent off!) and handed over three months of shoveling snow from drives and sidewalks and delivering newspapers around the neighborhood, *honest labor*, collecting his pennies, nickels and dimes, his grubby dollar and sometimes five-dollar bills, counting and converting them in his mind until the balance added up, copper, silver and paper currency equaled the weight of iron, in this case the classic one hundred ten pound set of weights, a five-foot long, twenty pound iron bar with sleeve and collars, an assortment of ten, five, two-and-a-half and one-and-a-quarter pound black cast-iron plates, and two shorter five-pound dumbbell bars, also with sleeves and collars, carried them back to the car piece by piece, loaded them in the trunk, covered them with an old blanket, and shortly afterward, the notfather, smelling of shaving cream and cologne, and he, smelling perhaps of incipient traces of the manly deluge of perspiration yet to come, creaked and rocked the five or ten miles back home again. Odd, the notfather said, confiding as he had never done before in the notson, another sign, perhaps, of the door of manhood opening another inch. The car feels different today, maybe the shock absorbers are going bad. The notson stared out the window and said nothing. Later that night when everybody else was distracted with paying bills and sorting, sort of, the laundry (the notfather and notmother), with doing homework and playing video games (his presumptive and statistically probable rank of siblings of that day and age, that is to say, so many brothers and sisters, elder and younger according to a certain distribution by gender or gender variant), he went outside and, soft, boyish biceps and triceps already sore and aching from his earlier effort, carried his new set of weights piece by piece and pound by pound up the back steps, into the kitchen and down to that dim, dank and largely unfamiliar basement beneath the silent condemnation of the notfather and the notmother who, yes, of course, by now knew he was *up to something,* but who said nothing then, not to him, reserved their commentary, judgment, until later that night lying side by side like anchored enemy war ships in their cold estranged marriage bed, and then they unleashed their fusillades, cannonades, attacked each other, Oh, you idiot. Why on earth did you let that *stupid* boy buy that junk? What are you talking about, you lunatic? I didn't *let* him. He did it on his own. I didn't even know. Well, regardless, the man who sold it to him should be shot. Yes, shot. But don't say anything about it to the boy. No, don't say anything to him. Because he might get angry. And act out in public. Because he's going through—don't say it!—*ch-ch-ch-changes*. And besides, maybe he'll get over it. Yes, and maybe he won't! The notmother's ice-cold condemnation returning, the notmother who took any opportunity whatsoever, found enough cause or casus belli in all things large and small to launch into Old Testament prophecies of doom, catastrophe, floods, plague, scorched earth, the sky's going to fall, women are going to lie down with women and men lie down with men. *No way!*

And so that stupid, that errant boy went down into the cellar with his thin little stick arms and his bony ribs and soft belly, knock-kneed, gangly, wide-eyed, intimidated, okay, let's say it, *frightened* by the dreariness of that dank gray basement he had seldom had reason to visit before, the wooden rafters draped with dusty cobwebs, the glare of the single bare light bulb hissing its disapproval in the cold damp air, shelves laden with ancient cans and jars of fruit and vegetables gleaming in the dim, diffuse light, something that looked like a human embryo, the fetus of the notorious sheep child or some other monstrosity that had been stewing in formaldehyde for the past century? Or only spicy pickled pears? The institutional gray cinderblock walls and poured concrete floor. The constant trickling of water somewhere. It goes on day and night, the trickling, seeping, and that horrible smell, like brackish bayous, raw sewage, and no wonder, that Twenty Thousand Leagues Beneath the Sea sump pump thing submerged in that dreadful black hole of Calcutta located next to the cement wash basins where it is at least conceivable that some time in the future a very disturbed individual (okay, a psychopath, but please, let's not get into the shaming game) might wash clean the internal organs he (seldom a she) has skillfully removed from his latest victim.

And so he began, with no idea in the world how to begin, with an iron bar that in itself was almost too much for him to lift, a meager pile of weights, plump, black, cast-iron disks, *plates*, gleaming dully like the pocket change of a troll or an orc or some other chthonic creature. He knelt on the cold cement floor, still in his school clothes, with unusually studious intent tried to decipher the exercises in the instruction pamphlet that came with the weights, illustrated by ancient black-and-white photographs of men in handlebar mustaches, bare chests, black tights, their bodies muscular, hard, carved out of marble, stone, shown in different acts of lifting barbells. And then he attempted to make his own body conform to those contortions, unaware that the manual and the exercises he endeavored to imitate were grossly outdated, obsolete, that he was learning how to drive a horse-drawn buggy when everyone else was driving flying cars, that he was invoking old gods, practically antediluvian, Eugene Sandow, Charles Atlas. *The guy who held the world on his shoulders? Dude, that's the Gold guy.* He didn't even grasp that *reps* simply meant the number of times or repetitions you performed a particular exercise, or that each group of repetitions comprised a *set*, a term he vaguely associated with algebra, to which he did not apply studious intent. He knew nothing about proper breathing or technique or even the spacing of his hands on the bar. Just grab it any old way, yank it to his shoulders and heave it overhead. After each *set* he knelt on the floor, examined again the photographs, the written instructions, tried to better understand the esoterica of each exercise, some of them utterly unfathomable, impossible to figure out. They had odd names that suggested different ends of the spectrum of gravity's rainbow: butterflies (sunlight, spring breezes), dead lifts (corpses), rows (your boat), presses (shirts?), curls (hair? ribbons and bows?), squats (poop!), clean and jerk (I don't know—skin, gut and cure the meat of game animals?), snatches. *Ha, don't let your mother—okay, not your mother, that maternal impersonator—don't let her hear you say that, boy. She'll wash out your mouth like a cleaning lady swamping a public toilet.* The notmother who came snooping around, *sneaking*, to catch him at, to see exactly *what he was up to* down there. He heard the cellar door squeak open, the top stair's wooden tread creak beneath the notmother's formidable weight, he saw her silhouette, also formidable, and the poisonous gleam of her eyes when she stopped midway between the second and third steps, paused to peer, *glower*, at him in the dim light, to communicate, silently, unspoken, her severe disapproval, *condemnation*, before she turned, retreated back up the stairs, watching over her shoulder for fear, perhaps, of the notson, that little worm, that larval nothing, turned,, grown into a bloodsucking, brain eating zombie banshee monster screaming up the stairs after her.

Undeterred, however, by either the arcana of the exercises, or matronly concern (persecution), he carried on, pressing the barbell overhead, curling it to his chest, attempting the more difficult lifts as best he could. But what the heck was that burning in his arms? They felt rubbery, numb. And *ouch, ouch, ouch*, the next day he felt as stiff and achy as a banged up old buckaroo who'd just ridden his pinto across the West Texas desert. But not a sign of pain or distress did he show to his teachers and classmates in school, not even when Coach Tyrannovich, *cruelly*, punishing them all to punish him, he suspected (how do you spell early-onset *p-a-r-a-n-o-i-a?*), made them climb the ropes to the ceiling of the gymnasium and run extra laps around the track. Not a wince or a whimper did he allow escape in front of the notfather or the notmother, neither that morning eating his porridge plain, nor later that evening over the dinner table *after* the groaning, shuddering, black exhaust spewing old yellow school bus dropped him off at the corner and he walked the last half mile home, *after* he watched a truly stupid cartoon on TV (mythological super hero Hercules saves dumbass adolescent centaur from evil sorcerer) while consuming a peanut butter and jelly on white bread sandwich and glugging a glass of whole milk, and maybe after that a disturbing sci-fi program he didn't really understand that actually gave him a headache trying, although that may have been the notmother frying (incinerating) liver for dinner, *after* he trudged back down those creaking wooden stairs *into the dungeon gloom* of that damp, dismal basement and again knelt down on the cold hard cement floor and again struggled to decipher those strange exercises even as he struggled to lift those insignificant weights over his head, despite the complaints from his already stiff and aching little biceps and triceps, even then, perhaps the first, signs, indications, of that indomitable will, determination, of that, yes, *obsession*.

And every day after that day he came home from school and he went down into that damp stinking basement and he heaved and jerked and pressed and curled and dutifully attempted to execute the most arcane maneuvers, and gradually he decoded the language of iron, deconstructed the components of each exercise by actually putting his numbskull brain to use for once, reasoning, *ratiocination*, oh, *that's* how it works, but also by his growing familiarity with the physicality of the iron, by his propinquity to the iron through repetition, psychomotor conditioning, the body's tendency to align itself in the most efficient and least injurious way, in the process abandoning exercises whose purpose he doubted or that ultimately proved too difficult to master, focusing on those where he felt certain inherent strengths, the curls like lifting buckets of water from a stream, the overhead presses like raising high the roof beams, the squats, limited to the weight he could heave over his head onto his upper back, like—what else can you say?—squatting to take a shit but with another person sitting on your shoulders, the deadlifts like hauling a drowned body out of the river (note to concerned citizens: proper authorities have been alerted to a suspicious pattern of references to dead bodies). He learned to take a deep breath before executing each repetition and to forcefully exhale at its completion. He learned to space his hands approximately shoulder width apart and equidistant from the center of the bar. He learned how to bear down, focus, to *demand* of himself that he perform hard *work*, to acknowledge, understand, that it was work. Beyond that he had no real sense of goals or progression, no sense of where he was going or how to get there. He saw no correlation between the algebra, geometry and trigonometry classes he sat through, eyes glazed, thoughts far away, his sophomore, junior, senior years, and the trajectory of an inert object of a given size, weight and shape (i.e., an iron bar loaded with cast-iron metal plates) through intersecting horizontal and vertical planes. He knew nothing of the classic Olympic lifts, knew nothing about records, contests, who had lifted how much where or when. His approach basically heave and shove and yank, grunt and groan and lift as much weight as he could as many times as he could today, tomorrow, the next day. A country bumpkin, unlearned peasant, performing his quotidian chores, manual labor, in the stables, in the fields, in that bucolic land of yore (but not his), ignorant of automobiles, flying machines, of the net, the web, the cloud.

Combining the allowance grudgingly and niggardly disbursed by the notfather (accompanied by a lecture on the importance of proper money management skills—apparently the less you have the less you have to manage), with his earnings mowing lawns in summer and shoveling snow in winter, he purchased a pair of twenty-five pound plates, and then two more, and finally the huge, black, train wheel-like fifty pound plates. Calling upon ancestral carpentry skills that must have skipped over the notfather's generation, he built himself additional equipment out of old lumber, a wooden bench and a rack—why not a rack? What boy wouldn't like to have his own medieval torture device? But no, not a machine to break the bones in his body, not intentionally anyway. A rack to support the loaded barbell while he positioned himself under it to perform squats, or bench presses when he lay on his back on the bench he, personally, had crafted and slowly lowered the bar to his chest as if he were the sole defender of truth in the face of perfidy, groaning *more weight!* even as the growing pile of ~~stones~~ iron crushed his ribcage, collapsed the bellows of his lungs and burst his heart. But no, he, *hero*, overthrew tyranny, pushed the weight off his chest, locked it out at arms length, and then repeated this effort *six-seven-eight-nine* more times.

At some point it occurred to him that it might be a good idea to record, keep track of, his progress, to know when he achieved each milestone, some kind of chart perhaps, but sturdy, official-looking, projecting a certain gravitas. He found a steady supply of material in the cardboard boxes the notfather's shirts came in, the notfather who went to work every morning in a brand new starched white shirt and came home in the evening in a wrinkled white shirt with yellow sweat stains front and back that was more likely to end in the trash bin than the laundry hamper due to the fact that the notmother, frequently in the grip of a debilitating depression (boxes of chocolates, a stack of romance novels, white wine by the case, *sippy sippy*, and all day in bed), just as frequently allowed her housekeeping duties to lapse. More expedient, then, any reasonable person would agree, for the notfather to buy several boxes of shirts at a time. Glossy white on the outside, pristine as a field of newly fallen snow, they practically cried out for calligraphic intervention, but, alas, the ink of his ballpoint pen smudged on the smooth surface. On the other hand, the boxes were matte gray on the inside, a bit dull but the ink held fast. He cut the bottoms from the boxes with the notmother's (unwittingly made complicit) sewing scissors, with his ruler and ballpoint pen constructed graphs with vertical columns listing each lift in the order of his priorities, e.g., press, curl, squat, and horizontal bars where he noted the weight lifted, sixty, eighty, a hundred pounds, and how many sets (three, four, five) and repetitions (five, ten, fifteen, twenty), eventually adding space for comments: good, bad, great, tired, etc. Unfortunately, every time he changed his routine, which he did often as his theories of the proper way to lift the iron continued to evolve—all wrong, of course, completely misguided, uninformed, no different than reading tea leaves or divining from the flight of birds—he had to abandon his current chart, which, if not exactly lapidarian, was largely indelible, and start another, methodically drawing new lines and columns, neatly printing, in the new order, the exercises to be performed, entering after each session the weights lifted, one hundred, one twenty, one forty, his comments, whether positive or negative, good, bad, *great!*

It was like a drug, was a drug, every additional five pounds he lifted overhead another brick in the monument he was building to his own delusions of grandeur, every black cast-iron plate he slid onto the bar *skriiiick bang* another gold ingot in the vault, the steadily growing dragon hoard of his wealth and power. Yes, *heroic, wealth* and *power*, the words he used, how he perceived his relationship with the iron, a spiritual calling, warrior's code, kingly. Just to be in proximity to the iron, to touch, handle the rigid cast-iron plates, to close his fingers around the iron bar, infused, invested him with a sense of power. He imagined himself older, bearded, with a mighty physique, like Hercules, in one of those short, um, skirt things guys wore in ancient Greece? Okay, that sounded weird (*skirt?*). Maybe just bare-chested, in a pair of tight jeans, and boots, definitely boots (work? cowboy? those swashbuckling knee-high boots the Three Musketeers wore?), and walking two giant mastiffs, no, tigers, Bengal tigers, on leashes, around the high school track during the Homecoming Parade, and everyone, the cheerleaders waving pompoms and all the people in the stands, would see, look at him, how *great* he was. Ridiculous, of course, pure adolescent fantasy. No *grown* man or woman would take such an idea seriously … um, unless they saw it on TV, a commercial for men's cologne? ladies' razors? a six thousand horsepower, double rear-axled, all-wheel drive with twin mounted eighty-eight millimeter deck cannons that the meat eater, meat getter, he-man of the house is dying to have? Mind manic, fed by too many sugary caffeine drinks, Slurpees, slushies, mocha loca lattes *wheee*, his dreams of glory soared even higher. He imagined himself a great potentate of industry, he'd own palaces, a private spaceship, fly around the globe in minutes for urgent meetings with kings, presidents, prime ministers (not sure what those were). But always this inchoate vision of himself doing something not just important but great, in a nutshell, saving the world, which somehow involved his ability to lift more weight over his head than anyone had ever lifted before. Exactly how he was going to accomplish all this irrelevant, a minor detail, leave it to his cabinet members. He knew it could be done, that he could do it, because he wanted it to be done. That simple. Ignoring his own sophistry, ignorant of the meaning of sophistry. No more unrealistic than discovering a secret charm in a cereal box, or receiving a magic potion from a wise old wizard who lived in a red and white capped, mushroom-shaped (*Amanita phalloides*, of course) cottage in the forest and who knew all the curative, restorative and even poisonous properties of all the genera and species in the plant kingdom. But in exchange for what? Money? His soul? Because there had to be some kind of payment. Nothing is free in this world, right? Ah, but he hadn't learned that yet, had he? Still a naïf, innocent, babe in the woods—*run! It's the green man!*

Above all else he sought to prove the equation that brute strength equaled invulnerability, that he could fend off bullies, oppressors, death itself. In this at least he agreed with, conceded to, the general consensus of what manhood entailed, brute strength, invulnerability, the ability to pulverize stone in the mortar of his rage, to forge his loneliness and fear into cold unfeeling iron. Knowing full well it wasn't true, that deep inside his slowly building corpus fortress he was still crushed beneath his own cowardice and fear, that his castle keep was vulnerable not just to catapults and battering rams, mangonels, trebuchets and ballistas (boy child, that's what he retained from medieval history), but words, pointed words, barbed, mocking, hateful words. He walked the halls in school, sat in class, rode the bus to and from school with that useless strength brooding inside him while his eyes darted about like mice in a shoebox, constantly on the alert for the next assault, a hand on his shoulder, a sucker punch planted square in his face when he turned a corner in the hallway, an elbow in the ribs, a leg stuck out to trip him, a spit wad launched across the auditorium during study period, a simple snicker or taunt directed his way in the cafeteria, his peers, male, mean, cruel, bullies looking for a fight, for someone they could mock, humiliate, put into flight without a fight. But that wasn't even his greatest fear, the fear that penetrated his shield of invulnerability, filled him with an ache and yearning beyond anything he'd ever felt before at the very same time it weakened him like kryptonite, threatened to bring him to his knees. When he saw a young female face, a pretty face, even if only pretty to him, a face glowing with warmth and intelligence, a face that might smile, show some small kindness, but then, if she even glanced in his direction, even by accident, he looked away, *embarrassed*, what if she knew he was looking, *staring*, at her? While inside himself, this body, his, he longed for, *desired* something he knew nothing of, *physical contact*, which might possibly be defined, named in a single word, which was what? *Touch?* Meaning to hold hands? Or hug? Or even *Kiss?* How did one kiss, what did it feel like? *Her hungry mouth pressed against his. His hot burning lips.* Or was the word he was searching for more profound, animal-like, atavistic, that he, yeah, kinda knew something about, well, not exactly, a word he never, hardly ever, used, said. *Fuck.* But, oo, yuck, why would he even want to do that? Was there an explanation in the physics class he paid no attention to? Magnetic attraction? Quantum entanglement? But no matter how strong this strange attraction, despite the words the other boymen used, yea, insisted he use by their collective will, by the social template they modeled, he never thought of a girl like that, never dissected, butchered into *What're you having today, sir? How are the tits and ass? I'd recommend the pork loin.* But how to call, to describe that thing, that place between her legs, he could only barely begin to, couldn't really imagine, what it looked like, how did he, his body, connect to that? But not like that, not that far yet, as we said, still an innocent, a naïf, the boy needs a mentor, teacher, someone to explain to him how these things work, to encourage him. But whatever you do, don't ask the notfather. Good God, Martha (or Clementine or Victoria), are you out of your mind? Let the boy learn the way I did, in the locker room. But even if there were someone, wise, experienced, a mentor, *wizard*, just try to tell this stupid kid, explain to him, this total blockhead, the facts of life, set him on the straight and narrow, the road to success, hard work! duty! your life for your country! Forget it. Punk's not even listening, too absorbed in his illusory little world, on cloud nine ten eleven because of that bomb set off inside him by that vital, virginal (presumptive, who knows, maybe, maybe not in these liberal—libertine?—times) female presence, by something that made her more than just a *girl*, the soft skin and the eyes and the mouth and the soft plump pillows of her lips he, yes, *yearned* to press his mouth against and something else, not perfume, not yet, or maybe just a hint, an experiment, a friend let her try, but that fresh young female scent exuding from god knows where or what part of her body, something to do with green meadows, fresh cream, the scent of lilacs blooming in a dooryard, of peach and cherry blossoms carried on a spring breeze. Really? *That?* From *him?* Did someone say *romantic? poet?* But what if, just supposing, yes, yes, impossible, of course, purely conjecture, for the sake of argument, but what if a girl *did* look at him, who knows, maybe even flirted with him, met his eyes with her eyes, her lips, soft, ripe, parted with longing, even if it was only in his mind, he only imagined it, they were in class together, she brushed past him, maybe her skirt made contact with his leg, okay, his *pant* leg, her bare forearm touched his wrist, golden down brushed his skin, nothing more, and still the thrill, something he'd never felt before, a warmth and tingling, an electric current infused, flooded, the salt seas, the oceans, his entire being, he was a fuse, black powder, his whole body, his brain sizzling, his face flushed red, hot, aflame, his legs rubbery, weak. And what if she actually did look at, spoke to him, directly, in his eyes, even smiled at, said hello, acknowledged him, his existence, briefly raised him up out of the primordial swamp, the slime, an anonymous amoeba, splat of protoplasm, yes, you, boy, I, a girl, am speaking to you. No! impossible! A monster! He was a monster! He had to turn away, avoid her gaze, avert his horribly disfigured face, his hunch-backed, twisted body, *Quasimodo! leper!* Okay, not that bad, overly active imagination, his mind can't sit still in its seat, but nevertheless, regardless, whatever the truth, however you want to say it, too bashful, too shy, reserved, too afraid to talk to her, to say hello in return, how are you, would you like to take a walk, hold hands, get something to drink, see a movie, kiss in the dark in the park, wander across the meadow in the warm sun and the bee hum, in the smell of sweet green grass and the fragrance of wildflowers and lie down naked and kick and bleat like a goat and laugh like a nymph, a satyr, but no no no, not that, not yet, maybe not ever, a *monster*, how could he even think of such a thing, this force, need, obsession that drove him home and down into the basement to take off all his clothes and lie naked on the cold cement floor with the damp frigid air stinging his flesh, a young ascetic, practicing for a lifetime ahead of wandering in the desert (a notion possibly derived from a cult following TV series about a Shaolin priest), even more extreme than that, living in a cave, an anchorite, hermit, growling like a beast at anyone who came near, but whatever you do, boy, *Don't touch that thing!*

No, don't think about that, he couldn't think about that, okay, just for that he was going to lift like that, na—*don't say it*—ked, just to prove to himself, to deny, because he had a workout to complete, he had to stick to his routine, he had to accomplish everything he planned to do that day, he had to finish all the sets and reps and nothing less, he had to breathe in and breathe out and count every rep to himself *one-two-three-four-five-six-seven-uhh-eight-uhhh-nine-argghh-ten*, he had to infuse and penetrate that cold iron bar with his own warmth and desire the way he would a young girl's body if if if he was a country boy out in the boonies, in the hoot'n holler'n hills and lush green valleys with a country girl, dairy maid, shepherdess, dryad and he knew how—to penetrate a body that is, female preferably, gender *girl*, with his, this, *thing.* Although such a proposition was impossible at that time. There was to be no girl for him, no young woman, temptress, nymph, dream lover. Prevented, prohibited, not only by his own bashfulness, his own certainty that he was some sort of monster, but because he had been consecrated in the concept of sin, of thou shalt not, dirty, filthy, how dare you, denial, because, surrogate, proxy for that thing he denied, he had become consecrated in the iron, because somehow, somewhere in the struggle, in the conquests and failures of one, two, three, four years he became more determined than ever, developed a will, a purpose, he had to increase the weight on the bar, he had to add more weight to that weight, he had to struggle and strain, he had to push himself harder, he had to take a deep breath and get one more rep, *fiiive!* he had to exhale and expel the hot ruined air from his lungs even as he struggled to breathe in again *siiix!* his breathing more labored with each additional rep, *sehhhhven!* counting to himself in his head (the notfather, remember?) and then out loud in a harsh, aspirated whisper *ayyyyyyt*, gasping for air before he began the next rep, *huh-huh-huh*, *niiiine*, encouraging, cheering on, giving himself a pep talk, come on, you can do it, one more, *huh-huh-huh-huh*, *mmmmmmmuhhh*, *ten!* His whole body, all the muscles in his body, rigid, rock hard, engorged with hot blood and the iron bar engorged with hot blood, unbearable, to have it so close, to feel the need to touch and only himself to touch, as if by accident, *I didn't mean to, God*, until he couldn't stand it anymore, he had to take that blood engorged iron bar in his callused hand and, a few quick strokes, not necessarily pleasure, desperate, release himself, explode, then collapse, sink to his knees on the cold hard cement floor, supplicant, penitent, condemned *off with his head!* like that, all alone, depleted, desolate, his body, *soul*. When he should have climbed up those creaking wooden stairs, climbed up out of that dark, damp cellar, that hole in the ground smelling *stinking* of cess and decay, of seeping bone water and graveyard earth, climbed up out of and abandoned forever that (say it) *dungeon* and plunged into the hot red matrix of the sun and the green pungence of the grass in the meadow, in his nostrils so green-O, in the softness and warmth of her body joined with his *oh oh oh*. Some future his. Maybe never his. An ugly, stupid jerk like him? A monster? And only then feel the cold and emptiness in his body, in his chest cavity, chapel, hollow, the cold and ache in his bony knees jammed against the cold hard cement floor, shiver and hurry to put his clothes back on, to cover himself against the ensuing guilt and shame. How could he do such a thing? And beneath the very eyes of God? How could he possibly? It was bad, it was wrong, a *sin!* In gym

class they had a *health and hygiene* day, watched a movie, it
didn't say much, didn't really explain, just enough to confuse,
make things somehow bleak, threatening, *disease*, maybe even
worse, *pregnancy*. And what if the notmother and notfather
knew? Oh that stupid, that worthless boy! If only you had
spoken to him when I asked you to, when I begged and
implored you to inform him, to discuss with him those horrible
and unmentionable although quite necessary, in fact, natural,
although how can anyone describe those horrible activities as
natural, those unnatural acts of abuse to the body, this sacred,
God-given vessel, a God who would never, *ever* … But why
me? Why should *I?* Because he's *your* son.

Because despite the proscriptions against it (church and
state, family and society), no matter how much he himself
proscribed against it, there were occasions, okay, numerous,
when he committed further atrocities of asceticism and rites of
purification, when he lay naked on his bed on a cold winter's
night with the window open and God hovering right over him,
kind of treading water and watching him so that he couldn't
touch himself, mustn't touch, couldn't even think about
touching, his aching priapus, yearning, untouched, he had to put
all his thoughts, energy into something else, he had to think
about the iron, not just the iron but a great iron bridge built of
trusses and girders looming up in the night, and he had to lift
that bridge off its foundation, he had to hold it up high against
the black night sky so that the great ship of humanity with all
fifteen or twenty billion (projected) souls on board could pass
below to safety. But that wasn't, wasn't right, now, now he was
standing *on* the bridge, his naked body, his arms, shoulders,
buttocks and calves frozen, *welded* to the iron girder behind
him, the bitter cold wind howling around him, but he couldn't
move, he could only look down at the black river rushing
between its snowy white banks far below. But why night? Dark,
lonely, desolate night? Why not during the day, it must have
been day, a cold gray day, iron gray, because there was a crowd
of people, a large crowd of people down below, and they were

all staring up at him, they all felt so sorry for him, for his pain and suffering, their faces, their eyes were dark with sorrow and remorse, like a charcoal sketch of a nation in mourning, because he was going to do it, he was going to sacrifice for all of them, he was going to give his life. But wait, maybe there is such a thing as redemption, maybe even a god, because then she came, the girl, the most beautiful girl he'd ever seen, and she was naked too, he could see everything, her breasts, belly, the dark pubic patch, somehow his mind filled in all the details of things he'd never actually seen or experienced, well, okay, maybe he did see, a glimpse, in a magazine he found in the garbage can behind old Mr. Gruber's, and she knelt in front of him, she took his cold iron rod in her soft warm hands and, impossible to believe, to conceive, how did he know? imagine? maybe he saw it in that magazine, she put it in her mouth and it didn't matter whether he wanted her to or not he couldn't stop her because he was frozen to the iron girder and it felt so good, so unbelievably good, her warm mouth and tongue, her soft lips, and the burning, sweet, somehow he knew exactly what it felt, would feel like, never having had that experience, maybe never would, *monster monster monster*, okay, but if you do then you can't do it again for a whole week and you have to make up for it tomorrow, you have to do two extra sets of everything, you have to … touch touch touch, *explode.*

But now you'll get the wrong idea, you'll think all he did was fantasize and *abuse* himself, that monastic game of denial, refusal and spasmic flagellant release. But that isn't true, he worked hard, he suffered for his art, his craft, gave himself entirely to the iron. He was a knight errant, Spartan warrior, Shaolin priest, he learned to endure hardship, pain, the blisters on his hands that broke and bled and burned before they turned into horny callous, the strained muscles, aching joints, the mental stress of pushing himself to the maximum every workout. Anything and everything for his mistress, lover, right? Although he most certainly did not think of the iron in those terms, never would it have occurred to him to equate the cold hard iron with a woman's soft warm body, he didn't have the least concept of a *lover*, of intimacy, a relationship, much less *mistress*, coy, alluring, jilted, scorned, seeking vengeance. And yet, like that errant knight, uncourtly, false lover, he tested his commitment again and again.

In that bleakening time of year when autumn's flaming glory had faded, when old souls had been remembered, a dutiful holiday of thanksgiving and overindulgence had passed and winter descended like a great bird of prey with iron gray skies and an iron cold grip, he had an epiphany, he heard a voice in the night, an angel descended a burning ladder with a message, a suggestion. Or maybe, more warriorly, it was the ancient call of the ram's horn, the clash of sword against shield echoing across the ages that stirred his heart to action. But maybe, more prosaic, it was simply that, elevated to the status of junior in high school (some time travel may be required), he decided to get more involved, meet some people, beef up his college resume, make his mark before it was too late. After all, time flies, tempus fugit, Helios' winged chariot rolling across the celestium waits for no man. To put it briefly, bluntly, in twenty-five words or less, *seven*, he decided to try out for wrestling. Not to be confused with *wrastling*, that atavistic, free-for-all, anything goes, country boy grappling not all that far removed from the ancient Greek pankration, that, yes, he may have engaged in a time or two with other youth, guys in the neighborhood, buddies, kind of. But not that. Rather, the highly technical and physically grueling art of unarmed, hand to hand combat with an opponent of approximately the same size and bodyweight involving throws, take-downs, locks, grips, holds and pins while excluding any eye gouging, punches, kicks, fists or elbows to the face or knees to the groin one might associate with the classical and country boy styles. But oh, impetuous youth, what was he thinking? He quickly realized that he hated everything about this endeavor. He hated the rancid sweat smell of the mats. He hated the regimen and discipline Coach D'Agonistes imposed on him. He hated the intimate contact with another male body. He hated the agonizingly slow-motion, stamina-draining struggle against his opponent. He hated that his strength could be overcome, defeated by the applied principles of science and technology he eschewed, ignored, paid no attention to in the classroom. He hated going out into the cold black night after practice and a shower, sweat still flowing from his body, his damp, clammy clothes clinging to him, the frozen air penetrating his coat and enveloping him in its gelid grip. He hated riding home on the rattling, banging, unheated *activities* bus stinking of exhaust fumes and not infrequently stale puke from some kid who made himself sick *giving it his all*. He hated getting home late and finding the cold slop the notmother left out for him, pork 'n beans and mashed potatoes or a hamburger in a small white lake of hardening grease with mashed potatoes or a plate of boiled to death hot dogs, sauerkraut and *mashed potatoes* even though Coach D'Agonistes said they should only eat lean meat, fresh green vegetables, whole grain bread, and cut out starch, potatoes, white bread, fat and sugar. *Nonsense!* the notmother scoffed. *The man's an imposter! He knows nothing about proper nutrition!* He hated that, already worn out, exhausted and, yes, a tad *frustrated*, even, one might say, *depressed*, not to mention this TV show he really wanted to watch (the Shaolin priest) going on unwatched in some alternate dimension, he still *had* to go down to that damp, cold, stinking basement and lift, make himself lift, weights, the iron, waiting for him, cold, black, gleaming like a poisonous viper. His spirit, drive waning further, dying, as he loaded the fifty pound plates on the bar *skriiick bang*, stared for a moment into the burning white glare of the bare light bulb for some glimmer of hope, inspiration, before he bent down, placed his hands on the bar, here we go, now, *lifffft*. Nothing. He couldn't do it, couldn't move it, not an inch, not a centimeter. He sat down on the wooden bench, his head drooping between his shoulders, doubly defeated, defeated on the wrestling mat, defeated by the iron. Compounded by, added to that, homework undone, never to be done, procrastination turned into inaction when he trudged back upstairs, collapsed on the sofa in the corner in the blue glow of the TV, escaped into that flickering black-and-white medium of fantasy and delusion, and, *yes!* only missed the opening scene, the moment before the arrow struck the hero in the back. Wait, what? Impossible! Will he die? And then the notfather's voice thundering down from the notparents' sanctum sanctorum above, *Turn off that blasted nonsense and go to bed!* And how many more days of denying to himself, the truth, obvious, forcing himself to obey, commit to that unholy contract, *dope, nobody's making you,* before he decided, made the decision, painful, that physical torment in his brain, lying awake tossing and turning, no matter what humiliation, ostracism, directed at him by the other kids, *loser, quitter,* he wasn't going to, didn't, show up for practice the next night? And guess what? No one noticed, cared, said a word.

And now what? Back on the straight and narrow, the true path? Focused entirely, never again would he betray, the iron? On a clear winter day, the sun's cold white incandescence burning in the pale blue sky, the whole world white, frozen, buried in snow, a wonderland, he and his neighborhood buddies (see above) down by the old mill stream, the pond on old MacDonald's farm, particularly fascinating the thick sheets of pale green ice on the surface of the pond, and, who knows, that show on TV, the Shaolin priest (of course he survived), modeling, a mentor to (surely not the producer's intention) an impetuous youth, adolescent male, this thing that came over him, *compulsion,* his whole body carbonated, ready to explode, he undertook to prove or disprove some confused theory of immovable mass met by inexorable force by smashing his knotted fist through a six inch thick block of this ice, although just in case, he wisely (so he thought) chose to perform this feat with his left, or weaker, hand, looking up first with surprise and then shock and then pain when he realized that it was not the block of ice but his hand that he had shattered. Well, not that dramatic, not shattered, *broken*, and not his whole hand, a bone, the external *metacarpal*, at the base of the joint with the *phalange* of the little finger, aka *pinkie*. Of course he didn't know that yet, not exactly, specifically, in those terms. At first he thought it was nothing, tried to tell himself it was nothing, but, no denying it, something didn't look right, the pain wouldn't go away. Even worse, having to report his folly to the notparents whose faces appropriately registered not sympathy, not compassion, but rather a somewhat theatrical, wide-eyed, gape-mouthed incredulity and then outrage because this stupid boy! this imbecile! moron! this complete idiot! *your son*, had disrupted the routine, the status quotidian, not to mention the inconvenience and expense. Someone will have to take the boy to the doctor! And think of the cost! *My ducats! My dollars!* (sic) On the other hand (*ouch*), the offending and offended hand now ensconced, encased, entrapped in the plaster cast (*A Fall On the Ice*, the community daily rag reported, the doctor, of course, knew otherwise), he couldn't help but notice a change in the family dynamic, the notmother's crooked smile, smug, malevolent, that barely suppressed satisfaction *I told you so*, the notfather's deep, heartfelt sigh of relief because despite the doctor's bill and the, let's be frank (or Bob or Brent), annoyance, at least now the boy will have to stop this nonsense.

But of course the boy didn't stop. He put on his thinking cap, ate a can of tuna fish for added brain power, a can of spinach for strength and stamina, and, despite his inability to focus in physics and trigonometry, he rigged up a contraption of levers and pulleys that allowed him to pursue his ~~madness~~ interest, albeit from a different approach, the fixed and rigid arcs, angles and lines of mechanics applied to the soft machine of the human body, his, and possibly even in this process he caught a flash, a mere glimmer—already lost—of another machine that lay somewhere in his future. *Shhh.*

The world turned, the seasons changed. Our hero (in the narrative in his head anyway) did not fail to notice the first breath and intimation of spring in the air. The sun broke through the clouds in Michelangelesque glory, bright green patches of flattened grass appeared out of the melting snow, the swollen purple buds and bare black branches of the maples and oaks gleamed in the spare brilliant light of winter's receding. His injury by now healed, cast removed, that pale, thinner, frail hand and that slightly atrophied arm brought up to standard with a regimen of dumbbell presses and curls, he came home from school and in yet another burst of adolescent exuberance, the sun shining, the temperature soaring all the way up to fifty degrees Fahrenheit (it's practically a heat wave in northern climes), he hauled his pile of iron up out of the basement and out in the front yard and, *oh hubris*, took off his shirt, his shoes and socks and, bare white chest expanding in the brisk air, bare feet firmly planted in a patch of splatted flat green grass ringed with a dirty gray crust of snow, he loaded the bar with the two train wheel sized fifty pound cast-iron plates, a couple of tens and fives, more or less his own bodyweight, more than he'd ever lifted before, slung it to his shoulders, took a deep breath, and pushed, pressed, raised it over his head like a monument to his own existence, actually shouting to himself in his brain *I did it!* and all the angels above, the heavenly host, screaming a joyous ode *He did it! He did it!* and that cute blond passing in the red sports car he noticed at the very moment he locked the bar overhead actually turning to stare at him, O mighty warrior, *he did it!* his face flushed with exertion, with victory and something else he didn't know yet, couldn't have suspected, that careless, that foolish boy, despite the wisdom of ages, the superstitions of elderly relatives sweatered and swathed in solemn black and brown wool in the middle of summer even though it's a sweltering hundred degrees *beware of drafts! the evil eye! the full moon!* translated into modern medical language, germs, bacteria, *disease* borne upon the chill spring air, sent searching by an inadvertent sneeze, a casual squeeze of a doorknob, a turn of the faucet in the boys' room at school, the touch of the flush handle on a urinal, searching, seeking, viral little Argonaut, for an immune system weakened by lack of proper sleep, the absence of a healthy diet, by worry and anxiety, whether it's the undone, never to be done homework or yet another bully he can't make himself stand up to at school or the notfather roaring down at him through the ceiling, the celestial firmament of carpet and planking, *You blasted moron! You worthless idiot!* or the notmother's increasingly vocal proclamations of doom and catastrophe, *The sky is falling! The end is near!* as well as her endless spying and snooping (is it him, the true one, my own notson, bringer of the apocalypse?). There she was this very instant, peering at him through the kitchen blinds, he saw the contempt, the gleam of hatred in her eyes, he saw her lips moving, muttering incomprehensible curses, incantations. He still didn't suspect anything that evening when he lay in bed, finally turned off the light, unable to sleep, restless, twisting and turning the night away, all these issues, concerns, didn't really notice the itching and scratchiness in his throat, didn't see anything unusual about the soreness in his arms and shoulders and back. Four-five hours later, finally fallen asleep, just, and it's already time to get up, get ready for school, but … s'up? Yesterday's flush of victory turned to fever, his nose, mouth, sinuses clogged, his head throbbed, aches and pains all over his body, shivering convulsively, a nauseous revolt taking hold in his stomach. But neither the notmother nor the notfather said, the boy seems to be under the weather, ha, ha, yes, under the weather, maybe you should take him to a doctor, maybe you should make him some chicken soup, maybe we should just ignore him, yes, ignore him. As for staying home from school? Nonsense. Toughen up. *Back when I was a kid* … The next two weeks he coughed and sneezed nonstop, drained nasty yellow-green slime and snot, alternately sweated against a fever, shivered against a chill, but he missed, skipped, was absent not a single day of class, *soldiered on*, to which his teachers and classmates must have thought but didn't say, Thanks a lot! Worse, winter returned with *a fury* a cold hard blast that added to his suffering, increased his shivering, shuddering misery. Further punishment for his impulsive act, he was too sick to lift weights, every movement, even picking up a five pound plate, produced a deep muscle ache, like a sword stabbing, plunging. All of it a conspiracy, of his own mind, body, of the elements, of a pantheon of gods on Olympus who mocked and reviled mortal pretensions, to ruin him, unnerve and enervate and prevent him from achieving his goals, as of yet imprecise, unstated, hadn't really thought about that. He didn't even begin to suspect it might be something else, a buzzer going off in his head, that little man in the control booth responsible for self-preservation warning him that he just might be on the wrong path. Wait, what? *Shhh.*

And so our young Spartan learned, had further inculcated in his brain, the old refrain, do not complain, do not expect solace, sympathy, *care.* When his head throbbed like a coconut being crushed beneath an elephant's foot—could it be the blackened, carbonized actually, liver and onions (long before Cajun cuisine made the scene) the notmother placed upon the dinner table that night?—or his stomach roiled like a barrel of cod-liver oil tossed about in a stormy sea—a product of the notmother's French phase? Shrimp and asparagus hollandaise *made with real mayonnaise* (out of a jar, out of date, thought it tasted funny, the notfather said, *urrp!*)?—or cramped and burned as if Torquemada was twisting his intestines with a pair of red hot irons—the notmother's attempt at kimchi (the Asian wave)?—he stifled his moans and groans and rocked himself to sleep in his solitary sick bed. When he strained a muscle in a sloppily executed overhead press or dropped a five pound weight on his big toe, left foot, he limped when he was out of the notparents' sight, clenched his teeth when in. And not once did the notfather ever say, Hey, what's wrong, buddy? Got a charley horse in the ol' hamstring? Pull a muscle in the ol' throwing arm? Here, let me rub in some of this Tiger Balm.

Just to note, record, for whomever might be keeping track (Santa Claus? God? The Feds? Anybody (and therefore everybody) with access to your e-ID?), that as he aged, matured, not that those two qualities necessarily have anything to do with each other, as he became more Spartan in his physical needs and resistance to suffering, his ship of state increasingly restricted itself to a narrower strait, a Corinthian Channel, one might say, in the waters of life. The iron grown from a simple interest, an avocation or hobby, to the single most important thing, the one and only, not just the focus in his life but, yes, say it, *obsession*. Maybe it was always an obsession, from the first time he wrapped his fingers around the cold iron bar and felt that infusion of energy, that gravitational pull inside his body, his brain, possibly something like a magnet must feel tossed into a pile of iron filings, except that he was both magnet and iron, he had to draw together, attract and assemble all those disparate particles of iron into a single mass, more than anyone had ever lifted before (However much that was—did he even know? No.), and he had to raise it over his head and hold it there, steady, unwavering, as if he himself were an iron beam, for the whole world to see, and he must accomplish this goal no matter what obstacles were thrown in his path. So convinced of the rightfulness and attainability of this goal that he foresaw no insurmountable obstacles, no impossible mountains to climb, no course-altering setbacks, only success, glory, fame. Keeping in mind that he had no coaches or trainers, no school bands, cheerleaders or pep rallies to assist and support him in his quest. Nor did he have the slightest idea of the relationship between physical strength and physical well-being, specifically, proper nutrition. After all, how would he know, how could he guess that all this time the notmother had been serving him poisoned food at the dinner table? *Taste this before I present it to the king.* Everything they ate saturated with lard, bacon fat, grease, margarine, butter, salt, sugar, corn syrup, the grayish ground beef, the chicken in assorted, not necessarily related, pieces, the fish frozen, thawed and cooked into an unrecognizable, pallid mush, the fruit and vegetables mostly canned, rarely fresh, and if they were the notmother cooked them to death. Absolutely zero sense of the value of food. That, one, it should be healthy, healthily grown and raised and healthy for you, and two, yes, it should taste good. But no, those are not considerations for ravenous animals or people who act like ravenous animals, just eat, gobble, masticate what's put before you and be pleased, *thankful*, to have that.

But the hell with all that, the negativity, the notmother's can't can't can't, and full steam ahead, into the breach, *hasta la victoria siempre* (huh?). He wasn't going to let anyone or anything stop him. He'd show them all. They'd see. Hmm, hold on a minute, *they?* A little *paranoid*, you say? Suggestions of mental instability? Not just obsession but *madness?* What about that counting thing? Wasn't supposed to mention that, was I? When he drank at the water fountain he counted to himself one, two, three, four, five, six, when he peed in the urinal in the boy's room he counted to himself seven, eight, nine, ten, eleven, twelve, when he entered the school, pushed through the glass doors of the foyer, walked straight forward thirteen, fourteen, fifteen, sixteen, seventeen, eighteen, nineteen, when he turned right and walked down the hall, twenty, twenty-one, twenty-two, twenty-three, the composite tiles beneath his feet alternating checkerboard-like from charcoal black with bone white highlights to bone white with charcoal black highlights, he counted the steps, twenty-four, twenty-five, twenty-six, twenty-seven, twenty-eight, to his homeroom, 112, somehow tangled up in the cabala and numerology of graphs and charts he carried in his head, how many sets and reps he did yesterday, the day before yesterday, how many he would, hoped, planned to, do today, tomorrow.

Madness, I say again. And don't ask how many years it might take to undo that madness, don't suggest that it was madness, he didn't even realize himself that it had become an obsession and maybe madness until the notmother and notfather tried to separate him from that madness. I don't mean like in the old days with whippings and beatings and threats of imprisonment in the attic or the insane asylum, prefrontal lobotomies, Thorazine-induced catatonia, electroshock therapy (it's back in vogue! all the rage!). They didn't know it was that bad yet themselves, they had no idea. But the signs were there, the evidence mounting, his insistence upon, resistance to any suggestion of change in his routine. Even if it was just a miserable one week summer vacation the notfather had been promising himself the last ten years, even if it was just to go visit poor old Granny in the country one last time before they planted Granny in the strawberry patch, even if it was just a single day, a glorious Sunday afternoon in October the autumn of his senior year when the air turned crisp and cool and smelled of wood smoke and the world was ablaze with color and the notfather suggested a drive in the country, the whole family, to rejoice in nature's beauty and bounty, to see the leaves changed from verdant green to a palette of orange and red and yellow, and maybe stop at a roadside stand along the way and buy a jug of apple cider, some decorative ears of Native American corn and a big orange pumpkin. And of course, he, the boy had to come along, couldn't leave the boy home alone, never know what trouble the boy might get into on his own. The notfather wouldn't hear any protestations, wouldn't allow any objections. You're going and you'll like it! Now shut up or I'll break your neck! Because this daytrip was his, the notfather's, sole opportunity to corroborate the commonly held notion of the family on a—what else?—family outing, even if the only evidence they had of such a thing came from the TV where examples of such family activities seemed not only incomprehensible but so alien they might have been beamed from Mars. He sat in the back seat, fuming, fretting, squeezed between his putative siblings, fatass and bagofbones, trapped, not moving, trying not to touch, to become infected by contact with indolence, sloth, closing his eyes to, putting on the blinders, refusing to see the whole world resplendent with the funereal raiments of the sun king, to witness the glorious dying of the light, to … trapped, in other words, between the repugnant flesh of his presumptive siblings and the walls closing tighter inside his skull, all this energy swarming inside him without a pressure gauge, safety valve to release, turn it loose, let it go. Only that gradual dissipation, entropic, he could *feel* the strength slipping, ebbing, from his body, feel the particles of iron breaking, freeing themselves from their molecular bonds, like a swarm of bees exploding from a hive and evaporating into the atmosphere, feel the leaden weight of kryptonite crushing him into the car seat. He was like Antaeus, torn, separated from, his mother earth, raised above, out of reach of her warm embrace, helpless. If only he could retain a modicum of his strength, do something to prod his muscle memory. Every time the car stopped for a bathroom break or to read the plaque on some roadside monument or the family was having lunch under a rustic (rotting) park pavilion, he had to break free, run up and down the mountainside with a log balanced across his shoulders until his legs were weak and rubbery, he had to heave and toss around boulders in a dry stream bed until his arms burned and cramped. *Idiot! Fool!* If only he had allowed himself to relax, let go, to free himself from the tyranny of the iron for just that one day and revel in nature's beauty, in the beauty of a girl his age, black hair, bangs, cute face (freckles, soft, they looked soft, pink lips, *green?* eyes), who may actually have been sneaking glances at him when they stopped at the picturesque overlook. But no, our young man of iron, our Spartan warrior, spent the entire day denying, cancelling out, refusing to see, enjoy, *the ineluctable modality of the beautiful*, only the iron waiting for him, black, gleaming like a madman's grotesque smile in that dank, gray basement, in that prison cell, solitary confinement of his own mind, even as this glorious autumn day, God's gift, gratis, to mankind, passed into afternoon and then dismal evening gloom and the melancholy, miasmic purple and orange swirl of clouds on the horizon before darkness and night finally fell and the headlights came on, knowing it was too late now, irrevocably too late, that by the time the notfamily car pulled up the drive outside the notfamily home and everyone piled out of the car and inside, grunting and growling in anticipation of the quick fix dinner, hamburgers, the notmother burnt black in a boiling lake of bacon fat in a black, grease-caked frying pan and everybody gobbled smothered in sweet, piquant ketchup and tangy mustard wrapped in puffy, pillowy white buns, between bites of burger shoveling handfuls of greasy potato chips into their mouths, snorting and chomping, he was too, hungry himself, desperate, ain't gonna be nothin' else on the menu, *fucking animals*, all of them, oughta be shot, put in a zoo, in the barnyard, *moooo*—after all that he'd be too tired, drained, enervated, freighted with that indigestible lump in his stomach, to make himself go down to the iron. And then what? Lie awake that night, in the darkness, in that hollowness, vacuum, empty space. Mulling over the failure and loss of this day. Nothing. He had done nothing, accomplished nothing. He was nothing.

This darkness, this sense of *worthlessness* that came over him, unforeseen, unexpected, this crushing weight of hopelessness and doom pressing down on him, the product of lunar tides, the full moon at night *owooo*, of events both cataclysmic (a huge zit that appeared on his nose) and mundane (the war on TV day after day after day after …), even worse in winter when the darkness and gloom closed in earlier every evening and the thought of going down in that damp cold basement filled him with dread, when wrapping his hands around the cold iron bar made him shiver as if he'd been doused with ice water, triggered detonations of pain, minor, warning signals, a dull ache in his lower back, a sharp stab in his left deltoid, suggestions of future, more serious, complaints? Too far on the distant horizon for him to care? Even worse still, this great black-winged wraith of despair that descended upon him with the advent, arrival of that special time of year, holly and mistletoe, the Yule log burning on the hearth, the notfamily enjoying, making merriment, reveling in this one day of the year when even they, monsters all, *animals*, put on their false faces, smiled and *acted* as if they were so happy together when they sat down at the communal table and ate, devoured, massive quantities of turkey, cranberry sauce, sage and chestnut stuffing with giblet gravy, baked sweet potato pie topped with marshmallows, cornbread, sweet rolls, dill pickles, green olives stuffed with red pimentos from a jar and rubbery black olives from a can, for dessert, mincemeat pie, figgy pudding, hand churned ice cream, the notmother miraculously revived, raised up from her own valley of despair, reanimated for this one special day of the year, everybody gorging themselves to their heart's content and beyond, to the extent of utter insensibility, bellies swollen, bloated, aching, belts, buttons, zippers undone, groaning, barely able to move, sulfurous and nitrous gases bubbling and stewing and beginning to breach the rectal gates of the corporeal fortress like volleys of cannon shot, and yes, he did, participate in, partake of, eat, gorge, stuff himself, food instead of, a surrogate for, a paucity of, love, but even on that festive occasion, that day of merriment, joy, *unto us a savior*, he would not allow himself that pleasure, indulgence, until he first went down into that damp cold dungeon, performed his daily penance, demanding of himself even as he heard the laughter and merriment (canned? the radio? TV?) overhead *don't think about that*, forcing himself even as the strains of music penetrated his ears *forget about that*, reminding himself that first and foremost he must always think of the iron *Rudolph the Red-Nosed Reindeer.*

And all that time the whole world in tumult, the millennial, centennial, perennial war *over there*, the war here at home, MRAPs and APCs in the mean streets, gunshots, explosions, his cohort, *peers*, teens toting guns, teens killing teens, teenage alcoholism and drug addiction, teen pregnancy and gang activity, but don't say *shit* or *fuck*, don't say *bigotry, racism*, don't say *greed, corruption, c-c-cap-cap-capitalism*, those words somehow worse than the actual acts, deeds, the unspoken philosophy that all are not created equal, that a select few (selected by whom? God? Yes, of course, on good terms, BBF) are entitled to more, much more, than all the rest. But not for him any fine lines of distinction, no shades of gray, no need to question, know, seek out facts about who or what or why. His solution simple. Smash them! Kill them all! Either they fall in line or we annihilate them! Again, not sure who this *they* is. These sudden tirades he launched into in Social Studies class to the horror of his teacher, in homeroom to the shock and surprise of the small group of students he might have called his friends *if only he didn't act so crazy!* at the dinner table at home before the stunned notparents. He himself stunned, surprised at these outbursts, at this alien force that seemed to arise out of some unknown reservoir inside him like a malevolent jinn out of a soot blackened smudge pot instead of a golden lamp, that somehow conflated the glory of the iron with *power*. But not just the power he wielded over, the power he derived from, an insignificant little iron bar. He was going to lift the whole world over his head and hold it there according to his own grossly uninformed (*the EEG says the patient is brain-dead, Doctor*) concept of order, a perfect young tyrant, dictator in the making, might even grow up one day to become president of this great nation (you never know), completely delusional in his sense of (un)reality and his (mis)understanding of how things really worked (or didn't), entirely removed from the real (debatable) world around him, didn't pay attention in class, didn't read the newspaper, never opened books or magazines, never discussed current trends and issues with his teachers or peers, much less with the notparents, almost certainly never surfed the web or texted.

The iron his only anchor, his tether to the earth. And his ball and chain. When other boys, young men his age, were twisting the night away at the sock hop in the high school gymnasium, or hurtling down the back roads in their hot rod jalopies at a hundred miles an hour with a beer in one hand and a girl in the other and nothing on the wheel while the car careened along by itself into the black forests and ravines of the night with a song of love and heartbreak blasting on the radio as they crashed through the guardrail, or, more safely, maybe, parked along a lonely farm lane for some hot and heavy kissing and petting and maybe even just about to *do* it when *Aieeeee!* a

bloody hand slaps on the windshield, i.e., whatever boys and
girls his age did, were supposed to do (homework? calculus,
chess and badminton clubs?), he was down in that lousy
stinking basement banging and clanging like a rogue pile driver,
a little humanoid steam shovel run amok. He didn't need a
hotrod, jalopy, bulldozer or other machine, he was the machine,
he was the force, the momentum and drive, the controlled
explosions of internal combustion, pounding pistons, the black
narcotic sump of oil pumped out of the ground and refined into
liquid sunlight and ignited by the primal fire of thunder and
lightning. He got that machine going and drove it as fast and
hard as any drunken teenage kid full of moonlight and
moonshine and heading toward that fatal collision not with a
tree trunk or bridge abutment or over a cliff into a ravine but
into the abyss of madness, into the concrete wall of mental and
physical exhaustion, of whatever it took to achieve, accomplish,
win this goal *victory*. Not even a machine, not that modern.
More like a caveman beating a saber tooth tiger to death with a
rock or a bone or his bare fist, because in his mind it was still
raw strength, power, that atomic explosion of youthful energy
and lust for life channeled, directed, forged into that dead black
iron. But don't say that! Never say that! The iron is not dead!
You are not dead! *You are not dead!* And yes, sure, believe if
you want that his was a glorious and heroic struggle to raise up
the molten iron in the middle of darkness and create a new era
in the cosmos and light the way forever for all generations to
come. Believe it was that and not yet another all too familiar
tale of a lost, lonely young man, a boy still, struggling to make
sense of life and the world spinning crazily around him.

Once again the cogs and gears engage, the world turns,
the seasons change. The air filled with the scent and perfume of
rebirth and rejuvenation, renaissance and recreation. The sun
shone, flowers bloomed, spring sprang sprung anew. He
graduated from high school with the usual mortar boarded and
gowned pomp and circumstance, marched in a file, two by two,
his partner a varsity cheerleader who never gave him a second

glance in homeroom but now as they marched along *step one, step two* professed with breaking voice all sorts of sentimental nonsense *we're growing up, we're going out into the world* that he dismissed with a cynical sneer. No, no longer a boy but a young man dreaming of flight and escape from the notmother and notfather and the constraints of home and society without any idea of how to escape, his only horizon a whole summer of iron ahead of him, a gladiator, Spartan, Roman Centurion's idea of summer vacation, a steamy sultry paradise of sweat and flexing muscles, the clang and bang of iron and steel in his arena, training hall, for all he knew and was concerned his only occupation from now until the end of time. A halcyon vision that inspired him to carry his entire collection of weights, dumbbells, barbell, cast-iron plates, DIY bench and rack up out of that hole in the ground and out to the garage, an old car barn actually, a vestige of the transition from equine transportation to internal combustion (appropriately for our little hot rod), when horsepower went from hay and oats to oil and gasoline, from domesticated draft animal to—him? *beep! beep!* A dim, drafty structure, somewhat shabby, rundown, long unused tools stacked in the corners, the rafters and cabinets clotted with dust, cobwebs and rats' nests, uncertain containers—rotting cardboard, corroding tin—of rodent and insect poison, petroleum products, soldering paste, a glass phial of fascinating but insidiously toxic quicksilver that beaded up and rolled in the palm of his hand, completely unfathomable, metal in a liquid state, not even molten, melted by the forge of his body, the heat of his passion, but cold, heavy, *metallic*, and exuding a seductive hint of death. All of those things he noticed closely because, displaying an industry that shocked the notparents, not, of course, understanding his intent, he forced open and pushed aside the old folding door, creaking, rusted rollers, springs and levers, swept and cleaned, tossed out, rearranged and transformed this musty old barn into his gymnasium, traded the stink and decay of the, yes, true, *cooler* basement dungeon for, yes, the heat and dust but also the vista of sunshine, green grass, trees and blue sky he looked out upon as he pursued the art of iron, lifted weights, *bang clang.*

Every day he went out to the garage clad in a loin cloth, okay, a pair of shorts, tattered, faded, cut-off denims, plaid bermudas, his old gym shorts *Go Tigers!* Otherwise, yes, pretty much naked, his bare feet leaving damp footprints on the dusty cement floor, his bare skin glistening, pores opening like spillways, gates in a dike, the saltwater of his own internal seas flowing from his forehead, chest, from his back and under his armpits, the sweat burning in his eyes, in the torn callouses on his hands. The heat made him torpid, every lift a monument of the will, after each set collapsing on the bench, his head drooping, dripping sweat, a small dissident voice he'd never heard before urging him to turn his back on the iron, go lie in the cool shade of the giant old oak tree on the corner like a hillbilly hayseed, or take off all his clothes and lull like a Pannish satyr in a cool, clear stream in a sylvan glade where she lay in her own nakedness and desire, drops of sweat beading on her breasts, her eyes feline, half-closed, what would it be like to touch her, to place his hands on her breasts, to press his body against hers, to—stop it, sir! You mustn't think about that! He couldn't think about that, he had to concentrate on the iron, he had to get up, stand up, finish this last set right now, *this instant.* He stood, Prometheus unchained, Samson preparing to bring down the temple, shook his arms to limber up his muscles, to ready himself for the final attempt, bent down, grasped the bar in his hands, began to exert effort, *uhhh* ... but no, huh-uh, at the least resistance he realized, knew, he couldn't, wouldn't, wasn't even going to try. He sat back down on the bench, picked up his chart, wrote down the date, beneath that the weight on the bar and next to that the number of repetitions he had anticipated completing. It wasn't lying exactly, not cheating, he was certain he could do it, lift that weight, it if wasn't so hot, if he didn't feel so sluggish, if his mind was clearer. Tomorrow, tomorrow, he'd lift this weight, and it'd feel lighter and easier than it ever had before.

III

HIGHER EDUCATION

AND SO IT WENT, would have gone, on, endless, eternal, those idyllic days of summer, the golden glow of youth, the movie playing in his head. And yet, and still, impossible to deny, the light had changed, the breeze carried hints of cooler weather on the horizon, autumnal whiffs of wood smoke and falling leaves. Time, he realized with a sense of melancholy and not a little foreboding, to transport his iron hoard from his garage gymnasium, high raftered, airy and wide open in summer, but drafty, un-insulated and freezing cold in winter, back down into the damp, stinking but, true, also slightly warmer basement. Ironically (that word again), immediately upon making this transition, another change, completely unexpected, unforeseen, occurred. One evening after the burnt offerings and vegetable slop the notmother prepared *double trouble, boil and bubble* for dinner, after an extra slice of cherry pie (store bought) all around, the notmother and the notfather approached, trapped, him in the *living* room in the flickering blue light of the TV in the armchair in the corner where he sat slouched in the shadows like an animal peering out of its cave. They had something important to say, an announcement to make, *ahem!* This fall he would be going away to college. Yes, of course they understood, it must come as quite a surprise. But they had given it a great deal of thought and decided that in this day and age education was the way to go, or at least the way for *him* to go, that is to say, for them to get him out of the house, which, of course, they didn't say. They had settled on a respectable little red brick institution overgrown with a hundred years of ivy in a quiet little college town shoved out in the country and surrounded by abandoned coal mines and inbred farm children where, for a relatively modest donation to the Chancellor's favorite cause, himself, an orangutan might matriculate. Classes were scheduled to begin immediately, he should put his things in order straight away, he would be leaving first thing in the morning. This arrangement was obviously more to the notparents' advantage than his, it gave him precious little time to resist or raise any objections to their arguments. In so many words, this nonsense of the iron had to stop, he had to forget these wild dreams of world conquest and learn something useful and maybe one day actually get a good job in an office building or a bank lifting stacks of paper, preferably cash, and maybe raise a family of his own. Because we're getting older now. Yes, older. And it would be good to have grandchildren one day. Grandchildren. They can listen to our nonsense. Nonsense. And support us in our old age. Old age. Because he never will. No, he never will. Even though the illogic of this train of thought clearly never occurred to them.

When the notmother and notfather heard him clanging and banging down in the basement later that night they smiled and nodded to each other. No need for concern. The boy was going through a ritual separation from that nasty pile of junk, the way he might say goodbye to a pet dog or a stamp collection. When he next came home again—not too soon, one would hope—attired in tweed and puffing cherry flavored tobacco smoke out of the solid briar the notfather had presented to him earlier that evening, extolling the virtues of pipe smoking as a college appropriate activity, he wouldn't even remember that pile of scrap metal he left to molder and rust down in that damp, smelly basement. Maybe now I can finally give it a good cleaning, the notmother said, even though she hardly ever ventured down into that frightful hole herself and certainly had no intention of cleaning it. Yes, a good cleaning, agreed the notfather, who himself had not visited this subterranean chamber since he attempted to fix something years ago and obviously failed, which probably explained that constant trickling sound and the limited, intermittent at best, hot water supply in the bathroom and kitchen. They were both, however, a little surprised to find the notson already up and out of bed the next morning, fully dressed and ready to go, all his bags apparently packed and loaded up in the car late last night beneath a full moon or else in the predawn hours before the first chirp of birdsong or vampire slaying ray of sunlight. This too they took to be a good sign. Any residual fears they had entertained of the boy putting up resistance had been for naught.

On the contrary, he seemed eager to begin his college career. Oh, he was going to make them both so proud. If he did well he might even proceed directly from college to the job and never come home again. They might even enjoy some of his prosperity themselves, remuneration for all the years of unforeseen costs, not to mention the mental anguish, *torture*, this ungrateful wretch caused them. It wasn't until much later, after the notmother had winced and squinted a great deal and finally managed to squeeze out a single teardrop, although it may have been a stray dab of collagen, and said a final word, not to him but rather the notfather, Oh, George (or Stan or Dave), you go on with the boy, you know how these separations distress me, after the notfather and notson had climbed into the notfamily car and backed down the drive and pulled away from the house, the neighborhood, the remnants of his childhood, youth, and the poor old internal combustion beast had banged and thudded over every bump and pothole in the road for the last fifty miles, only after all that did the notfather finally speak up. Say, *son*, what've you got in those bags anyway? Hmm, what a perplexing question. Did the notfather mean what did he, the notson, have in the suitcases and laundry sacks, golf bags and racquet cases he had loaded up and packed into the trunk and back seat of the notfamily car just like any other kid going off to college? *Nothing*, he replied. The notfather tugged at his scalp and muttered, Well, it's a mighty heavy nothing if you ask me. It was the first metaphysical discussion they'd ever had, indeed, probably the only discussion they'd ever had, as if the much-touted father and son bonding that had eluded them for the last eighteen years of their mutual but exclusive existence had suddenly taken hold. He felt a wild and disproportionate surge of sympathy for the poor old notfather, who, yes, could be, had been, a mean sonofabitch, but who was also a rather pathetic wretch, a coward really, who had spent the better part of his life hiding his head in the sand and trying to get along without bucking the system or calling attention to himself. Surprisingly, the notfather, too, seemed inclined toward leniency and adult reasoning. Look, son, why are you bringing along all that junk? Don't you see? You're going to college now. You won't have time for that nonsense. Besides, you're going to ruin the car. And he nodded his head solemnly and seemed to understand. Yes, perhaps it was unwise, certainly something to keep in mind in the future. Because he knew and the notfather knew it was too late now, they weren't going to turn around and go back home, certainly not at the risk of facing the notmother's wrath. Why on *earth* did you allow him to take that junk in the first place?! But I didn't *allow* him, I didn't even know until we were halfway there.

There. Those ivy beleaguered walls of those hallowed halls of higher *we measure success in inches* learning, institutional red brick, tall leaded windows, Monticello columns, chipped and peeling white paint, a general sense of decrepitude one couldn't put one's finger on immediately. The notfather offered to help him carry his bags into the dormitory but a single tug on a suitcase handle confirmed his earlier suspicions as well as his infirm physical condition, which he expressed with a hand on his lower back and the monosyllabic ejaculation *urk!* I'll handle it, the notson said with manly self-assurance, and after quickly unloading everything on the curb and demurring at the notfather's offer, sudden, surprising, startling them both, of a cup of coffee before departing, began to move himself and his belongings into the dormitory, a modern, two story yellow brick building recently built thanks to the generous endowment of a rare alumnal success story (before, that is, his arrest for fraud, conspiracy and embezzlement), where, upon entering his room, number 108, for the first time, he was unable to avoid an awkward introduction to his new roommate. It was immediately clear they had nothing in common but, young gentlemen now, they gentlemanly agreed, tacitly, to a détente, sealed with a quick handshake, a formal exchange of names, the roommate's forgotten as quickly as it was uttered, Tom? (or Jack or Jim), and his, well, this might be a good opportunity to correct a small matter of neglect, i.e., should we finally, at long last, give him, our *hero* (dubious), a name, an identifier to distinguish him from the rest of the protoplasm? Stephen? Karl? Paul? Yevgenni? Pliny the Younger? Something related to his obsession, like *Eisen?* Or *Stahl?* Naw, best leave things as they are. While his new roommate unpacked his high school trophies and pennants, gilt framed photograph of the girl back home, conservative button down oxfords, chinos, docksiders, shaving kit (graduation present from Uncle Harry (or Henry or Hank), with a fifty-dollar bill and a pack of ultra-sheer condoms tucked inside), and all the other vestiges of adolescence transitioning into adulthood, *he* began to extract from his bags and suitcases the two train-wheel sized fifty pound plates, four oddly plumpish twenty-fives, a bunch of tens and fives, his orcish pocket change, and finally, from a rigid, cylindrical fishing rod case, the iron bar with sleeve and collars, all of his dragon hoard he had managed to pack and transport, and little else except a limited wardrobe and toiletries. Of course his roommate had not failed to notice these proceedings, watching with an increasingly wary and then worried expression as the pile of iron accrued. But mum's the word, right?

Later that night, after the roommate had taken a last look

through his stack of newly purchased textbooks, logged off his computer, pried his way between the starched white sheets of a bed made immaculately and militarily tight by the sausages-and-potatoes lumpenprol maids, Olga and Irina, who swept and mopped the floor and changed the linen once a week in their gray socialist-state industrial uniforms (we'll see more of them later), said nighty-night to the cellphone tucked next to his pillow and turned out the reading lamp, our young hero, neither Stephen nor Fred nor Werther, who, long used to pursuing his ferrous if not feral obsession in privacy, had been itching, champing at the bit, *raring*, for the roommate to avert his gaze as it were, now felt an overwhelming urge, okay *need*, to get his quotidian fix of iron. Years of the notfather's tyrannical demand for decorum (silence) had taught him not only to be respectful but discreet, one might even say *stealthy*. Still, it was impossible to avoid some clanking and banging and scraping on the linoleum floor as he loaded a fifty pound iron plate onto the bar *skriiiick, bang*. The roommate turned in his bed. NotStephen waited a moment, then slid another fifty pound plate onto the other end of the bar *skriiiick, bang*. The roommate turned again. NotFred waited another minute before sliding on a twenty-five pound plate, *skriiiick, bang*. A lunar crescent gleam appeared beneath the roommate's right eyelid. NotWerther slid another twenty-five pound plate on the bar, *skriiiick, bang*. The roommate clicked on his reading lamp, threw back the covers and sat up in bed. What are you doing? He (*Outis?*) shrugged like *who, me?* grinned *bashfully*, like a serial killer caught dragging a corpse into the woods. *Nothing*, he said. That word again. Which might have been an opening for him and his roomie to engage in a chasm-bridging, friendship building metaphysical discussion in an epic all-nighter that eventually drew the entire floor into their room for an intellectual battle royale that quickly deteriorated into a no holds barred, biting, gouging and kicking forensic free-for-all with spilled packages of Skittles and empty cans of RedBull everywhere, which, of course, didn't happen. The roommate spent the rest of the night thrashing about in bed while he clanged and banged as quietly as he could.

Henceforth he endeavored to lift when his *roomie* (such a *quaint* term, ga ga, goo goo, my little man) was in class or involved in a social activity (not even two weeks and he already had *friends!*), when unavoidable, he lifted weights, bang, clang, while said roommate bent over his desk *trying* to concentrate on his studies, white noise machine aspirating like a flameless dragon, sound cancelling headphones poaching his brain in a wallow of pop schlock. The roommate had initially speculated that he, unnamed, unsung hero, must be some sort of eccentric genius. He hadn't attended the first week of classes, indeed, didn't seem to know classes had begun despite the sudden burst of activity early one morning, alarm clocks going off up and down the hall, cadres of young ephebes springing out of bed at seven a.m., heading to the showers and scrubba-dub-dubbing themselves squeaky clean among clouds of steam, spraying on antiperspirants and deodorants, brushing and flossing those pearly whites whiter, pulling on preppie button-down oxford collars, pressed slacks and docksiders, slacker Ts, surfer shorts and huarache sandals, and out the door with books, laptops, EyePhones®, and backpacks, while he scratched his head like a country bumpkin who just got off the Greyhound in Times Square. When he did go to class, finally figured out, deciphered the computer print-out, not entirely unlike one of his weightlifting charts, this class at this hour in this room in this building on this part of campus, he sat at his desk, stared out the window, daydreamed of the iron, of the empire he was going to build, of the fantasy she-goddess he was going to meet, although apparently not among his female classmates, *co-eds*, somehow more virtual than real, on a pedestal, so they thought, acted, or maybe, *maybe*, he placed them there, unapproachable, not by him anyway *monster*. As he had done in high school, he dutifully carried his books to class, worried and procrastinated over the composition he had to write for Monday, the biology test he had to study for on Friday, the Algebra homework he had to turn in tomorrow, in the end never wrote a word, read a page, worked an equation, his only focus, devotion, the iron.

Discounting his roomie's disapproval (which he mostly did), he assumed his treasure trove would draw no further scrutiny, but upon returning to the dorm earlier than usual one afternoon he found the previously mentioned maid staff, Olga and Irina, mopping around his weights and complaining to each other in a heavy Russian accent that occasionally devolved into the real thing. Why this student is havink all this junk? Is breakink my back. *Да, это правда, девушка* (you said it, girl). Leaving behind a damp floor and muttering more Slavic anathema (later in life he would learn that *дурак* and *сукин сын* simply meant *fool* and the slightly harsher invective *son-of-a-bitch*), Olga and Irina rolled their mop buckets out of the room and slammed the door behind them like actors leaving a stage (which, of course, they were). Fortunately, their grumbling seemed to be the extent of their discontent, at least for now. Of course neither they nor the roomie could possibly know he had only managed to haul *some* of his weights here in the initial trip, a situation he intended to remedy over the much-touted *long weekend* in early October, designed to allow homesick *frosh* to flee back into the expansive bosom of their families for four days, despite the fact they'd been in daily contact, indeed, multiple times a day, with their hovering, helicoptering, whirly bird parents *got a sighting, Foxtrot Tango, daughter at two o'clock, uh, roger that, Victory Tango, heading in*, there at a touch, an instant, the daughter app, *tap tap tap,* or, the EyePhone® never on mute, ever vigilant, *briiinnng* in the middle of class and the professor be damned, whereas on his home front all he had heard was *quiet*. For the price of a case of beer, he enlisted the aid of an older guy in the dorm (Bart? Bert?—he had a mustache) who not only owned a pickup truck but who also lived commodiously close to his nothome, and thus, following a thankfully brief reconnection with the notparents, he returned triumphant to school at the head of his lost legion, the remainder of his weights, as well as a commercial weightlifting bench and racks bought during a quick stop (negotiated for the additional cost of a bottle of peppermint schnapps) at a sporting goods shop. When *roomie* walked through the door later that day he discovered the young ironsmith cum wildcatter had assembled on his holdings, claim, patch of sod, just say it, his half of the room, something that resembled a small oil derrick, crude, yes, primitive by any standard, pretty sure, however, that it would have made Colonel Drake proud.

Roomie wasn't the only one distressed. One afternoon as the good Colonel's young imitator was in the middle of a set of heavy squats, grunting and groaning and struggling to push out the desired ten reps, six, *sevvven*, huh-huh-huh, *ayyyt*, he heard someone fumbling with the doorknob, the door flew open and in burst the aforementioned *Mädchen* (because the pun doesn't work in Russian, that's why), Olga and Irina, along with Junior, the country bumpkin heehaw janitor who *fixed thangs*, obviously expecting (hoping) to catch him in some ungodly and bizarre act with a sheep or an extraterrestrial, but what they did find him doing seemed even more bizarre and ungodly than anything their provincial brains were capable of concocting, and they didn't like it one bit, they wanted it to stop. *Demonic worship! Hedonism! Idolatry!* And off they marched to complain to the Head Resident, or Dorm Mother, as she was known among the young men under her care (or even *Mom* among her most obsequious suck-ups, upon whom she gazed fondly), the stern, bespectacled, seventyish-something Ms. Gretchen Grimble. Is impossible to clean around this pile of junk! We are not changing this hooligan's linens three weeks because of this obstacle! That's right, ma'am, the young feller's a dadblame nuisance! *What?!* Outrageous! I'll get to the bottom of this! Send the rascal to my office immediately! (Apparently everyone was in an exclamatory mood, that or it was the case of mislabeled caffeinated water the supplier accidentally delivered.) Citing building codes and dorm regulations, Ms. Grimble informed him with a malevolent gleam in her eyes that

she was sorry, so terribly sorry, but the weights had to go. But
… but … but … he sputtered like a worn-out lawnmower
engine … the iron was the only thing that mattered in his life, it
was his soul, his heart's inspiration, his *raisin deter*. Although
not a diligent student by any means, two books *bzzzzzt!*
Misplaced modifier! (in murderous red) from his English
Composition and Rhetoric class fascinated, *enthralled*, him, his
dictionary and his thesaurus, both of which he consulted for the
most poignant (pompous) and passionate (pretentious) words he
could find with precocious *precious?* little concern for their
precise meanings. A feeble five-watt light bulb went on over his
head. Couldn't I (uh-oh, that sounds weak), that is, couldn't *we*
(that's better, strength in numbers, now define your terms), me
and the other guys in the dorm, I mean, couldn't we turn that
little unused storage room in the basement into a weight room,
open it up for everybody to use? The gleam in Ms. Grimble's
eyes grew brighter, more malevolent. I'm so sorry, she repeated,
smiling at him over her glasses like an officious iguana, but I
think the idea of a weight room in the basement … is a terrific
idea! The Resident Assistant on his floor, Roland Strokemore,
aka stoolie, rat, priss, disgusting little sycophant, having walked
in at that very minute without realizing where she, Ms. Grimble,
his *boss*, had been going with that thought, not only finishing
her sentence for her with his usual over the top game show host
cheerfulness (eyes robotically bright, smile glacially white) but
expanding upon his misunderstanding with waxed enthusiasm.
It'll give the guys something to do, keep them out of trouble …
teach discipline … hygiene … physical *fitness?* The cheery tone
in his voice diminishing, *waning*, word by word as, too late, he
realized his fatal mistake, confirmed by the Arctic glare Ms.
Grimble now directed at her impetuous protégé, for the moment
possibly even hating him, before, that is, she remembered who
her true enemy was. The malevolent gleam returned to her eyes,
suggesting the elements of some devious scheme arising in her
mind. Her thin lips tightened into a hideous rictal smile and she
actually hissed like a basilisk, Yesss, maybe it isss a good idea.

Of coursse, it will have to be approved by *Dean Dong*. The name reverberated like a heavy iron bell in the cloistered confines of Ms. Grimble's cheerless gray office. Her smile broadened dangerously, almost clown-like, sending hairline cracks through the powdered porcelain facade of her face, and a hideous B-movie horror film cackle (see link) escaped her lips. After all, regaining her composure, *decorum*, the redoubtable Dean Dong had never let her down before.

Then, there he was, rocking on his penny-loafered heels on the plush Persian carpet in front of the Dean's large mahogany desk in the Dean's richly appointed office with equally plush upholstered chairs and sofas and matching mahogany cabinets, bookcases and shelves, on the walls gilt-framed pictures of various men in the muttonchops and van dykes, military uniforms and formal morning coats current some time in the last two or three centuries, the dean himself a serious man in a serious gray suit, tailored, expensive, only the best, his grave face never troubled with the lines of a frown, much less a smile, seated behind his desk, disinterested, turning a pencil in his pink, manicured fingers, glancing out the window, while he, the petitioner, supplicant, his face red, flustered, his eyes, mind, locked in some kind of looming tunnel vision as he struggled to get out his words, I, that is, he, and some of the other guys in the dorm, wanted to turn the unused storage room in the basement into a weight room, it'd give them something to do, keep them out of trouble … teach discipline … hygiene … physical fitness—his argument augmented (plagiarized?) by the helpful laundry list given him by Roland Strokemore. Finished with his spiel he stood at parade rest, eyes front, chin up, arms behind his back, feet slightly apart, a good little soldier boy awaiting his fate. But wait, was it possible, his oratorical skills somehow hitting the mark? Witness the change in Dean Dong's demeanor, the slight tilt of his head, the arch of his brow, causing a wisp of probably once platinum blond but now oddly banana yellow hair to detach itself from his carefully combed but noticeably thinning bouffant, his attitude mellowed perhaps by the bottle of scotch, single malt, aged seventeen years, he kept in his desk, attested to by the equally yellow tinge in his eyes. Why not? he said as if he were agreeing to a night at the opera. And what could Ms. Grimble say when he returned that afternoon with a note from the good Dean, approving the weight room in the basement. Capital idea! The lad's got something here! (Clearly the scotch talking.) For which she would never forgive him, them, the Dean or the lad.

And so it was that his dragon hoard, junkyard, metal works was transferred into the depths, the nether regions of his dormitory with the understanding that he alone would hold the key to the "weight room," which initially seemed like a good idea, his weights, his key, right? but quickly proved a nuisance, untenable, throughout the day and even at night, *knock knock*, Hey, Dude, can I borrow *the key?* Finally he stopped locking the weight room door, left it open to everybody, told himself it'd be okay, his weights would be safe, I mean I guess. His was an athletic dormitory, not the dormitory itself obviously but its inhabitants, most of them past masters of various ballgames, large hollow rubber balls and hard little rubber balls, fuzzy, furry and feathered balls and oblong leather balls. They all had trophies of their high school triumphs, victories, they wore maroon and slate or black and gold or blue and white letter jackets (a habit that would die by their sophomore year when the ostentatious display of adolescent feats no longer commanded respect among their peers and certainly not their superiors). But this was a brave new world made of brave new friendships regardless of one's previous caste or social standing, Brahmin or untouchable, preppie or nerd. As much as the thought of these crotch scratching ex-jocks putting their greasy masturbatory mitts on his weights filled him with repugnance— he could actually feel sebaceous, *seminal* traces in the knurling of the bar *what is that stuff?*—he also reaped an unexpected benefit: if not exactly popularity among his new cohort, acceptance. Didn't hurt that *roomie* was quickly becoming a BMOC, already had a girlfriend, invitations to fraternity smokers, his cool friends hung out in their room. Everybody lounging on beds, chairs, sitting on the floor, half the time in their underwear, jockey shorts, boxers, some kind of male bonding process, that ol' homoeroticism ever lurking (keeping in mind what those badass Spartans did to their little boys, just saying), talking about the stunts they'd pulled, drunken parties, orgies in swimming pools, running from the cops, their sexual experiences and prowess, double entendred references to genitals and various pieces of sports equipment, balls, bats, clubs and putters, *big rack but a short stick*, the air's getting steamy and thick with the funky, musty smells of male excretions and secretions. He'd never been involved in conversations like these, never hung with guys like these, never (as we know very well) actually hung with anybody. He tried to follow their lead, emulate proper manly demeanor. Various cellphones, EyePads, laptops, security cameras, drones and other electronic devices may even have recorded evidence of him tossing the old pigskin around with his new buddies in the quad (there's always a quad), the lads all sweaty, faces flushed, spirited shouts of bravado and camaraderie, lively but polite *right* commentary on girls passing by. Also worth mention his attendance at a fraternity kegger where he was observed imitating a piece of furniture, clear plastic cup of beer in hand, talking to no one, no one talking to him, and grinning so hard the back of his head hurt, until, the beer long gone warm (discovered he didn't like the taste), he saw a chance to escape. An all night card game (royal flush in hand he folds against a pair of eights). A panty raid, a bunch of guys shouting, laughing, swarming the girl's dorm, doors banging open and shut, girls in various states of dress and undress, *eeeee*. A secret drinking foray (blurry images of a male form upchucking neon red cherry vodka into a trash can *blorrrph!*).

Yes, a lousy poker player, couldn't cut and shuffle the deck, couldn't bluff, but in the public arena, as we've also seen, he mostly kept his cards close to his chest, played it quiet, cautious, hesitant (thanks, *Dad*), lest he overstep some unspoken rule or boundary. On rare occasions, however, he emerged from his watchful silence like a missile launched from under the sea, exploded out of the ocean's pacific blue waters and slammed into the midst of his unsuspecting victims like a ton of TNT, his fuse lit by carbonated beverages and candy confections purchased from the machines in the break room, his mind on fire with sugar, caffeine, adrenaline and endorphins, the young dictator, tyrant, future king of the world emergent, he burst out of his quiet turtle shell in angry tirades, ranted and raved against perceived injustices in the world he knew nothing about. Those terrorist dudes from, um, *Tabascostan*? Those illegal immigrants, the, uh, *Phlebotians*? Those rapists, murderers, drug dealers sent here to steal our women and undermine our way of life? Kill them all! Nuke the whole damn country! The other guys are going, whoa, what's up with this dude? Maybe *somebody* should, like, notify the *authorities?* Hey, anybody else notice the, um, tail and horns? Hee hee, just kidding, *sort of.*

One day he heard cheering in the rec room, distinct from the breakroom, a pool table, ping pong table, TV. The Olympics were on, men's gymnastics. The camera briefly switched to men's weightlifting. He'd never actually seen Olympic lifting before, never seen an Olympic barbell. It was huge, the size of a semi-tractor axle, and loaded on each end with half a dozen cast-iron plates as big as train wheels. Six hundred pounds! the announcer said. A world record! A big blond Russian guy in a bright red weightlifting suit lifted it over his head like it was nothing, the bar actually bent beneath the weight, but it happened so fast, he didn't see, didn't understand, the actual mechanics of the lift. And then, instead of carefully lowering the bar back to his shoulders and then the platform, the Russian guy just let it drop and it hit the platform and bounced back up in the air and nearly knocked him over. But, *Xa! Xa! Xa!* no harm is done, everythink is okay. Big grin, hand raised to acknowledge the cheers. And just like that his, the young ironsmith's, spirits soared with visions of Olympic glory. He had seen the torch on the hill, the stairway to heaven, his ticket to fame, to the future, to fortune, in short, in a word, okay, one, two, three, four, five, *six*, a specific goal to focus on. He began to make elaborate calculations, projected ahead to the next day, week, month, year, if he could add five, okay, ten pounds to each lift every month that'd be a hundred and twenty, okay, make it one-fifty a year, and if he could keep that up for the next two, three years, by the time he graduated from college he should be able to lift four, five, six, um, six hundred and fifty? Anyway, more weight than anyone had ever lifted before, in fact, vision soaring higher into the wild blue yonder, he'd lift so much no one would ever surpass him. He sketched a fairly respectable picture of a barbell loaded with the amount of weight he planned to lift, tacked it to the door of his clothes closet so he saw it every time he dressed or undressed, reminded himself morning and night of the goal he'd set, the work that lay ahead. If the iron had been an obsession before, now it was going to be—more of an obsession. Little did it matter that he wasn't actually attempting to perform any of the Olympic lifts, which, truth be told, looked funky, uninteresting and *difficult*. Despite his epiphany and visions of Olympian triumph, he steadfastly continued in the old way, grunting and groaning like a draft animal, like a dwarf of myth and fairytale blindly hacking into the mountainside with his pick and sledgehammer in pursuit of a phantom vein of gold.

Despite his primitive methods he quickly grew bigger, stronger. You look *huge!* a wide-eyed dorm mate exclaimed (got a bottle of that caffeinated water?), encountering him in the hallway, headed for the shower, white terry cloth towel wrapped around his waist, still pumped up from a session with the iron, his muscles engorged with blood, his ego equally inflated, yes, huge, a giant, the Incredible Hulk burst out of his nerdly Bruce Banner shirt and pants. His weight gain due to the abundance of food available in the dining hall. In the morning he trudged up the hill for breakfast, bowls of oatmeal, platters of bacon, scrambled eggs, French toast, endless glasses of whole milk.

Afterwards dragged himself to class or, just as likely, back to his room, to bed, slept until lunchtime. Sloppy Joes, Spaghetti-Os, bean burritos, BLTs, bowls of cottage cheese. A guy in the dorm whose mother *brriiinnng, mothership contacting male offspring—sorry, gotta take this* owned a *health food* store (*nota bene*: the first time he'd ever specifically heard this term, encountered this concept—later he'd hear it repeated in a sing-songy pop tune performed by the spacey glam girl duo, the PopTart Twins, *Woo-hoo! Inka dinka doo! Healthy food that's good for you!* Immediately followed by the notmother's outraged voice, frosty as a package of frozen spinach, echoing across the floral patterned, oilcothed fabric of time and space, *Infidels! Culinary imposters!*)—anyway, to get on with this tale (who's wagging whom?), this guy *sowwy, that was my mommie* had informed him of the importance of protein, but exactly what constituted protein he had no idea, he still knew nothing about nutrition, the value of a balanced diet, amino acids, vitamins, minerals, trace elements. Just eat and eat and eat like tomorrow there'll be nothing to eat (it happens, you know). For dinner he gobbled fried chicken, barbecued ribs, fish sticks, meatloaf, macaroni and cheese, stuffed himself with sweet yeasty rolls, odd fluffy pillows of white flour, fat and sugar slathered with butter, glugged glass after glass of whole milk. Thanks to the intensity of his workouts, the freshman fifteen (petitions are circulating to raise the bar to fifty) went to his biceps and triceps, pecs and delts instead of his gut and his butt.

In the evening he sat at his desk, in the yellow light of his desk lamp, to all appearances, a studious young scholar, the famous Lucubratius, he of elucidation, explication, exegesis, but disabusing anyone of such a mistaken notion, a quick camera glance over his shoulder revealed him *not* reviewing biology notes or Venn diagrams, but meticulously recording the results of today's session with the weights in his lifting journal, which he now maintained in an eleven and a half by nine and a half inch spiral-ringed, blue-lined notebook, carefully printing in their respective columns in blue ballpoint pen the number of sets and reps of each exercise, which he had committed to his memory like an electronic tabulating machine as he lifted, press: five, six, seven, *ayyyyt*, uhh, *niiiine*, uhhh, arrgh, *damn*; bench: *sevvven*, uhh, *ayyyyt*, huh-huh-huh, *nnniii*—shit. Adding comments, highlighted in pink or yellow or blue (putting to use those magic markers whose ink had never stained a page of his largely untouched textbooks) according to the degree of success, the moderate *good* (pink), on rarer occasions the more exuberant *Excellent!* (blue) Could have gone even heavier! On down days, spirits flagging, the unenthusiastic *okay* (yellow) or worse, ***Blah!*** in funereal black. But what was blah? Because he failed to meet his goal with the iron today? Or the homework once again postponed, put off, his dread growing as the clock *murderer! assassin!* mercilessly hacked away at the rapidly diminishing chunk of the space-time continuum separating redemption from surrender, abject capitulation, when he knew his homework would never be done (note passive) and the almost relief that came with that realization? Or the dark tumult of clouds threatening rain just when he was thinking about going out for a walk around campus, maybe wake himself up, clear the cobwebs from his brain, hit the books later? *And then out onto the dreary road go, solitary, alone, the tracks of his passage erased by the relentless rain*? His thoughts wandering off on another tangent, ballpoint pen close behind, in pursuit, his weightlifting journal transformed from iron-barred prison cell, rigid, officious, to public forum, agora, to sacred springs, forest grove, lines of verse that came to mind unbidden, *poetry*, mostly saccharine, sugar crystalizing all over the fucking page, sing-songy rhyme and meter, okay, not that bad, sure, simplistic, but also dark, fantastic, mystical, trying to turn today's failure with the iron into something more than it was, yes, redeem, through the medium of words.

Sometimes he woke early in the a.m., one, two, three, trudged back down to the basement, returned to the weights, started again, staring into the bare light bulb as he pushed the bar overhead, bleary-eyed, dazed, because he had to succeed, he had to accomplish and achieve what he had failed to accomplish today and if he could not, then punish himself for his failure, add to it greater failure still by ruining himself for the following day, enervating, exacerbating mental and muscle fatigue, creating sleep deficits that caught up with him in bouts of collapse when he slept the entire day, barely left the room, pulled himself up from his lethargy, slumber, only to make a trip to the john or the dining hall for dinner and even then the food repulsive, greasy, a cold, rubbery bolus he couldn't force down his throat. These alternating states of depletion, of utter paralysis, stasis, when he couldn't make himself move or do anything, and hyperkinesis, that manic, frantic need to move, walk, go, to get out of the dorm, away from the stultifying campus life, to pound the pavement into town, past the single movie theater RIALTA, past the shops, stores, restaurants and diners on Main Street, glancing in the windows, at the diners, shoppers, mannequins, sometimes a face staring back, a forkful of mashed potatoes just entering his *her?* mouth, that sudden uncomfortable intimacy through a pane of glass, quick, look away, run, flee, too much noise, too many people, whatever he was searching for not here either, hurry on then, boy, stretch out your stride, escape into the country, a lonely stretch of asphalt, in the melancholy of autumn, walk and walk and walk beneath a leaden gray sky clotted with steel wool clumps of clouds, the smell of wood smoke hanging in the air, throngs of paper bag brown leaves swirling around his feet, the cold November air grabbing at his throat like a frigid pair of hands. Sometimes walk until two, three in the morning, until he was exhausted, trembling, weak in the knees and falling asleep on his feet and there was no choice but return to the dorm, to his room, and still unable to sleep when he finally lay down in bed, stared into the dark, restless, because of this wildfire still burning in his brain, this urgency for something more or other than what existed now, *freedom*, yes, freedom, but from what?

This sense of entrapment, *claustrophobia*, amplified in winter, sitting in the classroom in his hard wooden chair at his hard wooden desk, wrapped in the warm, sleep-inviting blanket of heat issuing from the steam radiator hissing and ticking next to him, inhaling the cloying, mind-numbing smells of wood polish, floor polish, the other students, his classmates, in rows of colored puffy parkas, heavy wool coats, outside the leaded windows the early darkness closing in, the ghostly white slump of snow burying trees, shrubs, walks, buildings, cars, the professor's voice, aged in whiskey and pipe tobacco, droning on, verbs and adjectives, the battle of something in the year something, a spaceship landing on the planet something, *zzzzzz*. After class, snowball fights in the quad, festive lights in dorm windows, joyful carols and solemn hymns everywhere, everybody excited about heading home for the holidays, right? Everybody but him, poor *orfink* (cf. Popeye). Dreading the return to that dreary abode, the notfather's tyranny and anger, the notmother's snooping and sniping. Worse than that, worse than all, having to abandon his weights for the duration of this long vacation, impossible to haul them home and back to school again.

  Of course the notfather and notmother would never mention how peaceful and quiet it had been since they got rid of—er, been separated from—the monster officially recorded in government documents as their son. Of course not. No need when everything about his first day *home* reminded him of how unwelcome he was. While the rest of the house was as warm and toasty as an oven, his room was cold and drafty, ice had formed on the inside of the window panes. He had forgotten about the uncertain plumbing, the lack of hot water or, for that matter, any water, not just to drink or bathe, but to flush the damn toilet. The first night at dinner, the kitchen filled with the acrid, nauseating stink of burnt bacon grease, an inedible plate of *aubergines très frites* in front of him (~~carbonized~~ caramelized eggplant parmesan, the *Ladies At Home Journal* recipe said), he was also reminded what a *willfully?* terrible cook the notmother was *but why? to get even? with whom?* And that day and every day thereafter he bore on his shoulders the absence of his weights, locked in that room in the basement of the dormitory, unused, inutile, gleaming madly at their private joke, *haha, we're here and you're there*, tugging at him like a distant lover, this odd quantum entanglement, although he did notice, yes, incontrovertibly, an odd concurrent lightness of being the longer he was separated from the iron, which he attributed to a rapid loss in mass and bodyweight with the equivalent loss *murder?* of his appetite, even that annual holiday feast, the fabled *Christmas dinner* (insert appropriate religiously oriented meal), a complete failure, fit for the landfill before it ever hit the alimentary canal, sabotaged by the notmother's cavalier application of salt and a sudden Pollyannaish infatuation (change in meds?) with garlic (*begone all ye witches, warlocks!*). Another concern nagged at, dogged, his thoughts. He knew, didn't need a counselor to tell him, the counselor *didn't* tell him (*Was* there a counselor? Engaged with another student, maybe? Prissy Praseworthy, homecoming queen, swimsuit model, self-esteem issues, Now, Prissy, this treatment may seem unorthodox …) that he had finished the first semester in, *ahem*, precarious academic straits. No ifs, ands or buts, his ship was taking on water, if not downright sinking, a matter he of course neglected to mention to the notparents, convinced, *determined*, he would remedy this situation upon his return to school. Go to class, hit the books, do his homework, maybe sign up with a tutor. Uh-huh.

And it's true, he was more determined. Revived in body and spirit after this enforced moratorium, his mind on fire with desire for the iron, peace serving only as preparation for war, etc., *Spartans, Xerxes approaches!* he hit the weights with even greater dedication, spent hours in the dormitory basement, essentially reclaimed ownership of his iron hoard from the public at large by the simple act of possession (legal definition), both possessing and possessed by (the canonical definition). Dorm residents who headed downstairs for a workout with the weights found a grimacing demon *gargoyle* hunched over the barbell. He snarled when anybody asked for a turn *they're mine,*

mine, I tell you, scoffed at their puny human efforts *bwa-hah-
hah,* accidentally *forgot* and locked the door behind him when
he left. This more or less sealed his estrangement from the other
inhabitants of the dormitory. His roomie, it should be
mentioned, had apparently taken advantage of the holidays to
find a different living arrangement. Now he had the room to
himself, his hermit cell. He became even more withdrawn,
avoided chance encounters as much as possible, glowered and
muttered to himself as he skulked down the hall to the shower
or back down to the basement, suffered the long dark nights and
winter gloom in lonely solitude, absent the reassuring chatter
that often crisscrosses the Transatlantic void separating young
men, each from each, in their bunks, in their berths, in their
separate voyages toward manhood.

Ah, but as winter gave way to spring and the snow
melted away beneath the bright warm sunshine and the first
green shoots emerged and the breeze carried the scent of peach
and apple and cherry blossoms and the birds in the trees madly
sang their ode to joy to no one in particular, and he felt some
corresponding thing inside, a primal urge, a lust for life and joy
in living, that compelled him to abandon his ascetic cell,
anchoritic cave, go out into the light, to walk, move, get away
from, escape again the din of civilization, to plunge into the
nearest sylvan glade, to marvel at the velvet soft, emerald green,
deeply dentated leaves of an uncurling wood fern, or a
mushroom, the deadly but psychotropically transportive (if you
survive) red and white mottled death cap pushing up through
the crumbling black humus, or a waxy pink and purple lady
slipper with its belly swollen like an odd pregnant bird, and yet
… and yet, in spite of, or maybe because of these beautiful
things he felt that old melancholy returning, that sense of
something inside himself, soft, fragile, a membrane, or an as of
yet medically unidentified organ, being torn asunder, because
now, just now, when he should have followed that vernal urge
to new horizons of the mind, when he should have thrown off
the shackles of family and society, of church, state and

institutionalized education, he couldn't get away from, couldn't escape the one thing that really weighed him down, couldn't get away, that is, from himself, his obsession with the iron, because *bang, clang*, he *had* to abandon this edenic escape, *had* to go back to the dorm and down to the basement, *had* to put his hands on the bar and raise up again the iron even now when he had missed lunch and dinner and it was getting late and he, his whole body, felt kind of rubbery and vibrating inside. *Had* to. This confused resentment, this undercurrent of anger, unfocused, somehow they, yes, *they* again, the world out there, responsible for this burden he carried. He began to *act out* more, don't give a damn how much noise he made when he dropped the weights on the floor *clannnng* or slammed them against the wall *bannnng* until the building shook as if it had been hit with a wrecking ball (slight exaggeration). Oddly, not a complaint about damages incurred did the custodial staff raise *он разрушает все* (he is destroyink everythink. No reports from the RA regarding his anti-social behavior *acts like a Caveman! I'm a Cave, Caveman! I'm a Caveman!* No summons to the office of the head mom, Ms. Grimble, to address this untenable situation *under threat of force*. However.

One night, deep in a troubled slumber, in a murky dream, kind of like a film clip, ominous, Tarkovskian, *water*, he had a premonition of disaster, triggered perhaps by an event in the waking world around him, a distant rumble in the plumbing, a dull clang and bang, almost an ache, as if the whole building suffered from indigestion. The following day he went down to the basement, opened the door to the weight room and stopped, stared, stood frozen, trying to process, fathom, exactly what was wrong with this picture, what it was he wasn't seeing, even as this boiling hot wave of comprehension gushed through his brain and finally he did see, understand, raised his hands before his face in Biblical supplication, too stunned, startled, incredulous to speak or cry out, *My daughter, my ducats!* All gone! Alas, it was true, the room empty, completely bare, his weights undeniably gone. Oh why did he decide to leave the door unlocked? Oh folly, oh hubris. How could he be so dumb, so stupid, to tempt the fates like that? Sputtering, enraged, in a state of shock, he staggered upstairs and down the hall to Ms. Grimble's office to report his loss. The redoubtable lady, made of stronger stuff in those days, listened with an air of indifference and a barely restrained smile that once again threatened to crack the brittle, rouged and pancaked ceramic surface of her face. Oh, but of course she was concerned. It was awful, really, a tragedy (*boo hoo* crocodile tears), nothing like this had ever happened before in her dormitory. A police officer came, a local yokel in uniform. He wanted to know if any of the guys in the dorm were using drugs. *Drugs?* What did drugs have to do with his weights? He wanted to know if any of the girls went around without underwear. How the *fuck* would *he* know? He wanted free tickets to the basketball game that night. Talk to the dean, why don't ya? He wanted to know everything and anything but this annoying business of stolen or maybe it would be more accurate to say *misplaced* barbells. Whataya mean *misplaced?* But of course he didn't say that, didn't say anything, refused to reply to these rude, invasive and probably even unconstitutional questions, simply shrugged, shook his head no, no, I don't know anything, kept his answers to himself, unspoken.

In shock and despair, he staggered up and down the streets and alleys of that dismal little college town like a Frankenstein monster, head slumped, seeing no one, nothing, the sun setting in a red and gray murk, the glare of streetlamps coming on, the electric buzz of crickets, cicadas and nighthawks in the warm night air, the bums and winos collapsed in sagging heaps outside dive taverns and bars, the gang of kids breaking into a parked car, the lights burning in the attic windows of neurotic madmen, in the garrets of students pulling all-nighters, the silhouette of a young woman just beginning to undress behind a curtain—*hsst!* Someone whispered to him out of a dark alley. He recognized the speaker. It was the one and only, the sole campus revolutionary. Wearing a black trench coat, thin as a walking stick, face ravaged by acne, a couple of hairs sprouting on his chin, as conspicuous in his madness as our young ironsmith was in his. What do you want? he asked. *Nothing*, the revolutionary replied. Hmm, this was a familiar but as of yet unexplored topic. Turned out the revolutionary had an interesting piece of information to pass on. Toying with a live hand grenade—he kept pulling the pin and myopically sticking it back in—he casually mentioned that he had just hacked into the students' files in the Registrar's Office. One file in particular interested him, a file marked Top Secret, *your* file, containing several high level communications, *damning*, apparently a plan, *conspiracy* (and you thought *he* was paranoid). Ms. Grimble had enlisted the aid of the college president for precedent, as well as the ROTC staff for strategy and, if necessary, armed support, and the football team for added beef, and of course the Dean of Underwear whose duty it was to make sure everything was spotless, no telltale and embarrassing stains left in the boxers and jockey shorts, in the silk and cotton and satin panties he himself held in evidence from the boy's nocturnal raids and sometimes, *shh*, fondled and pressed to his face for a deep inhalation of naughty and nice traces of peepee, caca and forbidden jellyroll. And finally the help of the chemistry department just in case any dangerous materials might be involved. What if he was building a bomb! Indeed, it was this remote possibility that had originally attracted the revolutionary to his side. He squinted *where is that damn hole?* stuck the pin back in the grenade, finished his tale (everybody has one, vestigial, prehensile, yesterday, when I was young, etc.). Ms. Grimble's goon squad had converged upon the weight room at 0600 hours, a time they had determined the subject would most likely be asleep in bed (confirmed by a reconnaissance patrol), dismantled and hauled his iron out the service entrance where the town's sole scrap metal dealer waited with his banged up two and a half ton stake bed, rust to rust, as the saying goes. Maybe the revolutionary thought he might set off some kind of chain reaction, that this gorilla would vent his oversized simian wrath on the college campus, knock down a few buildings with his Hulk-rage. Didn't happen. (Of course it didn't happen. This isn't a fucking comic book.) He felt violated, betrayed, he plotted retribution, revenge, he'd show them, get even, *they* would pay for this, his anger smoldering, like a fire burning underground, consuming blue-black veins of coal, damaging, *injuring*, not his enemies, oh no, but his own soul. Finally the fire burned itself out, he gave up, defeated, paralyzed, by his loss, by his sorrow and impotent rage, by his inheritance of the notfamily will to failure, the prophecy of doom, in his bloodstream, genes, *DNA*.

And that actually might have been a good thing. Without that weight and burden, without that insane discipline he had imposed on himself, anything could have happened. He might have lifted up off the ground altogether and blown away like dandelion fluff. He might have overcome his grief and found a new path in life free from rules and regulations, restrictions and regimentation, free, i.e., from the iron. Oops, now I've let the cat out of the bag, wasn't supposed to say that. Look, is that a Tyrannosaurus Rex? But rather than salvation, a redemption song, he only saw this loss as retribution by the gods. Why did they want to punish him? Was it a lesson in humility? *Hubris?* Because he had lost his way with the iron? Wasn't committed enough? There, you see what I mean? All the wrong questions. He couldn't even begin to guess what the real problem was.

He began to sleep late, then later, ate dinner for breakfast and breakfast for dinner, haunted the streets at night, spent what daylight hours remained in brooding pastoral peregrinations, meandering Emersonian cordials, wearing his mourning weeds, his gloomy mien, *memento mori*, among, in contrast to, a shadow upon, nature's rainbow palette. By now he was a student in name only, attending classes a thing of the past. One day he received an official-looking document in the mail, which, upon opening, informed him that he had effectively dis-enrolled himself from the university and therefore would have to vacate the premises immediately, and furthermore, since there appeared to be few if any records of tests taken, papers handed in, in sum, toto, a grade average as close to *absolute zero* as theoretically possible, there was really no point in his returning next year *and don't let the door hit you on the way out, Sincerely, Dean Dong,* who, mulling over this letter with a tumbler of single malt before he signed, wondered, could this really be that earnest young man who stood before me, pleading his case for—what was it again, some sort of sports equipment? Oh yes, of course, a condom dispenser in the dorm.

IV
FAIL AGAIN BETTER

TO ADD TO HIS IGNOMINIOUS DEPARTURE from college, he now had to return home to the utter scorn and contempt of the *n-n-not*parents. It was that nonsense with the weights, the notmother said. I don't know why you allowed him to take that junk with him. I didn't allow him, the notfather replied (whined). He smuggled it without my knowledge. To *him* they said, How could you be so *stupid?* Did you think the sole purpose we sent you to school was so you could lift weights? Well, *duh.* Now what? While his former classmates were gone across the ocean to Greece or Rome or the Amalfi Coast with dear old Dad and *Mumsy* with whom they were really quite chummy, *best friends,* he was spinning his wheels and going nowhere in this little rube, rhubarb, hicksville town (or village or hamlet). But he had a plan, primitive, tactical rather than strategic, but nevertheless a plan. With unusual alacrity he found a job, gofer at the local car dealer *Hi! I'm Bob Bonobo!* changing tires, washing cars, driving a truck to the warehouse to pick up parts. He'd never had a real job before, he perceived it as some kind of theater, all the world, he the hero, never thought, conceived, that world out there might notice him. One day, end of work, in the locker room changing out of his uniform, a couple of mechanics, older guys, married, kids, the patriarchal paunch starting, whistled with admiration, gave him a few friendly jabs, Hey, *Ahrnold!* Charles Atlas! *Huh?* He didn't even comprehend at first, torn

asunder from his precious weights, his iron lode for, what, a
month? two? it never occurred to him that, in the eyes of others,
yes, he *the monster!* might, did, kind of, sort of, look like,
resemble, no, not Herakles, but a young Adonis, *maybe?* One of
the mechanics, Slim (or Lennie or Bruce), a handsome guy with
a shiny black *little dab'll do you* hairdo, stoked his ego even
more, asked him, the *obvious* authority, if he had any advice on
fattening up his wife. You know—cupping his hands under
imaginary breasts, patting his butt. He should have said, Are
you out of your fucking mind? Fatten her up? Are you gonna
say that ten, twenty years from now when she's a two hundred
fifty pound blue ribbon moocow? (Yes, he wasn't, had no idea,
PC.) Instead he said, *Protein.* He said milk, eggs, cheese, dairy,
meat. On another occasion (just to give another example, where
his mind was at), a coworker, guy his age, pudgy, slope-
shouldered, fancied himself buff, referred to the two of them as
two hundred pound studs. He, ego stroked again, thought, wow,
really, *me*, a stud? The two hundred pounds stopped him short
though, gave the lie to the studly part. More like one sixty-five,
max, and rapidly trending downward. All his reserves of
kinetic, frenetic energy expended on the job, on the appearance
of doing his job. He was like a whirling dervish, a human top,
spinning around the car lot, through the mechanics' bay, the
parts shop, twirling a tire iron, splashing soap suds, stocking
parts. He was on fire, he had to move, go, do. Driving to the
warehouse to pick up parts, he clutched the steering wheel in
both fists, leaned forward in the seat as if he could will the truck
to go faster, as if he were the engine, the mill, motor, the pistons
pounding up and down in their cylinders, cam shafts spinning
madly, *happily.* He burned up hundreds, thousands of calories
making the job more than a job, a mission, challenge. The
notmother and notfather were certainly impressed and perhaps
not a little bit bewildered by this newfound industry. They
looked at each other and said, Well, that's something. At least
he has a job. Yes, he has a job. Although *what on earth* is he
doing down in the basement at night?

And what exactly *was* our troubled little steam shovel doing back down in that stinking dungeon, that cold, empty forge? He longed for the iron, of course. He sat on his wooden bench, poring through a monthly magazine he had discovered (thanks, actually, to the guy in the dorm whose mom owned a health food store), dedicated exclusively to the iron (later he would also discover that the glossy covers of muscle-bound bodybuilders were treasured among the gay crowd, which probably explained the *queer* looks the postman gave him): letters to the editor, anecdotes, contest results, profiles of bodybuilders, power lifters, Olympic lifters—distinctions he had been completely unaware of, advertisements for protein supplements, lifting gear and equipment, *barbells* (exactly how he heard it in his head, italicized). With an old broomstick, he began to practice the Olympic lifts as they were explained in the magazine, imagined himself lifting an enormous barbell overhead, the bar bent beneath the weight, the huge cast-iron plates clanging together. Afterwards he sat on the wooden bench and read over again, tried to better understand, the mechanics of these lifts. Sometimes he heard the cellar door squeak open, the top step creak, sensed the notmother's imperious reginal eyes peering down her nose into the basement, trying to divine what he was up to, condemning, hating. *I don't like it. Not one bit*, she complained to the notfather later that evening, after the ritual burnt offering, the news on TV, *hundreds killed*, two frigates anchored side by side in their cold Atlantic sea berth, marriage bed. Maybe he's studying to make up for what he missed in college, the notfather suggested, not convinced himself. Or maybe he's taking a correspondence course, he mused, no less dubious, when the notson mailed off an official-looking envelope.

One afternoon said notson came home from work to find a tractor trailer pulled up in front of the house and a fat little man in a brown uniform, curled mustaches and a bowler derby plopped down on his cue ball head busily unloading cardboard boxes and wooden crates with an electric lift at the rear of the truck. The notmother, dressed in a faded floral housecoat, stood by clasping and unclasping her hands, her face ghostly pale, wrenched in tragic mask agony. I signed some papers, I don't know what for, she said in a fretful, tremulous voice. The little man, sensing proprietorship, came huffing and puffing up to him, his face red as a radish, his jaws grinding his anger into the words he wanted to say, to articulate, complain about this excessively heavy delivery, *I ain't gettin' paid to break my goddamn back*. No need. Ignoring the little man, reducing him even further in size by his utter indifference, he began to heave the cardboard boxes and wooden crates onto his shoulders and carry them, one by one, into the house and down to the basement while the notmother fretted and worried and gathered in her Valkyrian bosom a growing outrage that she compounded and saved for when the notfather came home later that night from another day of obscurity, tired and worn out and sensing something in the air beside the corned beef and cabbage. *Well, he's at it again*, the notmother said *frigidly*, her voice, her words, hanging in the air, frosted with contempt. What do you mean? the notfather said with immediate dread, even as he heard the Vulcanic clanging and banging beneath his feet. You know perfectly well what I mean, the notmother snarled. This business with the iron. A truck came today, a little man with cartons and crates. I had to sign some papers. And then *he* came, *your* son, *wonderful!* Or not. He hauled the whole pile of junk down to the basement. He's down there now. He's crazy, I tell you (*takes one to know one, nyaaah*). Talk to him, make him understand, it's all got to go, you won't allow it. He's *your* son. He, of course, was aware of none of this. Preoccupied with breaking metal bands, prying open wooden crates and extracting various pieces of iron and steel packed in sawdust and excelsior, he didn't hear the knocking on the cellar door, didn't hear the hesitant tread on the steps, didn't realize until he looked up and saw the notfather's pale, flaccid face hovering like a partially deflated helium balloon midway down the cellar stairs, afraid to come all the way down, afraid of the damp and the gray, afraid of the spiders, mice and other creatures, afraid of this hulking monster, not a little boy he could push around anymore, but a strapping young man with frightening strength and spontaneous outbursts of rage as terrifying as if the previously referenced *bzzzzzt! Jargon!* (his rhetoric professor's words echoing blood-red in his head) Tyrannosaurus Rex had burst into the house. *Son?* he said, clearly aware himself of the tenuousness of that word. You can't do this anymore, I—your mother and I won't allow it. Can't you see, *son?* It's dangerous, it's an *obsession* (*yesss, my precious*), it's going to ruin your life. You're an adult now. Storm clouds rumbled in his skull. His brain seethed with loathing and disgust. How dare this trembling, fearful blob of protoplasm that called itself his father violate, trespass upon his sanctuary, sacred training hall? He listened in silence, said nothing, his eyes gleaming like the oiled pieces of iron lurking in their boxes and crates, *threatening*. Finally the notfather turned, shoulders sagging, retreated, trudged back up the creaking wooden stairs, defeated, and he returned to unpacking his new weights, waves, hot ocean tides of excitement rising through his body, still not quite believing that he was in possession, the owner, of this great treasure, that he had worked for, earned, bought this dragon hoard with his own money, the huge black cast-iron plates like train wheels and the finely machined titanium steel bar *within one ten thousandth*, gun metal blue, with parallel bands of crosshatching, *knurling*, for improved grip, and stainless steel sleeves, like howitzer shell casings, on each end to slide the weights onto, and to lock them in place, heavy iron and leather collars like the knobby valves on a piece of nineteenth century steampunk machinery. Just to be in the presence of, in proximity to, this thing of metallic beauty infused, filled him with a gloat of power, at the same time intimidated, yes, *frightened* him. The bar was seven feet long, more than a foot taller than him, it felt alien and unfamiliar when he closed his hands around the rough knurling. He had to be careful when he picked it up, turned, rotated on the axis of his feet, not to crash into the furnace, the old chest of drawers, the luminous white, seldom used washing machine. He had to struggle to avoid crashing the great iron plates into the rafters when he drove the bar overhead *BOOM!* And then the notfather's inner tyrant rose again. Stop that racket down there! You're destroying the house! I'll call the police! (That was a new angle.)

Despite these minor obstacles his enthusiasm for the iron returned with even greater force. He couldn't wait *yearned* to get home from work and lift weights. He was still young, full of stamina, spunk, *beans*. Even after a day of labor he could go down into that stinking basement rejuvenated, his adrenaline flowing, his heroic dreams soaring to new heights. To add to this aura, mystique, to signify, sanctify his commitment to the iron, he sent for *his horses*, ordered through the mail, that simple, no magic involved, a super hero costume, a weightlifting suit, technically called a *singlet*, essentially a one-piece wrestling uniform, stretchy, spandex, dark blue, a pair of lace-up weightlifting shoes with high ankle tops and thick soles, and a weightlifting belt, wide, thick, brown leather, made from the hide housing the living thing, the moo and milk and chewing cud, with a heavy metal buckle like the Pilgrims wore on practically every article of clothing (oh, it's another myth?). He bought a block of gymnast's chalk to improve his grip on the bar, made wrist straps from pieces of denim cut from an unsalvageable pair of blue jeans to further augment his grip, allow him to lift even heavier weights. Voodoo accouterments of the sport to give himself moral support, to feel like a warrior girding for combat. He gradually learned, weeks, months, to perform the ceremonies, rituals that would become reflex, pulling on his lifting suit, lacing up his lifting shoes, stretching out his quads, hamstrings, spinal erectors, some unidentifiable movie soundtrack, soaring, *heroic*, playing in his head as he began to warm up with the empty bar, judging how his workout would go by how light or heavy it felt, picturing in his mind the lifts he wanted to accomplish, the effort it would take as he began loading weights, gripping the heavy iron plates in both hands, sliding them onto the stainless steel sleeves, *striiiick, bang*, his concentration tightening, centering, honing in on that moment when he finally strapped on the wide leather belt, adjusted it so that it sat at the base of his spine, encircled his waist just above his *gluteus maximus* (solemn, focused, gladiator not spectator, he saw no connection to the circus), inserted the tongue through the steel buckle, cinched it tight, then rubbed the chalk block between his hands, clapped them together, once, twice *here and now*, sent white dust spraying everywhere as he stood over the bar, centered his feet approximately shoulder width apart, his breathing slow, rhythmic, every breath must be measured exactly right, must be in sequence with the actual process of the lift when he bent down, closed his hands around the bar, closed and opened them, gripping the bar, squeezing it lightly, turning it, turning it, each turn tightening his thumbs and fingers for a fraction of a second, just enough for callused flesh to test iron, to *interface* with the ridged reticulations of the knurling, no, not there, not yet, squeezing and releasing, squeezing and releasing, searching for the perfect placement, the perfect alliance, *melding*, of iron and flesh, this simple act excruciating because his success or failure depended on it, *there*. His hands tightened, he gripped the bar like a motorcycle rider driving over a cliff at the same time he lowered his body into the pulling position, pushed his hips and butt down as if he were sitting on a low stool, okay, say it, as if he were squatting to take a shit, his spine arched inward, indented, shoulders back, head up, eyes focused on an imaginary point that happened to coincide with a can of creamed corn on the far wall. And then he began to apply pressure. At first everything seems to happen in slow motion, the weight separates from the concrete floor like a diesel locomotive beginning to move on the track, like a moon rocket lifting off the launch pad *we have liftoff*, but almost in the exact same moment, molecules, atoms of iron still clinging to the cold cement, everything is moving faster, the bar gathering momentum as all the muscle groups in his body coordinate and contract like the hydraulic system of an earth moving machine, calves, quads, glutes, lumbar, spinal erectors, latissimus dorsi and trapezius (the anatomy lesson he has already learned), weight and mass accelerate along an essentially linear trajectory that requires his body to continually adjust and align itself in a simultaneously peristaltic and serpentine motion around the bar as it slides up his shins, over his kneecaps, rides up his thighs, a faint *ding* as it comes in contact with his metal belt buckle, whispers past the spandex covering his abdominals, pecs, his shoulders shrug, his elbows pull upward, the bar passes half an inch in front of his face in fact almost skims his nose as he rises on his toes and his body extends itself fully like a frog leaping *green flash* from a lily pad, the momentum of the weight and the tensile dynamics of the bar combine and the bar continues to travel upward, reaches its apogee even as he drops again into that primal position, the squat, catches the bar across the front of his shoulders, receives and supports it on his deltoids, for an isolated fraction of a second, discrete, his entire body compressed, all his muscles, coiled, piston, spring-like, before he rebounds, struggles to rise again, stands erect with this weight, pauses, a full second, two, taking rapid deep breaths, *huh-huh-huh*, then dips, bends his knees slightly and, second stage firing, explodes upward again, glutes and quads, delts and triceps forcing the weight overhead as he drops beneath the bar in a forward lunge, spine bent backward, vertebrae creaking, muscles straining, the bar locked out at full arms' length, then stands again, brings his feet together, holds the barbell overhead, steady, a trophy, laurels, golden wreath, a libation and offering to some approximation of God, the only one who sees his triumph, victory, in other words, unbeliever, ye of little faith, *no one*. Maybe that's the way it went, on the best of days, in his imagination, actually maybe not quite like that, his timing off, his technique not so hot, still mostly push and shove and less finesse. He let the weight drop back to his shoulders, lowered it to the floor, exhaled, expelled the hot ruined air from his lungs, collapsed on the wooden bench, almost as quickly jumped up again, shook his hands, wrists, his feet, rolled his head on his neck, stared up at the dim white glare of the single bare bulb, trying to keep his muscles loose, his mind focused, staring at the bar, concentrating on it, preparing in his mind for the next attempt which must be heavier still, *striiick, bang*, which must encompass even more mass, more energy, a greater part of the universe. And with each lift tighten his focus that much more, squeeze and turn and handle the bar, perform set after set of presses, benches, squats, five-six-seven-eighhht-niiine-*ten!* And do that again and again until it was impossible to go on, he could lift no more, not another pound, not another rep, the transference of heat, energy, complete, the cold iron invested with all the warmth of his body and soul, whatever soul that was, helium balloon, empty hot water bottle, construct of psychoneural processes, and he sat back down on the wooden bench, dripping sweat, all his pores open, releasing the toxic stream of heavy metals, contemplating his workout today, what he had accomplished, or not, all duly recorded later that evening in his spiral-ringed notebook, his weightlifting log, ledger, in the system of accounting he had developed to tally and record every repetition, every pound lifted, commenting on the degree of success, whether more difficult or less than expected. Because even if he hadn't actually succeeded in lifting the weight he desired, he could at least succeed in plotting its course, in projecting and extrapolating it on some graph of future potentials if he only did this or that compounded by so many days, weeks and months, a kind of physics evolved out of dreams, fantasies, delusions, the movement of a heavy object, a given mass of thought, of concept, translated into iron, along a linear path transecting horizontal and vertical planes of daylight depending on gravity and his ability to overcome it, depending on the sunshine that morning or the thunderstorms or snow showers that evening, *white roses blossoming in the purple velvet of night, when Thor struck his hammer, Zeus tossed his bolt of lightning*, not even realizing where he was going, what he was doing, that strange impulse again, his pen off on its own, continuing to move over his graph, words all over the page, descriptions of strange mythical creatures, goofy cartoon images of ancient heroes sprouting among, desecrating, subverting his rigid system of accounting, carefully crafted, lined, laid out columns, figures devolving into the anarchy of cursive, syntax, spontaneous, not an ironsmith, mechanic, but a revolutionary, romantic, *poet*. His weightlifting chart become a platform, dais, stage for verse, spiritual and political treatises (completely uninformed, unfounded, of course, tirades really, the kind of stuff tyrants spout, that gets presidents elected). He wrote word upon word, as if the word were reality, the weight lifted, his kingdom come. A subconscious attempt to turn dross into gold? To make something more out of less? And in saying less, acknowledge, accept, that he hadn't yet, may *never* achieve what he wished, hoped for, expected? His folly, grand delusion, finally made clear even to himself? Never! Or rather, yes! Fool, why hadn't he seen before? It *was* folly to believe he could ever achieve what he hoped for, dreamed of, his *goals*, if he continued as he was now, inertial, day after day, wasting his precious time and energy on earthly, *temporal*, matters, completely irrelevant, like a job and a paycheck. If he wanted to succeed he must devote everything he had, his *life*, to the iron.

He quit his job, stopped going to work, did nothing but lift and read and think about lifting weights. He essentially lived in the basement, declared it off limits to the notmother and notfather, to the speculative, supposed brothers and sisters in the notfamilyland above, not by any words, promulgations he made over the dinner table, proclamations he tacked on the cellar door, but by the Vulcanic clanging and banging and the hot foul blast of sulfurous and nitrous fumes when anybody opened the portal into that inferno, forge below. Even if it was only to go downstairs for a jar of pickles or an old *Ladies At Home Journal* with that special recipe the notmother wanted to consult for a sawdust and cornhusk casserole tonight. But no, they didn't dare go down there, didn't dare disturb his sanctum, he snarled and growled at them like a beast, a *werewolf,* if they even started down the steps. Even when the plumber came, banging around with his lunchbox and his pipe wrenches and puffing on his stinking cigar to see if he couldn't plug that leak that had plagued the household plumbing for the past quarter century (all eyes on the notfather, seen assiduously staring at a spot on the ceiling *spider?*). I don't mean to offend you, Ma'am, but that *animal* you have down there, *your son*, he wouldn't allow me, he threatened me with an iron bar.

Caveman, troglodyte, *monster*, that's what he'd become, demonic, chthonic, *k-thunk*. When he did go out on the street, rarely, he avoided people as much as possible, glowered at those he did encounter out of the caverns of his skull, snarled at them and muttered under his breath. One night, restless, unable to sleep, he went for a walk, maybe by accident, maybe design, *subconscious* (nothing is accidental, *hat gesagt der gute Doktor*), he canine wandered, following his nose, ears, distant smells, sounds, to a nearby town, to a popular youth spot, non-alcohol, under twenty-one, all these *kids*, people his age, laughing, shouting, dancing, having fun. He stood in their midst like a sentient doorpost, feeling lonely and apart from everything and grinning so hard his head hurt, trying to show, pretend, that he was having fun too, but it wasn't fun, the vise continued to tighten in his skull, squeezing, he had to get out of here, he turned to leave, flee. The door wouldn't open, it was blocked on the other side. He heard guys snickering, laughing, *some jerk's trying to get out*. Hot red rage surged through his brain, molten. He put all his might against the door, threw it open like Samson bringing down the pillars of the temple, strode down the stairs like Moses through the parted waters of all the bodies he had cast, knocked aside, the people who had laughed, his detractors, *jerk*. He felt a hand on his shoulder, turned, saw just in time to deflect the fist aimed at his face, saw the other fist preparing to strike, he had no choice, he had to fight, to launch a counterattack. But even if he was a monster and a snarling beast, he wasn't a killer, a murderer. Despite his violent outbursts, his uncertain rage, he didn't like *hated* to fight, couldn't strike another person, even in self defense. He tried to throw a punch but his fist ploughed through the air with a kind of slow-motion dream-like futility. All he could do was clumsily ward off and parry the other guy's blows, until he finally caught the offending fists in midair, pulled his opponent toward him and gave him a little squeeze, a hug he had never given anyone in his life, just enough to suggest the power and destruction that awaited anyone foolish enough to test his ire farther, ribs snapping, chest cavity collapsing, heart and lungs exploding—but no, just a suggestion of that. And then push the guy away, slink off, return to his cave, den, his dank, rank dungeon cell, and sulk over this, yet another failed attempt.

Not surprising that his increasingly anti-social behavior should be noted by the notparents. He only came up from the basement or down from his room for dinner or to sit in the blue glow of the TV, a dark, scowling presence—*sullen*, that was the word the notmother used, she actually said to him, *Stop looking so sullen*, she, the prophetess of doom, of royal condemnation of everything she disapproved, i.e., everything. And what was he scribbling in those journals—formulas for bombs? Coded messages to Russians? *Martians*? Maybe we should report him to the authorities? I don't think it's *that* bad, the notfather's timid reply. And still his obsession showed no sign of abating, he refused to do anything, look for another job, make plans for the future. And his appetite, he ate everything in the house. He drank milk by the gallon, wolfed down the notmother's burnt offerings of pan fried hamburgers and boiled hotdogs, methodically worked his way through packages of cheese *food*, peanut butter and jelly sandwiches, slices of stale white bread smeared with relish, mustard and ketchup, raw carrots, green tomatoes, ate everything in the cupboards, in the refrigerator, even the artifactual, botulism ridden cans and jars on the dusty cobwebbed shelves in the basement, like a cockroach scavenger, survivor, cleaning up, consuming, devouring any and all crumbs, leftovers, residual traces of anything that remotely resembled food. Five, ten, fifteen pounds, the weight he'd lost on the job returned, and five, ten, fifteen more. All the notmother did was shop for groceries. At least it gets her out of the house the notfather thought but didn't say. *Oy vey*, but at such a cost. One night he overheard the notparents whispering in their room, some kind of secret agreement, a conspiracy, pact, we gotta get this monster out of here, get him back in school, for his *own good*. They made him a deal, a bargain. If you can stay in school and out of trouble we'll pay for your rent and tuition (the chancellor, as mentioned before, willing to forgive and forget any offense for a generous contribution to his favorite charity *moi*), we'll provide you with an allowance, you can find your own housing arrangement, live however you want. We'll even pay to have your weightlifting jun— *equipment* delivered to your new residence. Hmm, maybe he should have smelled the subtextual stink of an eviction here, but, oh impetuous youth, what he smelled, heard, thought was *freedom*.

After searching the ads in the small-town rag, at last he found exactly what he was looking for. To let: spacious *downstairs* dwelling with kitchen and bathroom facilities. Rent negotiable. Contact Mrs. Dorothy (or Margaret or Joyce) Grumble (no relation to the aforementioned Ms. Grimble, even slantwise), who turned out to be the owner and live-in landlord, a stick-thin nonagenarian in black wool and white lace with steel gray hair tied in a bun, wire-rimmed glasses perched high on a patrician nose, and a slight stoop in her posture. Having met him at the leaded glass front door of this rickety old Victorian manse with its crumbling chimney and its widow's walk atilt, she led him poking her way with a polished walnut cane to a door on the side of the house, hung at an angle that suggested a steep descent and, indeed, upon opening revealed a flight of creaking wooden stairs that led him deep down to a large, high-ceiling basement apartment lit by a single bare bulb dangling at the end of a frayed cord, which revealed in its dim incandescence a faded, oval-shaped red and brown throw rug on the concrete floor, enormous spider webs stretching across the rafters, dust and cobweb covered cans and jars on wooden shelves, a huge, clunky old coal burning furnace converted to gas, two dirty, narrow rectangular windows above eye level that allowed in a minimum of additional light, a pile of boxes in one corner, including one with an unsettling resemblance to a coffin, exposed pipes, damp cement walls, the sound of water trickling somewhere, possibly related to the primitive water closet and green-slimed plastic shower stall set up in another corner, that or the humming, shuddering *ice box*, an earlier version *predecessor* of the perishable foods preserving, ice making, recipe consulting, universally app-adaptable refrigerator. Apparently Mrs. Grumble's deceased husband Horace (or Morris or Orville), handyman ordinaire, had crudely fashioned this dank, damp basement into what he smugly thought a man cave extraordinaire, especially after several eclectically mixed highballs. The young ironsmith, putative hero of this tale(?), took a deep breath and sighed, *Ahhhhhh*, just like home. Mrs. Grumble, who had been apologizing abjectly for the state of things, although in a practiced tone that suggested she really didn't give a damn, seemed genuinely thrilled to have this *nice young man* take up residence in her basement, especially considering the fairly generous rent he offered to pay her, sort of a bribe, really, to look or rather *listen* the other way. Fortunately, Mrs. Grumble was also quite deaf, so she was unlikely to be disturbed by the clanging and banging and occasional odd gong-bonging sounds transmitted by the byzantine tangle of ductwork leading from the furnace to the various heating vents placed throughout the house.

Thus began his Athenian idyll, physical culture and scholarship. He attended classes, did his homework, which, mostly reading, *literature*, didn't seem like work at all. On the contrary, he gladly, happily, somewhat incredulously, *right at home*, *second nature*, immersed himself in prose and poetry, in the world of heroes and heroic language and even—bells going off in his head, hundred watt light bulbs of recognition, of kindred spirits—invisible and underground men, fed on words and by words fed, kept alive, his faith, in fantasy, his dream of greatness, with the iron his maiden, mistress, or, no sissy he, his mighty sword, lance, his noble steed, a solitary knight errant on a quest for fame. This delusion, yes, say it, bwah-hah-hah, *madness*, enhanced by autumn's arrival, his favorite season, *inspired*, when chilly gusts sent motley clusters of red and orange and yellow leaves swirling down the street and everywhere he looked he saw girls in skintight leggings, in wool sweaters, girls with faces aglow, hair blowing. Oh, female pulchritude, Oh, double X chromosome, how he yearned to know one of those girls, to hold her in his arms, to kiss and caress and, yes, say it, that too, *fuck*, but no, even now, even to himself, it sounded too ugly, too harsh, that word, it had to be *truth* and *love, courtly*, even if the truth was he really wanted to fuck. Oh autumn, when the full moon hung like a swollen egg luminous and pendant in the bare black limbs of a great oak and the cold air gripping his throat and the smell of wood smoke were all somehow unbearable with their knowledge and the message they shared of life and time passing. And somehow he had to say all that, he was convinced *deluded* he could make, do, move all that, his *vital mission*, to lift all that up, to raise it *glory to God* with the cold, hard iron when he went back down into that cold, lonely basement.

Well, okay, the lonely part a pathetic fallacy, not the basement lonely but he. (Hee hee, not really supposed to mention that, were we?) But cold? Yes, decidedly, as he discovered with winter's first arctic blast, when the heat from the stodgy old furnace completely bypassed him, his subterranean dwelling, in its natural tendency to rise, ascend to higher heights, when his every breath enshrouded him in a white cloud of vapor, when he worked up a sweat lifting weights and the steam rose from his body like a dray animal pulling a sled in winter. An electric space heater part(ial)ly ameliorated the situation, the hot plate he used for cooking gave off a minimum of warmth, but, you know, sometimes you just gotta man up, tough it out. Besides, our heroic hero could claim,

DNA test pending, that he carried at least a few drops of Viking blood in his veins, Erik the Pink maybe, naww, the c-c-cold d-d-doesn't b-b-bother me. Of course, with winter also came colds, the flu, germs everywhere, hack, cough, sneeze *ah-choo!* Shivering beneath a pile of blankets, coats, sweaters and all his clothes on his mattress on the floor, waves of nausea roiling his stomach, too sick to lift, go to class, do anything but make it to the loo and further evacuate, eliminate, torture his rectum and throat, shit himself empty and puke himself dry. Only roused from his wretched sickbed by a faint rapping, tapping at his cellar door. Aching, moaning, he ascended the creaking wooden stairs, pushed open the portal of his rabbit hole, *eh, what's up, Doc?* and, lo and behold, found Mrs. Grumble, the dear old lady herself, a saint, I tell ya, the paperwork's already in at the Vatican, a simple matter of her vacating the earthly domain before she's canonized, who, perhaps having noticed the absence of any activity in the nether regions, the cessation of those strange metallic sounds, like the clanking of chains (Jacob Marley?), spirit messages from her dearly departed Morris (or Horace or Orville)?, or maybe it was intuition, her nurturing nature, years as a combat medic in that never-ending war *over there* (and coming soon to a theater near you), even now her watery blue eyes swimming in pools of compassion behind her wire-rimmed glasses, or, who knows, maybe picked up a touch of the bug herself, feverish, whatever the case, the cause, she, Mrs. Grumble, a decent lady, humble and good, stood now, or rather stooped, her body, thin as the walking stick she leaned on, cloaked in a furry Cossack hat, an unfashionably out of fashion full-length mink coat and authentic reindeer hide mukluks, an outfit she wore inside the house and out, whatever heat the furnace generated somehow eluding her too, bearing in her free hand, arthritic, blue-veined, wool mittened, a steaming pot of chicken soup. Bless her heart.

Winter brought with it another issue, less material (okay, that's debatable), not necessarily more spiritual—*pathological* perhaps?—the arrival of, dare we say it? *Christmas,* and with it the prerequisite return home for the holidays. For most, well, many, a time of bright festival lights, feasts, fanfare, family reunions. For him, only bleakness, darkness, the prospect of a month away from the iron in the ~~prison~~ bosom of the notfamily. But, you know, sometimes miracles do happen (kudos, Clarence). As he was steeling himself for this dreaded pilgrimage he received a letter from the notfather. Dear *son*, our ship has come in (but not yours). Your *mother* and I will be sailing to the islands for a well-deserved vacation. Why don't you stay on at school for the rest of the school year? Concentrate on your studies. I hope the check I've enclosed will cover your expenses. Love, *Dad. Yaaaaaay!* And given this reprieve, how much greater, then, his relief and, yes, joy, when winter's frozen, white-knuckled grip gave way to the balmy breath and verdancy of spring and not long after that summer arrived, bags in hand, from vacationing in warmer climes, and he faced not only the unavoidable return *home* but the perennial problem of transferring his foundry, forge, collection of iron to that unwelcomed and unwelcoming abode, to his surprise he received another letter from dear old Dad. Dear son, your mother and I are having the house remodeled, we'll be traveling out west, or maybe in Europe, or perhaps the Subcontinent. Please stay on at school (don't try to find us). I've enclosed a check that should cover expenses for the duration of your college career. Oh, ouch, ouch, please, spare me, no more, right? Alienation? Abandonment? Abdication of parental duties? Kidding. Kind of like tossing B'rer Rabbit in the briar patch. Only too happy to remain ensconced in his habitat, hole in the ground, in that stygian pit, that subterranean existence, banging and clanging and forging the iron, driven, determined, his only connection with the world above his regular attendance in class where he managed not to connect with any of his cohort, sulked in the back of the room, attentive, yes, but glowering like a gargoyle, or else trips to the grocery store where even communication with the clerk or cashier caused him pain, made him want to flee in panic.

Even when the wind changed and everybody on campus turned into free spirits in long hair and beards and strings of beads and called each other brother and sister and renounced the law of the iron will and he walked among them nodding his head *yes yes yes* in agreement and mouthing the words *peace* and *love* and believing that he believed what he said even as he trudged back down the creaking wooden stairs to his basement hideaway, yes, exactly that, hideaway, because he couldn't let anyone know what he was up to *down there*, because they wouldn't understand, because it was too cold, too lonely, too dark and heavy and bound to the earth, because they didn't want to shoulder that weight and that burden, they wanted to fly, cut their tethers and soar where no one had ever gone before, and how would he be able to make them understand, how explain that it was the same thing, that all his life he had wanted to soar, spread his wings, raise himself above the temporal, the things of the world, but the only way he knew how to do this was with the iron. And even then, as he had that thought, said the words to himself, in his head, *not* see the contradiction, fallacy, that he was tethering himself ever more firmly to terra firma, alienating himself further from his peers. Sometimes, rarely, he took hope, thought he detected the signs of madness in others, in the tics and grimaces, in the way they walked, talked, carried themselves as if they were constantly struggling forward through a dense medium or trying to keep erect beneath an immense burden. Then he'd discover he was wrong, their madness lay elsewhere, music or painting or quantum mechanics, yes, possibly equally as mad, but still other than, *not* the iron. Also socially acceptable.

Even when he did encounter someone, some nobody nothing nerd, skinny, pimply, four-eyed, who started pestering him to study together in their Modern American Lit survey class, or the hulking brute, more blubber than muscle, who loved, read aloud in an odd falsetto voice, Shakespeare, but someone *whom*, confusing his passion for words with his passion for the iron, he could encourage and entice, *seduce*, into following him down into that dank stinking hole, *C'mon, just try it, just put your hands on the bar, feel the iron and the weight of the iron*, playing the part of the lying, conniving, W.C. Fields drawling carney barker, sideshow huckster and master of prestidigitation, pushing and cajoling them, distracting them with excited palaver, talking himself dry, releasing reams and cartons of his philosophy on life and the iron and everything else he'd thought about and stored up in his brain over the past six months of seclusion with the iron, as if the words and the talking were the act itself and out of those words he could generate the reality of so many more tons of gravity reversed and lifted overhead when he had to go back down in that basement and raise up the iron the next day *alone*. Because none of them lasted, none endured, whether they were too weak, too puny, not just in body but in spirit, they had no desire, drive, ambition, they had no vision, yeah, sure, they put their hands on the iron as he instructed, they *tried* it, felt the iron and the weight of the iron and they thought but didn't say *this is fucking crazy*, and they left, fled back into the sunshine and fresh air, abandoned the sulphurous and nitrous smells, the soot and grime and machine oil of his foundry for their girlfriends, games, easy lives, telling him, maybe even telling themselves, I'll start back tomorrow, tomorrow I'll get it going again, *and then tomorrow comes and tomorrow, and then next week and next month until it's never again and they're reduced to their sad pathetic little stories, all lies, fiction, Yeah, I used to mess with the iron, I threw the weights around. Don't ever say you wanta mess with the iron, boy. The iron'll mess with you, grind your elbows and knees into bone meal, crumble your spine like a stack of stale soda crackers*. That old man again? The wizard of his fantasies, dreams? Or his own anger, resentment, his sense of abandonment each time he lost another acolyte, lifting buddy, possible friend. *The hell with them all, goodbye and good riddance?* In the end his anger held him in good stead, aided his recovery, each time that abandonment felt less, each time his determination grown more in proportion, the last man on earth, *übermensch.*

    But that isn't true either. There was one, a *friend.* Why
bother to give him a name? Just something to distinguish one
body from another. How did that happen? Unexpectedly, out of
nowhere, thin blue air, he rode in out of the west? Howdy,
pardner, my name's Tex (or Shane or Wyatt). I come from a
town over yonder, maybe you've heard of it, Krypton? Only
that he would have been the antithesis of iron, lead, gravity, the
heaviness, weight of darkness, solitude, *loneliness.* Not that. A
country boy, shepherd boy, true Adonis, summer brown and
golden-haired with a wide bright smile, who lived in the sun
and fresh air and never worried, never brooded, never lost
himself in the depths of despair, beautiful the way the ancient
gods must have been beautiful, the way ancient artisans crafted
their gods to look beautiful, with strong lean bodies, curling
locks and serene faces, full lips and yearning priapuses carved
out of obdurate marble and stone. He loved, yes, loved him, and
hated him, resented him for his beauty and his strength, because
he could abandon the sun and the meadows and the call of the
panpipes and the young maids who yearned for his beauty and
the joy he took in life and go down into that pit stinking of
graveyards, cesspools, of fire and brimstone, of burning coal,
gas, the incineration of myth and history, of all that went before,
and without any knowledge whatsoever of the science or the
craft of iron raise the bar over his head as if he were lifting a
drowning child to its mother or an offering to God and stand
like a rock without wavering or trembling and then not touch
the iron for another month or two months and only on a whim
go back down into that pit and lift even more weight than he
had before, while *he,* he struggled for every pound, ounce,
gram. But in the end this friend, yes, monster, *friend,* this gifted
athlete, demi-god, didn't use that gift given him, didn't pursue
the iron. He went back up into the sun and fresh air and bird
song, calling, Come, Come with me, I know a girl, she has a
beautiful friend. But no, he couldn't. He *had* to go back down in
that stinking pit, *had* to raise his loneliness and obsession over

his head day after day and hold it there for God to see and approve, God alone to witness his triumph, his solitude, his ~~failure~~. Wait, what? Not failure, *future!* But why? his friend said. It's cold and dark and damp down there and she is beautiful and her breath sweet and her body warm. Come with me, forget the iron for just this day, let's all go to the sea for a week, the mountains next month. *And there, you see? That's how it goes. A day, a week, a month. And then you forget and forget and forget until you've forgotten forever and your body has rotted and sunk into the earth and you are no more and nobody remembers you.* But he didn't listen. He stopped his ears against such talk, closed out the sweet enticing words, entreaties, the laughing voice and bright eyes. Let him have his happy life with the woman he would marry and the house he would build and people with all the babies that were to come, let him disappear into that life and never seek out or hear from him again. In the end he triumphed, overcame, he alone endured, surpassed his friend's best efforts, squashed, humiliated him, would have, with his great strength, victory, with all that he accomplished, was going to. Yes, and what was that? That cloud of delusion and dream he lived in, convinced it was as real and solid as the iron bar he held in his hands?

Even when, impossibly—impossibly! *monster, ugly, deformed*—that day finally came when he found himself confronting, touching, *tasting* for the very first time in his life the soft lips and sweet milk breath and swelling breasts of a young woman not much more than a girl herself. But how on God's green earth did that happen? Oh, I know. Assigned a seat next to her in his Romantic Lit class, instantly smitten by this cute sex kitten, *howl-owl-owooo,* the sly fox, the big bad wolf, he said smooth as silk, glass, Hi, there, sweetheart, little darlin', *honey,* what's *your* name? Well, no, not exactly, in fact, the opposite, not he who did the talking, au contraire. She gave him a curious glance, like, hmm, is this really a monster sitting next to me? and, minoring in anthropology after all (mythology?), *she* said, Hi, what's *your* name? He was utterly smitten.

(Already said that, dumbbell.) She was thin, willowy, a windblown sprite, hamadryad, out of the pages, poems, he held in his hands, with golden and honey tangles of hair, tendrils, falling around her face and her features finely defined, like spun glass, and her eyes the color of the sea, in pictures he'd seen, *aquamarine*. But what did she see in him? He was a monster, bashful, blushing, shy, but a monster nonetheless, horns growing out of his head, cloven hooves, that *tail*. So all the more stunned to find himself deep in the woods beneath the flickering canopy of leaf, sunlight and patches of blue sky with her, this otherworldly creature, *naked*, he wanted to stare at her, record in his mind what she looked like so that he would remember when—when what? But this is no time for questions, doubts, more important business to attend to. She, the temptress, nymph, beckoning to him? He, kicking and bleating, leering, laughing madly, a satyr? No, not like that, at all, totally unschooled, inexperienced, no idea whatsoever whether to guide or be guided, to allow himself to be soft, vulnerable, and still strong, to convert iron into flesh and flesh into iron, much less the concept of pleasure, his or hers, only that here now in her arms in her embrace with the ache and burning of the molten iron, that hot cauldron bubbling, erupting, too suddenly spent. And then, after this *attempt* to make love (exactly how does one *make* love? the way you make a fire, build a house? Oh, it's another *quaint* expression?), after this *attempt*, I repeat, go through all the confessions and agonies of the soul, divulge, show, put on display for each other to weigh, consider, possibly forgive, their deep, dark secrets, their petty crimes and misdemeanors? But no, the iron man, solid, stolid, say nothing, tell her nothing, reveal nothing, even if she did, why not? happy home, loving parents, oh, and she loved to smoke pot. *Gosh, you mean drugs?* And then ask again, What the heck was she doing with him? They were completely different. He was iron and stone, the mountain fortress, the gloom of wintry castle keeps. She was the spring breeze, the balmy summer evening, the sun's brilliance on the Aegean. As if he knew anything

about the Aegean or any other sea. As if he knew anything.
Landlocked from birth, a country bumpkin lumpkin. She
ridiculed the stupid, uninformed things he said, she mocked his
pursuit of the iron, laughed at him when he said he was going to
do something great one day. What have you ever done? What
have you won? Where are your medals, trophies, ribbons,
awards? She laughed at his heavy plodding step and gloomy
thoughts, laughed when he tried to lead her down into that dark
pit, to see, maybe to try it, the iron, *she*, a *girl*. She enticed him
to eat the lotus with her and learn its secrets, kief, hashish,
ganja, weed, *primo bud, dude.* And you know, maybe he did
take a toke or two, *but he didn't inhale.* If only he could let go,
allow her to lift him up from the earth and carry him away with
her on the wind to some island in the sun and live the rest of
their lives in a paradise crowded with palm fronds and orchids
and a brood of fat laughing babies. Ah, but when she talked like
that, suggested such possibilities, come with me on a magic
carpet ride, he recoiled inside, looked at her darkly, suspicious,
as if she were a witch casting spells in front of her like fishing
nets, allowed his darkness to spoil everything just when a key
might have turned, a door opened onto another world,
possibility, dimension, something other than this, say it,
obsession with the iron. *Other* but not exclusive of because he
could not *never* imagine a world without the iron. Because *love*
did not have the same credence as iron, did not have the same
mass, density. Because he had to be able to measure it
somehow, he had to give it weight and meaning so he could say
afterwards I lifted so many pounds, so many drams of love, or if
indeed she was nymph, hamadryad, then amphorae, measured in
the weight of honey, olive oil, wine. He was saying yes, yes,
yes and smiling so hard his head hurt at the same time another
voice in the back of his brain was denying everything, shouting,
no! no! no! Hard Work! Discipline! Madness! Iron! So how did
that work? He loved, yes, loved, said to her love, desired, felt
attached to, part of, wanted to be with her all the time, to touch,
feel, marvel that he was touching, at the very same time,

madness, *madness*, he felt that terrible urgency and need, he had to go this instant, back down in that stinking hole with the iron and forget her smile and her pretty face and her soft lips, forget the place filling up inside him with fresh air and sunshine, with life, laughter and love, and remember, remind himself, pound that mantra into his head, the iron is not dead, I am not dead, when, by his every action, he ensured the exact opposite, that living death, commitment to death, that slow death beneath the crushing weight of gravity. And then wonder why the next time he saw her she only looked at him sadly and turned away, wonder why the next time he saw her after that she was with some other guy, a tall, thin, willowy, windblown sprite with tangles of long hair and brilliant flashing eyes and wispy mustache over a soft sensuous mouth, wonder why after that he never saw her again or if he did it was always from afar and she looked happy and laughing like she was having fun and enjoying life.

O love, love and loss of love. She dropped him and let him fall the way he let the bar slip from his grip and fall *crash* to the floor because he couldn't, didn't, unbearably heavy, impossible to move, he just felt too damn bad, okay, say it, *sad*, to carry on as usual. How could he have known he would feel such pain? Or that such pain could exist? How could he have known that something as insubstantial as a smile, a caress, her soft lips and breasts, her simple presence, and the absence, loss, of all that, could crush him and knock him to the floor, crumpled, a lump of putty, melted wax? His grief shorn him of all strength, of the will, he had no appetite, no desire to eat or read or walk in the woods beneath the trees or in the meadow by the stream. He could do nothing more than lie on his mattress and groan and moan like a lovelorn ogre.

A knock on the door aroused him from his funk. Mrs. Grumble's watery blue eyes (allergies? tears of compassion?) peered down at him kindly. How did she know? Telepathic? A message from God (anything for a saint)? Was he that obvious? Oh, the poor young man looked troubled, his hair tangled, unkempt, dark circles under his eyes. Would he like to come up for dinner? He'd hardly eaten anything in days, a few spoons of peanut butter, half a green apple, a stale crust of whole wheat bread. He wolfed down the roast beef and baked potato Mrs. Grumble placed before him, consumed the slice of fresh baked cherry pie she gave him in a trice, and when she excused herself to answer the phone, it rings all the time, those dratted telemarketers (tinnitus, actually), he scarfed down the rest of the pie in three, four, five bites. Goodness me, I'm getting forgetful, Mrs. Grumble mumbled, taking the empty plate out to the kitchen. I wanted to offer the young man another slice.

His improved appetite suggested that if not entirely recovered from heartbreak, he was recovering. Still, something had undeniably changed, something to do with her, the loss he felt, the pain. But, dimwit, dunce, once again he misunderstood what that small dissident voice in his heart, in his head, was telling him. Instead of further self-examination, a new direction, way, path in life, he rededicated himself to the iron. Once again his will triumphed, he took the hollowness and aching back down with him into his basement and converted it into force, energy and drive, he approached the iron and raised it up again, one, two, three, four, five. Even when he was away from the iron, when he sat in class taking a test, or in the library (primitive structure for the storage of print information—Ed.) reading a book or writing a paper, the iron occupied his mind, he filled his notebooks with formulas, sketches, projections, obsessively, compulsively, reviewed, copied down, guestimated how much he lifted, was going to lift, yesterday, today, tomorrow. He went all day expending energy in trying to conserve energy for the next lifting session, thought about nothing but the weight he was going to lift today until the thought of the weight became heavier and more unbearable than the weight itself. *How many times can I say* weight *and still not know if I have explained correctly or you have understood correctly what that weight is, a weight that can not be called a weight in ordinary human language, not just so many pounds of iron but the real and undeniable reminder of mortality, of the crushing burden of life, a weight that must constantly be defined and redefined in your mind even in the process of lifting it, so that you are always surprised yourself to find that the weight is not what you remembered or expected it to be, that it has already, in a matter of seconds, less, in the time it takes for one thought to morph into another, become something else, sometimes an empty shell filled with nothing, air, that you can lift overhead like a broomstick, but more often than not an impossibly heavy object, an immovable mass. You never know how heavy the iron will be until you actually approach it.* Waiting for, anticipating that moment to arrive, that optimal time of day according to the stars in the sky, according to the clock ticking in his body, in his brain, on the shelf, according to his ability to withstand the waiting one more second. And still that waiting, that anticipation and yearning, countered by the raw fear, yes, fear, churning in his bowels so that he felt like he was going to shit himself for fear of the task ahead, for what he wished to accomplish and how hard he'd have to work to accomplish it. If he could just tell himself and convince himself that's all it was, just hard work, just a job to do like any other job, just get down there and do it and soon it'll be done and then you can go off and do something else, maybe have a little fun. But that isn't possible, is it? Never fun, maybe when he was a child, a little boy, he knew what fun was (probably not), but now, no, not fun. But stop it, don't think like that, the negativity, the inevitability, the *hopelessness*, just take it easy, take it as it comes, we're going to do it, we're going to get it done, succeed. Giving himself a pep talk for the effort ahead, for when that moment arrived, when he couldn't stand it anymore, he had to go down to the basement, do it now, clang and bang and drive himself to complete every set and every rep of overhead presses, curls, benches, squats, deadlifts. But not the old way, one, two, three, four, five, etc., a new method, recently discovered in his weightlifting magazine, the inverted pyramid, more reps and a lighter weight to warm up and then progressively heavier weights as the number of reps diminished and the effort required to complete them increased, eight reps, seven, six, five, forrr, threeee, his counting more strained, attenuated, his breathing coming in gasps, *huh-huh-huh* twoooo, groaning aloud as he made that final maximum endeavor, *uhhhhh*, one! Between sets massage the deep cleaving ache, nagging, chronic, in his biceps and deltoids with warm, penetrating balms and liniments and cool soothing ointments he'd added to his kit of voodoo accouterments, then press on (pun unavoidable) to the benches, the curls, the squats and deadlifts, arrive at last at the final set, rep, *huh-huh-huh*, squeeeeze it out, *arrrrgh*, done.

Yes, you're done, you've finished lifting the iron for today, so now you can begin to think about lifting the iron tomorrow and the next day and the day after that, a never ending continuum from now until the end of time. Because even when he was completely worn out and exhausted in body and spirit, devoid of any energy whatsoever, and the thought of approaching the iron again filled him with dread, he refused to admit to himself that he was worn out, that he was no longer progressing, that he had grown *stale*, because he didn't understand, fully comprehend yet, what staleness meant, an invisible nemesis, the descent into, result of, monotony, *unvarying*, routine, didn't understand or refused to admit to himself that he could fall out of love, lose his passion, not having had the experience of falling out of love, hadn't accounted, allowed for the possibility that the thing he loved could betray him, enervate him, that he was not only not making progress but growing weaker, as if each day he had been exposed to a slightly higher dosage of kryptonite. His dreams of glory beaten to the ground by fatigue and ensuing despair because he had not accomplished what he had planned, hoped to accomplish by now, because he was reminded of how much more he must accomplish. Sitting on the bench in the cooling embers of his defeat, staring into the bare bulb overhead, its pale fire draining him, sucking out of him the energy and will, telling himself he was no good, *worthless*. That hopelessness that descended upon enveloped him like a leaden cloud blanket when he doubted himself, his vision. Wasn't he supposed to be some kind of world champion by now? More than that, a world conqueror, not just the known world of a different time, ancient Greece and Rome, the Levant, the Magreb, Egypt and Mesopotamia, the Silk Road and all of Asia, but the entire world today, Alexander the Greater? He had always held those distant goals and dreams in his mind, assumed he was acting on them, but had he ever actually seen himself achieving, realizing those goals and dreams in a concrete manner, as a physical fact, a reality to supplant the current non-reality?

It should be mentioned, the defense wishes to admit in evidence, that there was a period, brief, when he, their client, searched through his mystical weightlifting magazine, so he perceived it, for news of upcoming competitions, and even told himself, okay, I'll go to this one, convinced that he would, he even sent in the registration form and fee. And then? What'd you expect? Of course he didn't go, his anxiety growing as the day approached, his fear not of failure but taking action (thanks, *Dad*), rationalizing, excusing himself, denying, lying, it's not important, I'll wait until I'm really ready. But when was that? When was he ever going to be ready? Only rarely did he attempt to perform the Olympic lifts, the mechanics of which continued to elude, in fact, intimidate him, the *clean and jerk?* the *snatch?* Hmm, sounds *erotic*. His Shakespeare prof, to whom, for reasons unknown even to himself, he had confided his interest in the iron, her response shocking, offending him, a *woman*, said *that*, about the *iron*, *mocked* it, *him*, she even *laughed*. She had no idea how hard, difficult, to perform, execute, the snatch, with that awkward wide grip that, yes, he understood, was intended to reduce the distance the bar had to travel but—and this was the part that scared him—then he had to simultaneously drop into a full squat beneath the bar and catch it overhead in mid-air at arm's length. A half-assed, sloppy   attempt   carried   weighty   consequences,   a   slight miscalculation and *yee-ow!* he caught the bar wrong, bent his hands backwards too far, the pain sudden, sharp, like somebody had smacked him on the wrists with an iron bar. Then they went numb. Did he break them? But wait, he could still move his hands, the pain seemed to be going away. Miraculously, the next day his hands, wrists, were okay and he forged ahead with the same disregard, resorted to the same old folly of heaving and groaning like an ox beneath the weight of the iron. Because no matter what obstacle, setback, heartache, staleness, injury, he must adhere to his schedule, his routine, he couldn't afford to miss a single day, because then his whole program would be off, he'd never succeed, never reach his goals, which even now he couldn't begin to define, some nebulous and unattainable quantity of gravity measured in grams, molecules, and bound together by the indomitable, unconquerable iron will.

But that's exaggerating again, hyperbole, he wasn't entirely an iron man, invincible, impenetrable, solid, stolid, locked away in his fortress of solitude, in that dungeon, cell, a hermit, mad monk, anchorite. He did come up for air on other occasions, in his weakness succumb to weakness, when his despair became too much, his loneliness, not just straying away from the iron but drugged, drunken debauchery, there's proof, evidence, somebody's always watching, snooping, recording every move, unbeknownst to him, of course, the rube, hayseed, techno ignoramus, cellphones, security cameras, drones hovering overhead, iris and biometric scans in soda and snack dispensers, *Hi! How are you today,* (insert customer name)? *Care for a candy bar or a soda,* (insert customer name)? selfies, wedgies (ha, ha), camera grabs, crotch grabs (ha. ha.), photo bombs, those winedrunk nights when he could no longer stand his own company and, his fortunes changing? fate intervening? serendipity? a classmate, casual acquaintance from Sixteenth Century British Lit, invited him to a party, who knows, maybe thinking to himself, this guy's pretty weird, maybe he'll be entertaining, a conversation piece, trained ape, and he obliged, King Kong unchained, he gleefully plunged into vats of wine and mead, joyfully puffed on opium and hash pipes, performed bravado strongman stunts, heaved a sofa with two occupants overhead, bent an iron fireplace poker with his bare hands, at some point, far more amazing, found himself talking earnestly to a girl, young woman, pretty, he liked her, maybe she liked him, what happened to that? Later still arguing some arcane point, red in the face, yelling back and forth, *But that's the point, that's what I'm trying to explain!* The conversation inevitably leading, well—budding rhetorician?—he led it there, to the iron. Even later that night, still filled with exuberance *madness*, actually leading his new buddies, young rakes, revelers all, tumbling down the steep, creaking wooden stairs into his cellar fortress roaring with laughter and shushing each other, *shh, my landlady! shh, hizh landlady, hmmmph!* even though dear old Mrs. Grumble couldn't hear a word they said, deaf as a donut. It didn't even bother him that his new friends— his *friends!*—laughed when they saw his shabby quarters. Apartment and condo dwellers, modern appliances, all the amenities that Dad and Mumsy's money can buy, they're looking around like, Seriously, Dude, you live in this pit? Ha! And what's this? Gathering around his weights, his racks and bench. An antique farm implement? A spent fuel rod from a nuclear core? He's arguing back, good-naturedly, no, you've got it all wrong, weightlifting is great. Repeating all the health benefits, psychological reasons, you know that old saying, I think it's Latin, *French? in corpore* sans *mens?* And then of course he had to demonstrate what this weightlifting was all about, wanted, *needed*, someone to see just how powerful, *strong*, he really was, without any warm-up proceeded to lift the heaviest weight he was capable of, in one foolish moment, a misplaced foot, his grip slipping, the barbell crashing to the floor, he *fucked up*, possibly even injured himself again, undid, ruined months' of close and careful planning. But oh no! It was nothing! Open another bottle! Laughing and shouting and telling himself it didn't matter, he was living life, having fun. And oh what fun next morning, sick, hung-over, that glorpy, gloopy nausea roiling his stomach, the municipal employee of the year, street division, pounding away in his head with a sledgehammer, a pain in his ankle whose origin he didn't remember, and of course the iron sitting there, oiled, shining, grinning at him, mocking, challenging him to put his hands on the bar and get back to work, to push and drive himself beyond all limits and endurance, to punish himself for his betrayal, until he was sick and vomiting and swearing that he would never again repeat last night's folly. Utterly disgusted with himself, his so-called *friends*, with all their blather and nonsense, mostly his, that had seemed so vital and wise last night. Resolving, promising himself, yes, naïve, who hasn't? that he'd never have anything to do with them again, never again allow himself to be distracted from his goal, purpose in life, the iron. No, he would not go under, succumb, *untermensch*, *cockroach*. Somehow he must not only surpass his previous accomplishments but go beyond, so far beyond that no one could ever approach his achievement.

V
YOU CAN'T GO HOME AGAIN

FOR ALL HE WAS CONCERNED he might have gone on like that forever, the perennial student, never quite finishing his education, lingering, switching majors, staying on in perpetuity, meanwhile finding a niche, a modest living arrangement, a job tolerable enough and that tolerated his growing eccentricities, sustained him into old age, sort of, dog food and white bread sandwiches, doctor's visits permanently postponed, declining mental faculties, unattended personal hygiene, turning into a stinking, drooling, wild-haired, wild-eyed old madman terrifying children, housewives, *hey Aqualung*. And then one day late in spring, the semester just come to an end, he received a letter in the mail, hand-delivered, Pony Express, *the only mail in years, the old nag could barely make it from one station to the next*. Dear *son*, we haven't heard from you in some time (and vice versa), although we know you must still be there as the checks we have sent have all been cashed. This is partly why I am writing. By now you must have finished your studies so we, your mother and I, are asking you to come home. Unfortunately, our fortunes have taken a turn for the worse. We're getting older and we could use your support. Look forward to seeing you again. Yourlovingfather and mother. The *loving* crammed into that brief valediction clearly an afterthought, possibly in case of some later legal ramifications, wills, estates, court-ordered institutionalization of *either party*.

Truth be told, he'd finished his studies long ago, more than fulfilled his degree requirements, he just needed someone to make it official, show him the door, give him the boot, a harbinger, messenger, *fly, O winged Mercury*. Still, it snuck up on him, caught him flat-footed. Curiously, coincidentally, he received another piece of mail, a manila envelope, a diploma contained within, his name in black Gothic script, another kind of eviction notice, Dean Dong's signature not so firmly affixed at the bottom in *delible* ink, erasable, untraceable, quickly fades away, you know, just in case of future purges, with the added personal endearment, *Here's your piece of paper, punk. Now get outa Dodge.*

   And that was it, no graduation ceremony, pomp and circumstances, only this, disaster, catastrophe, not just his *cushy* lifestyle come to an end, but, age-old logistical problem, how the heck was he going to get his weights back home? And then, disaster upon disaster, as if to throw both oil and tragedy on the fire—wait, what? *FIRE!* He smelled smoke. Ran upstairs, outside. Orange flames roared from the kitchen window. He ran around front, pounded on the door. No answer. With a single kick he broke the door down, ran inside. Flames were spreading through the back of the house. No sign of Mrs. Grumble. He galloped up the winding wooden stairway, noticing and not noticing the blue and white fleur-de-lis patterned wainscoting, the gilt-framed oil paintings, still lifes, fruit in vases, dashed from room to room on the second floor, finally pushed open a closed door at the end of the hall, entered a strange fairyland boudoir of faded wall hangings, draperies, cob-webbed crystal chandelier and mirrors, found Mrs. Grumble blissfully asleep in a ghostly white, canopied four-poster bed decorated with equally white crepe and ostrich feathers, kind of like a palanquin or horse drawn funeral wagon. Lifting her in his arms as if she were a broomstick, he hurried back downstairs and outside and lay her on the ground, still asleep, then ran back down to the basement and after a second-*two-three* of staring around in wild-eyed desperation, grabbed the empty barbell and clambered back upstairs to safety just as the whole house went up in flames. Then, sirens screaming, fire trucks arriving, EMS, people milling around. Was there anybody else besides the old lady? What about that guy in the basement? The tenant? He must have saved her life! He's a *hero!* He didn't hear, had already wandered off, started walking, his oversized magic wand, his rod and staff, slung over his shoulder, his wallet and a couple bucks in his pocket, a hundred miles ahead of him, the determination of a dead man in his eyes.

If this *were* a fairytale you can be sure he would have many trials, tribulations and adventures on his Hobittian journey afoot, all of which he would overcome with his wits and his trusty barbell, fire-breathing dragons, blood-sucking vampires, lobotomized, cerebrophagic zombies, giant robotic monsters, growling, bloody ogres, trolls, orcs, flaming pits, fallen bridges, boiling oil poured from towering fortress walls, county tax assessors—if it *were* a fairytale.

There were no welcome home parties, no banners and balloons, no tears of joy, no hearty hugs and slaps on the back, no gold watch, new car, fifty bucks from Uncle Pete (John, Al). When he entered the home of his childhood and adolescence after three, four, *five?* year's absence the notfather and the notmother only looked at him with weary contempt, recognizing him at last as the stranger he had always known himself to be, only a little less novel now. A degree in *Literature?* What the *fuhh*—dge? Where was the product of their investment? The service he could render? The thing of value he could tender on the market and make some money? The notfather speaking *in hushed tones* to the notmother later that evening. *Yesss*, money, the notmother whispered, hissed actually, having one of her *fits*, my *preciousss*. Capitalists both, more accurately capitalist dupes, thought they got a piece of the pie in the sky, chess, cheesecake, cherry, chocolate, key lime. Wrong. They both looked much older, tireder, weighed down, *freighted*, by the burdens of life, the vicissitudes, the Scylla and Charybdis one *might* even say, of fortune and misfortune. Look, *son* (there's that word again), times have changed, business has been bad, money's too tight to mention. We can't afford to support your lazy habits anymore. You'll have to fend for yourself. Oh, one other thing, we've rented out your room. This is your new (not)brother, Elmer (or Frank or Ray), who pays his way.

He didn't say anything, simply turned, took himself and his barbell down to the basement, which remained little changed from the last time he'd seen it, a bit more cluttered, a bit danker, ranker, the cobwebs in the rafters thicker, half a foot of water standing in the southeast corner. He set things in order as best he could, cleared a space for his barbell, unrolled an old mattress on the floor, then went upstairs for dinner. The notparents looked at him as if he were an antelope. Finally the notmother placed in front of him a piece of stale bread and a glass of water. He surveyed the table. The others each had half a boiled potato and a thin slice of cheese on their plates. In addition to this frugal fare, Elmer (or Carl or Steve) also had half a raw onion and a spot of mustard. But if the notparents were worried that he, their notson, was going to lapse into former habits, lounging in front of the TV and eating them out of house and home, they had no need for concern. He was determined to find a job, earn enough money to get out of here, find his own place, most importantly rebuild his armory, his arsenal of iron. For the moment, however, things looked bleak. There was no joy in Mudville, no jobs in Metropolis, times hard, the global market in collapse. And then, who knows, is there really a thing called fate? He ran into a guy he knew in high school, not a friend really, more of a tormentor, nemesis (note to self: not to be confused with *emesis*), but, past offenses forgiven, young men now, mature, *adults*. Hey, old pal, old chum. Long time no see. You say you're looking for work? A glint, gleam, *cruel, malicious,* in his eye (a figure of speech, both actually, *eyes*). My brother needs some *help* on his framing crew. Hard work, long hours, lousy pay. He came home at night sore, aching, his hands raw. The notparents said, well, that's something, he has a job, he can pay rent. Didn't change a thing in the family dynamic, he was still an outcast. In communal silence he ate his dinner, gained somewhat in proportion, everyone's portion having gained from his added income, trying to concentrate, to think about, to find the energy after this day of grueling labor to go back down into that pit and go to work again.

Wait ... *what?*

Despite paying rent and helping to put bread on the table, he managed to save a few extra pfennigs each week, acquired a pair of fifty pound cast-iron plates, slid them onto the bar, *skriiiick, bang, skriiiick, bang*, assembled his train wheels again, lovingly, oiled and shining, the excitement he felt, the anticipation, to experience that familiar resistance, to feel gravity's pull and that explosion of power and joy, white-hot, electric, in his brain when he overcame that pull. An aura, halo, luminous, glowing, enveloped him, he was that incandescent bulb glowing overhead, that acetylene torch in the sky, the sun, sending light into the darkness, evaporating the shadows, the basement gloom. True, the loaded barbell weighed only a hundred and fifty pounds, practically nothing, he could throw it overhead like a broomstick, but as soon as he saved enough money he intended to add to his iron reserves. This renewed hope, optimism, energized him, gave him the strength, the will, to go down into that dank gray basement, his dray horse stable, to return to his gladiatorial regimen, even after a long hard day of manual labor.

Once again he saw a bright horizon ahead, a future in the future, a path to success, yes, still not clearly defined, but somewhere in that general direction, *forward, men.* Then fate took another turn, the weather changed, first rain, then bitter cold. Snow covered everything, the wind lashed his face, the ground turned hard as iron, the cold penetrated his boots and burned his feet until they went numb. He banged his elbows and knees hauling unwieldy sheets of plywood, lumber, nearly broke his neck slipping on icy ladders and scaffolding. His work gloves offered minimal protection against the cold, worst of all when he hit his thumb with the hammer *yeowww!* And after a day of that, go back home, go down into that cold stinking *abase*ment and *make* himself, his body, mind, go to work again? Afterwards perform his minimal evening ablutions, stand over a pan of hot water collected from the streams constantly trickling down the walls and heated over an improvised charcoal burner, the damp cloth in his hand, washing the obvious places, under his arms, his asshole and crotch, his body streaming rivulets of sweat. In the process burning away and stripping off every ounce of accumulated and extraneous flesh, dark circles forming under his eyes, his jaw and cheekbones more pronounced, his strength waxing not waning. There's gotta be a better way, right? Enough's enough? Yeah, maybe he thought that, would have acted on that, looked for another job, better situation, be prepared, *maybe*, but he didn't, *inertia*, the boss said it first. I'm heading across the pond, the big water, whale road, for a much-needed vacation, you guys are on your own. It didn't take the notparents long to notice he wasn't going to work anymore. Uh-oh, they'd seen this show before. Now he had no job, no income, he was back down there banging and clanging with that *dratted* iron again, and what on God's good earth were they going to do when this beast demanded food?

He had his own concerns. As the pages continued to fly off the calendar like pigeons startled from their roost, and warm and then warmer weather returned like the breath of a lamb and then a lion, and he, his body, yearned to excel, to revel in his still youthful youth, alas, he was limited, bound, by the limited poundage of iron, no more challenge in lifting his single pair of train wheels, not even equal to his much-reduced bodyweight. This situation he planned to change. In the lush farmland surrounding this bucolic if nebulously located village our hero resided in, old MacDonald had a cow pasture and in that pasture sat old MacDonald's tractor and on this tractor same said hero had noticed two large iron wheels, which, he estimated, must weigh at least a couple hundred pounds each. He thought about

these wheels every day, became obsessed with them, *fixated*.
Finally one night, just after dusk, a waxing gibbous moon on
the horizon, he slipped between the strands of barbed wire
enclosing the pasture, strode across the minefield of briars,
brambles and dried brown cowpies and examined the wheels
close up. Old MacDonald had clearly neglected a regular
maintenance schedule. The bolts, collars, cotter pins and
washers that held the wheels in place had rusted solid. Maybe if
he had an acetylene torch. Maybe if he had an industrial laser.
The next day he studied the assortment of tools some handy
manly ancestor of the notfather's had left in the horse barn cum
garage, hammers, hand drills, mangels and pipe wrenches,
gradually reducing the possibilities to one, a rusty hacksaw
blade. Crude, primitive, *crazy*. Later that night he wandered up
the tree-lined, moon-shadowed farm lane, stepped through the
barbed wire fence, trudged across the overgrown field to the
tractor. He had no idea how long this might take. Hours? Days?
Just in case he placed large fieldstones under the axles so the
tractor wouldn't collapse on the ground, then knelt down next to
the left wheel and began to saw at the axle. Without a handle
the hacksaw blade dug into his hands, the night was hot, the
heat and fire of his exertion burned in his arms, in his hands and
wrists, sweat dripped from his forehead. A rooster crowed, the
moon was almost down, he'd barely cut half an inch into the
axle. He'd have to come back tomorrow, meaning tonight. And
he did. He came back that night and the next night and the next.
Each night he worked on the opposite axle, judging his progress
one wheel against the other. He slept less and less as he pursued
his obsession. Early in the morning he crept home hollow-eyed,
his hair tangled with sweat. The notmother and notfather did not
fail to notice his nocturnal comings and goings. Do you suppose
there's a girl involved, the notfather wondered aloud, not
without a little pride at the prospect of his (putative, purported)
prodigy's being a chip off the old blockhead. The notmother
pondered this possibility with sour-faced distaste. I should
certainly hope *not*. But what if he's up to some criminal

enterprise? the notfather persisted. The notmother pondered this suggestion with slightly less disgust and in a plainspoken Ma Barker drawl said, You think he might share some of the loot with us? At last the night arrived when he knew he would finish the job. He made the final cut on the right axle and the wheel came away from the tractor. He rolled it across the field, through a convenient gap in the barbed wire, and homeward over high hill and low dale, over deep ruts and stones in the road, an owl hooting, the moon a crescent, a dog barking somewhere, and finally up the drive and into the garage. He was already beat, his energy spent, but he had to finish the job tonight, and he did, returned to the pasture, cut the left wheel loose from the tractor, rolled it home, into the garage and, completely exhausted, sank down on his mattress for a deep sleep, his best in weeks, the whole day through and the next night too, until, his mind and body filled, flooded with sleep, he woke early the following morning, crack of dawn, rooster crowing, great balls of fire, time's a wastin', gotta get back to work, *clang, bang*. Taking up a sledge hammer, he knocked the rust-welded pieces of axle out of the tractor wheels and, splendid coincidence, if not magic, or at least standardized metric, or even, those wild and crazy bomb-throwing revolutionaries, American, the barbell sleeves fit perfectly in the wheels' empty center bores. Scrounging around in an abandoned junkyard, always one of those out in the country, he added various iron gears and wheels until he had a passable assembly of greater and lesser increments of weights.

Now the iron was all he had and no matter what he did it had to be for the iron. He lay down on his mattress at night demanding enough rest, don't anyone dare disturb his sleep, shoot the dog, strangle the cat, put a pillow over the baby's face, blow up the TV, but don't make any noise, not a sound, nary a peep or a squeak. Shut up! Be quiet! he shouted, pounding on the wooden rafters over his head with the empty barbell, the fallen saint Nick, *Satan*, in his infernal pit shouting back his own remonstrances at the notfather stand-in for the

aforementioned self-righteous ass Johnathan (fart face) Edwards
(*plbbbb!*). At dinnertime he stormed upstairs and demanded by
his glowering presence at the table something to eat. But none
of this slop! he shouted at the notmother. Good food! I want
only good food! But of course by now, without his income, his
poor parents were destitute, practically starving themselves.
Their adoptive son Elmer (or Edgar or Ted) had divorced
himself from the family. There was no money coming in and
very little to eat. They were almost in rags and couldn't afford
his extravagances. Just as necessity is the mother of invention,
hunger is the father of savagery. At night he snuck into old
MacDonald's chicken coop, went down the line of nesting
boxes robbing eggs from under the sleepy-eyed brooding hens,
cracked the bloodied, poopy, unwashed eggs between his teeth
and sucked the gooey mass down his throat, then wrung the
chickens' necks, tore off their heads and feathers and ate them
raw. He snuck into old Mac's barn, got down on his knees in
the hay straw and cow flop, took the cow's teats in his mouth
and sucked out the green grass sweetness, the milk and
buttercream, and then to satisfy his appetite he bit off a chunk of
hindquarters. *There's a monster among us!* the villagers cried.
He roamed the meadows and forest glades in search of edible
herbs, roots and tubers. He stood naked in a cold running stream
watching for the flash of scale and fin and then his hand shot
out and he tore the coldblooded creature from the even colder
water, sank his teeth into and devoured the gelid, still quivering
flesh. He waited for hours in the dim green light of moss and
fern and overhanging canopy of leaves, sniffing the air for the
scent of some fur-coated, hooved beast, ran down antler and
hoof, tore the tawny hide heaving and panting with fear out of
the green forest, broke its neck, tore off limbs, ripped loose
chunks of bloody meat, swallowed them raw. He leapt into the
air and with his bare hands tore out of the blue sky and pulled
down to earth the brown flutter and beating of wings, gorged
himself on venison, fish and fowl, swallowed whole and alive
the living flesh in the belief that he would obtain the strength of

that flesh. In another time and place he might even have hunted down, killed and eaten the flesh of his own kind and picked his teeth clean with tibia, fibula, femur and rib. *A monster!* Each day he dined al fresco, allowed his meal to digest, disseminate protein, essential amino acids, vitamins and minerals through arteries, veins, blood vessels and capillaries and finally infuse the raw muscle fibers aching to be fed, engorged with fresh nutrients in preparation for the next workout.

And, sure, he was making great gains in size and strength. The rare times he went out in public, took a stroll into town to see what that public looked like, he inadvertently knocked people off the sidewalk into the street, tore door frames from the wall when he entered the public library, the post office. Benches in the public park collapsed beneath his weight. Everywhere he went people stopped to stare at him in horror and awe. Little children tugged at their mothers' skirts and pointed, Mommy! Look! King Kong! No dear, that's not King Kong. It's just a gorilla. A very big gorilla. Okay, that's an exaggeration, more hyperbole, stretching the fabric, whole cloth, sail cloth, three sheets to the wind, to be perfeckly honesht an outright lie. No giant he, Brobdingnagian, Polyphemusian, Paul Bunion-Onion-ian, titanic. All in his head, *delusional*. On the other hand, yes, pretty damn big, although glimpses he caught of himself in shop windows, narcissistic mud puddles, revealed not a buff, chiseled, *shredded* superhero but a bulky beef cow. How had he lost himself inside this excess meat? How convinced himself that brute strength was the only path? All this size and strength was fine if he wanted to get a job cracking walnuts or hauling tons of iron ore up out of a mine, but what about his adolescent vision, somewhat vague, no clearer now than then, maybe even murkier, viewed through a glass, darkly, something to do with lifting, moving, calibrating the universe and raising up the world, a gift and offering to God? But, that paradox, irony again, the more his strength increased, the farther away his goals seemed, the more uncalibratable that universe, more distant that God. And yet he saw no way out of his dilemma but to work harder, lift heavier weights. *You add ten, twenty, thirty pounds, you think you're getting stronger, you think, tomorrow I'll lift two hundred, next week two hundred and fifty, next month three hundred, next year four-five-six hundred, you see the weight adding up in your mind, you think you're getting stronger but instead you're getting weaker. What is fifty or a hundred or even a thousand pounds next to God and eternity? You think you're Atlas holding the world on your shoulders, but you don't see the weight is crushing you into the ground.* Every day he had to lift more than the day before out of the insane belief that by sheer will he could take the universe in his hands and forge it into a perfect entity and raise it over his head and hold it there for eternity according to the ironclad contract he had signed with some unknown and unknowable god, according to the madness imposed upon him by the falsified memories of some corrupt, unaccountable and possibly even nonexistent old madman before him invading and taking over his body and his mind, until he found himself perpetrating an even greater madness than that which had preceded him, sowing even greater destruction and ruin, even now, when he knew, should have known better, his experience told him, he'd been pushing it too hard, too long. Yes, yes, I know how it goes. All right, you say to yourself, I'll make one more heavy attempt, I'll reach one more goal, I'll push myself hard this one last time, and then I'll take a break and put it aside. But even as you say this you deny, refuse to admit, you ignore your body's warning signs, those tiny telegraphers tapping away, conveying messages of danger from north, south, east and west, *Indians! Terrible Turks! Mongol Hordes!* you refute the rational arguments of a, yes, perhaps irrational *unsound* mind, challenge your own sanity with insanity, *unreason*, the slightest suggestion of a pause, hiatus, moratorium utter treason, betrayal, and you push yourself to this point tomorrow and the next day and the day after that until suddenly you don't go on, the whole mad process stops in the sudden shock and irrefutable evidence of your own mortality, disaster!

A day like any other, approaching the end of his workout, the final set, the bar lying across his shoulders, just beginning to rise out of the position of catharsis, evacuation, the full squat, just finish this last rep and who cares if it's a little sloppy, if your body isn't quite aligned properly, even though he can hear that old man's voice bitter with ages of failure and regret shouting *No! Not like that! You're not a goddamn ape squatting on the side of a mountain taking a shit. You're a man, the first man, heroic, rising up, struggling to lift yourself out of the clay, before your eyes the gift of God, the ineffable beauty, edenic, of this virgin planet.* But he wasn't thinking of that now, he didn't remember, he only had one more repetition, he only had to stand up one more time with this relatively insignificant weight and be finished for the day, he felt something give, just the slightest shifting of muscle or tendon, a kind of sigh, a susurration of tissue, membrane, separating, tearing apart like the dewy silk of a spider web, and then, suddenly, out of nowhere, the blue, a pain unlike any he'd ever experienced before, a thunderbolt in his back, an iron rod shattering, penetrating muscle and bone, crushing, destroying, cleaving. Somehow he managed to return the weight to the rack, let it crash down on the stands, then hobbled, bent like an old man, collapsed on his bed of straw, his dirty mattress on the concrete floor. It's nothing, he told himself, a pinch or a pull, a quirk or a jerk, even as the red-hot irons, pitch forks, continued to stab into his back. Denial. A lie told to the self by the self to convince, persuade the self. And the truth? Who knows? That all along he had been struggling to defeat himself, to force that final and irrevocable trauma, an excuse never again to have to make that effort, never again have to struggle like that in loneliness and solitude? Which might explain the strange ambivalence he felt, the slightest edge of perversity and even *pleasure* as the molten iron of his body began to harden and cool and he felt the muscles across his back stiffen. He told himself the pain was ebbing even as it worsened, told himself his injury was something minor even as its seriousness became more certain. Staring into the dark, in a cold sweat, his body riven by one electrical jolt after another, lightning flashes of pain exploding in his brain, an odd sense *premonition?* of lying on a battlefield, wounded. He needed to turn, change his position but couldn't turn because of the pain. He was exhausted and needed to sleep but couldn't sleep because of the pain. And yet somehow he did sleep, a minute, two, maybe five, before the pain tore him awake again out of a dream of frozen paralysis and immobility but it wasn't a dream, he woke again and it was morning and his body was cold and stiff as a board, a frozen corpse, rigor mortis already settled in, and with it the overwhelming terror and realization that this was not simply another tic or cramp, pulled or strained muscle, that this time he'd finally done it, gone too far, he'd never be able to lift weights again. He heard the notmother's angry, deranged voice, throat strangled with hatred and contempt, uttering, *hissing* at him, that long ago prophecy, Oh you *ssstupid* boy, you'll break your back, ruin yourself for life. How deliriously happy she would be to know her prophecy had finally come true. He lay on the floor all day, mumbling confused prayers, orisons for forgiveness, promising God, promising the notmother and the notfather, promising himself, his saner, more reasonable self, never, never again will I pursue the iron. Even as, impossibly, an even more insane voice burrowed even further down inside his soul whispered aloud its own dementia, not only *if* I lift again, but *when* I lift again. *The iron is not dead! I am not dead! Say it out loud, Grasshopper!* Insane, delusional, *madness.* What else do you call that?

That evening he dragged himself up the creaking wooden stairs like a broken nag, every step another dagger in his back. Like an eighteenth century automaton, stiff, clunky, he lowered himself onto his chair at the dinner table. Not a gesture did he make or a word speak, just sat there blinking against the unaccustomed light while the notmother and the notfather and the hypothetical notsiblings stared at him horrified and then at each other, so unused to his presence they spoke as if he were not there, as if those long months down in his dark hole had deprived him not only of speech but hearing and sight. Look, is it really him? Why has he come up out of his cave? Is the monster sick? Is he starving? In pain? Who knows? Just put in front of him a bowl of whatever slop the notmother made, boiled burdock root, stewed rats, and hope he doesn't go crazy and kill us all. He didn't know himself what he was doing there, whether, like a wounded domestic animal, he sought comfort, perhaps even sympathy from his ostensible masters. Was it even possible he was trying to tell them, Listen, this time I think I've really hurt myself, I think I should go to a doctor. But what kind of doctor would that be? Some quack in a grass skirt, in feathers and bones clutching the entrails of an animal he slaughtered with a stone knife while he danced around a bonfire chanting and moaning and threatening rain? Some modern shaman smelling of soap, of perfume or cologne, most certainly disinfectant, who spoke of trauma, damage quotients? We'll have to use the knife, it's the only hope. Oh, not to worry. It's all robotics now. And then the rubber mask over his nose and mouth and the sudden smothering cloud of ether flooding his nostrils, pouring down into the reservoirs of his lungs and inundating the convoluted software of his brain with dreams of a red rubber sun and a silver slice of moon, beneath the drowse the scalpel hot, searing, severing forever nerve and muscle tissue, hopes and dreams, and finally the pronouncement, that verdict and those words he both feared and secretly longed to hear, Never! Never again! But no, of course not, that wasn't his way, not the notfamily's way, he wasn't raised that way, wasn't taught to believe in that kind of magic, doctors, hospitals. If you got sick you either got better or else you curled up in a corner in an old cardboard box like a mistreated and unwanted mongrel mutt and waited for death to deplete you of the last gasp and secretion. Who knows, maybe if he'd had physical therapy, alternating hot and cold compresses, massages, injections of steroids, muscle relaxants, anti-inflammatories, opioid pain killers. Maybe if he had healthcare. But no, that wasn't his country's way either. You're on your own now, boy, man up, grow a pair.

Everything he had eschewed, everything he had pursued, everything he had struggled and sacrificed for the last ten years wasted, an entire decade. For *nothing*. His whole life, his ironclad order, the structure he had imposed on his existence, smashed, destroyed. Those Olympian gods again, tyrants, dictators, capricious in their dispensation of punishment and reward, turning their backs on him forever? No, he refused to hear, entertain such thoughts, he could never accept that, never believe that, even now, as the *cold hard truth* settled in, as the pain endured, crippled him. He tried to put it in another light, make a bargain with God, whoever or whatever this god was that he continued to invoke. He'd done something stupid, pushed himself too long and too hard, he understood that. *Next time* he'd be more careful, he'd pay attention to his body's complaints, he'd know when he was getting crazy and pushing himself too far. But now, now, shouldn't the pain have stopped by now? Every movement, simply lying down on his mattress at night or getting up in the morning torturous, squatting to take a shit excruciating. What if it was true, he'd never lift again?

Yes, yes, I know what you're thinking, what's *wrong* with this guy? Finally, at last, here's his chance, freedom forced from the madness of the iron. And what do you think's going to happen next? The sunlight's going to come pouring into his monastic cell? All that birdsong and fresh air he's been missing out on for years? You think he's going to start sniffing the daisies and greeting all the smiling faces with his own idiot smile, good day to you too, ladies? Watch the sunset before going to bed and wake early in the morning to greet old Sol's glorious Technicolor return? But this is greater madness still. You can never forget the iron. Because that's all there ever was, the iron and that sick miserable love of the iron, black and gleaming in that dark basement dungeon like water, like the gleam of water droplets osmotizing out of the gray cinder block walls, out of the cracks in the floor, the rivulets and streams seeping and trickling over mortar and concrete. *Yes, the flow of water, that is the point you must return to when you are injured, when you have lost your will and your way, when you no longer believe yourself capable, the sound of water trickling down through the ages, the source of life, as one generation passes on to the next, it is in that knowledge you must reside if you wish to live, if you wish to survive.* Yes, the old man again, wizard, sensei, master, of delusion, a young man's … delusions. Because it was just at that moment *precisely* when he was entertaining that doubt, when he was thinking that just maybe maybe maybe baby he had been wrong all those years, when he woke up one morning to a day as glorious as any day he'd ever seen in his life and he even said to himself there'll never be another day like this, that he thought, *maybe I'll lift today*, nothing heavy, just go light, just try it out, see how it feels. But there, you see, it was already too late, he'd already started thinking about it, he was already luring himself back down into that dank, stinking cave with flights of Valkyries shrieking overhead and visions of apocalypse filling his brain. But oh no no no, he'd learned his lesson, right? He must restrain himself, he must not plunge in, plough ahead, Piers, anchors away, me hearties, haul those barges, boys, hoist those bales. He went through the ritual of pulling on his lifting suit, lacing up his lifting shoes, stretched his hamstrings and quads, rotating his arms in their sockets. Put on his belt, pulled it tight, fastened the buckle and approached the weight, nothing much, just the bar and two fifties. He shuffled his feet a few inches together, a few inches apart, bent down, closed his hands around the bar, turned it once, twice, three times. That's enough, there, stop, just grab the damn thing and pick it up. And *oof!* that was heavier than he had expected, but *hoo!* it also felt better than he expected, no pain at all, okay, a little pain, the suggestion of pain, an odd stiff feeling, the damaged muscles, tendons, cartilage, nerves, whatever part of his anatomy was involved, fused, desiccated into a hank of beef jerky, slightly uncomfortable, *annoying,* certainly not enough to deter him, no more pain than he couldn't deny, dismiss, really, it's nothing, all better now. You know how that goes. You add a little more weight and a little more and not until you're almost at your maximum do you realize what you've done. But still it's just a little pain, it doesn't hurt enough to be debilitating, and it's only because you didn't warm up as well as you should, you're out of practice, you're timing is off, your form and posture bad. You tell yourself all the lies you can think of to dissuade the pain, to prevent it from being real, but it is real, and you learn to live with it and sometimes it gets better and sometimes it gets worse. Although there are those rare days, warm sunshine, a balmy breeze, when you really feel fine, when there's no pain at all and you indulge for a moment in that great big lie, Finally! At last! I'm healed, cured, well again, *fixed*. But the very next day it's chilly, damp and gray, your muscles are stiff and aching, your joints sore, and just the thought of the iron waiting for you fills you with dread. But you told yourself you were going to lift this particular weight today and this additional weight tomorrow and you keep on lifting until the nagging pain becomes the loud angry squeal of metal shearing from metal and you can not deny, can not refute, the pain makes useless the rest of the machine and you have to shut down the factory again, lay off the crew, sorry, boys, there'll be no work for days, maybe weeks. And only that, pain and injury, can make you stop this madness until you have recovered enough to return to madness.

And so you learn the seasons of pain, the longer, slower seasons of healing, the raw and torn calluses, broken blood blisters, hands opening and closing like horny red claws, bursitis, tendonitis, torn and pulled and strained muscles and ligaments, broken bones, nerve damage, is there a name for the damage you do to your soul? Your mind? Pain become routine, your immunity to pain grown stronger, pain a part of your normal existence, you can not grow, can not accomplish what you dream of, envision, without the pain you impose upon yourself daily in your struggle with the iron, you can not hesitate, proceed with caution because of an ache in your back, a knot in your shoulder. Besides, there's another pain, one that you can not account for with your anatomy of failure, and that is the pain of solitude, loneliness. You've been down in that stinking pit for so long that your proximity, your *propinquity* to your own self has finally overwhelmed you and your senses and you desperately want, need, to get out in the street in the fresh air in the bright daylight, moonlight, starlight, in a crowd of people, *friends*, and drink and laugh, get drunk and fall down in the gutter and howl at the moon even if it's just the luminous white LED glow of a streetlamp, get drunk and laugh and shrug off all those years of loneliness and yearning and empty yourself in the arms in the body of another human being, refuge, retreat for your flayed soul, to hold in your arms, embrace, the warmth and softness, the yielding flesh of another human being, to confess, admit, your weaknesses, fears, desires, needs. But there aren't any friends, there isn't another body. There is only you and the silence, you and this prison you have built around yourself. Because even if he did think, say, out loud, to himself, *in a desperate voice,* I've gotta get out of here *now* this *fucking* minute or I'll never do anything or go anywhere again in my life, the iron always pulled him back into that trap, that dungeon cell, shackled and bound by the manacles and chains of madness, obsession, delusion. What irony, again. He, romantic, *poet*, who had always talked of raising up and worshipping God and all of existence couldn't say, not even once, Dear God, what a beautiful day, I'm not going to work with the iron today, I'm going to allow myself the freedom to wander the fields and forests, the meadows and sylvan glades of panpipes and ram bleat, of horn and hoof and renewed lust for life. But no, couldn't, didn't say, not even once. *Because that is the curse of the iron, that it will root you forever in one place, you'll never move again, never travel, explore, you won't hitchhike around Europe with an exotic girlfriend/boyfriend, search for meteorites in the Antarctic, scuba dive in shark infested waters in the Pacific, climb El Capitan or paraski in the Alps, you'll never go in search of new horizons, ancient ruins, bound by some telluric bond, like a tree rooted in the earth, like an iron girder driven into the earth, you will remain here forever, fixed in this one spot. Because everything is the iron, all of your energy and concentration must be focused on the iron, you can't afford to expend any of that energy in pursuit of anything but the iron, that is the vow of chastity you take, not exactly abstinence, because there is nothing more exacting, nothing that demands more of yourself, your precious bodily fluids, your ichor, nothing more mind-blowing, orgasmic (ask Ahrnold), than the iron, first and always the iron. Because how can you shirk that burden once you've taken it on? How dare shrug off that weight you've been carrying for the better part of your sentient life and suddenly find yourself tumbling off the cliff and into the abyss, the void of everything and nothing that lies beyond your conception of being and existence as you have constructed it out of, entirely contingent upon, the iron? How turn your back on everything that mattered, the only thing, reason in your life? How even suggest such a possibility?*

This doubt and depression that came over him like a vast dark cloud, a tidal wave rolling far inland and inundating everything in suffocating darkness, making everything utterly bleak and hopeless. When the pure overwhelming joy of existence and the thought of its origin, source, and its inevitable end, irrevocable, forever, became unbearable. When simply watching a butterfly light on a chrysanthemum posed problems of infinite complexity and, simultaneously, ineffable simplicity, like the most sublime conundrums, koans, of the most sublime minds, all of which nevertheless must be reduced to a single sentence or thought to explain the phenomenon to another person. If there were another person. If he were not alone, crushed beneath this burden, unmovable, insurmountable, like a bug struggling to crawl out from under a rock.

Diviner, fortune teller, oracle, soothsayer, prophet of doom (thanks, *Mom*), he foresaw nothing but failure to the end of time. That deep enervating miasma of sloth when he lay in bed, on his mattress on the floor, blanket pulled over his head, hiding from the world like a child, his whole fragile being wracked with inarticulate fear and doubt. His only refuge sleep, that groggy sludge of semi-consciousness, of dissolution of mind into torpid numbness and protoplasmic non-self. And out of that primordial slough he must somehow resurrect, reassemble a self and a will to carry on, to fight the hopelessness, meaningless, find a path and a way, a justification to live. Not that he would actually kill himself. He wasn't thinking that, was he? Not yet anyway, not seriously, who knows, maybe, if it got any worse, if he sank any deeper into this pit of loneliness and despair. If only he could lift up and throw off this weight, burden, this whatever he was carrying on his back, monkey, elephant, stack of cannonballs, sack of sins. *There, that is what you are carrying on your back, that is the weight and the burden of your own existence, that is what you must shrug off and unshoulder if you wish to succeed with the iron.* Well, gosh, thanks, old man, but what sins? For being alive? This weight and burden of *myself?* This failed worthless self? If only he could shut out, eradicate that clamor and clangor of negative, denying voices in the clanging and banging of the iron, in the triumph of the will over emptiness and death.

Because, okay, there's that other mechanism that turns in the other direction, that rides that tiger, that says *not if only* but *what if?* What if he did succeed? What if he did fight and struggle and persist? Because tomorrow, tomorrow he was going to work harder than he had ever worked before, he was going to lift more weight than ever before, he was going to push himself until the iron oozed from his pores like sweat, he was going to eliminate all the poisons, the dead weight he'd stored up and accumulated in his body and become pure and clean, an ascetic, he was *going to going to going to.* Because now it had started again, he was rushing forward in his mind, in the hot rocket blast and propulsion, his thoughts all over the place, galloping, full speed, telling himself, saying, I can't bear it anymore, I want it to stop, it has to stop, but it wouldn't, couldn't, didn't stop, this conflagration in his brain, soul, in whatever organ it is that receives the word of God, gives hospice and comfort to the message of God, at the risk of one's own life, sanity. *Bam! Bam! Bam! Open up in there!*

Night after night he lay in his unwashed filth and drying sweat, twisting and turning, feverish, burning, caroming between depression and mania, bathed in the cauldron of his fears, desires, anxiety, in a frenzy and panic, calculating the years of prime lifting he had left to achieve this indeterminate goal he had set for himself, working and reworking in his mind the failures of that day, imagining the weight he wanted to succeed in lifting tomorrow if everything went well, if he hit it just right, the right time of day, right state of mind. If only it wasn't so damned hot, if he could get to sleep, get some rest. Alternately throwing off and tangled up in the wrinkled yellow sheets, yellow from his sweat, wrinkled from his writhing and torment, from the notmother never doing the laundry, from there not being any water to do the laundry, while the June bugs whirred and banged off the rafters and walls and hit him in the face and the mosquitoes buzzed at his ears and fed off his blood at their leisure and the whole night world outside simmered and broiled in that deep black humidity, in the Cyclopean eye of that tropical storm brewing in his mind. Until he couldn't bear it anymore, he couldn't lie still anymore, he had to move, go, get out of here. He jumped up from the mattress on the floor, lurched up the creaking wooden stairs and out into the hot humid summer night and walked and walked and walked, the moon following him like a ship's beacon and an owl hooting in a tree and a cat screaming and a dog barking and the pavement passing under his feet with this thing, not a thing, a nonthing, a feeling, concept still in conception, this nascent, incipient vision on the verge of exploding in his mind, all it needed, lacked, was a spark, a lightning flash, a sudden electric arc and in that moment it all came together, perfect, the image of a machine, a humming dynamo of iron and steel that would allow him to go beyond anything he had ever dreamed of before. He had to turn around right now, this instant, hurry, rush back home, go down into the basement and get this on paper before it was lost, before he forgot. He saw everything, clearly, perfectly, *pellucid*, how it worked and what its purpose was and how to build it, not just a machine but a fulcrum or portal, a point upon which all the matter and energy of the universe rested or an opening, aperture, through which it poured. In other words the answer to everything. *In other words God, which you are not, which you could never be, no man, to carry that responsibility, that burden on your shoulders, how many times greater than the greatest thing you can imagine must this god be.*

Delusional.

Because something was wrong, because after he did turn around and rush back home and down those creaking wooden stairs into that damp gray stinking basement and quick, quick, quick, just grab something, anything, picked up his lifting journal and a ballpoint pen and began to write down, scribble, trying to describe, struggling, desperate, to release this burning in his brain onto the page, to transform *reify* concept, idea, into hard fact, reality, iron or stone or the *word*, a physical act, manual, his whole body concentrated on that nexus of wrist, hand, those two-three digits, those dermal upholstered phalanges that gripped the quill, pencil, pen, stylus, *huh-huh-huh*, but, oh no, oh shit, oh *fuuuuuck*, because it wasn't coming out right, not what he saw, wanted to say, remembered, there was too much, it was different somehow. Because after the excitement and energy, the *mania* of his revelation, epiphany, had died away and burned itself out like the final blue and gold fizzle and flare of fireworks evaporating from the black night sky, and the final *ooo* and *ahh* of amazement had given way to an indefinite melancholy *aww*, everything, the edifice of his imagination, the weight and the burden and the whole world, teetered, tottered and finally collapsed, came crashing down upon him in his exhaustion and defeat and he said, admitted to himself, *impossible*, he would never be able to do it. And in that conceptual failure and forecast of *rain today* failure in the future, find relief, enough that it didn't matter anymore, all meaningless, his thoughts disintegrating into an insect swarm, gnats, mosquitoes, finally, he was falling asleep, he was asleep. Sleep, the only answer. *Zzzzzzzz*

And woke the next morning groggy, foggy, in a daze, last night's rush and frenzy, excitement and mad scientist Van de Graaff crackling lightning bolts of inspiration faded, his mind still trying to dredge itself up out of the murky sucking bog of sleep and dream. While that driven dynamo, Drill Sergeant Upandatem, Drill Sergeant Will Power, was already ramrod straight in his starched and pressed uniform and shouting *ten hut! he*, that slackadaisacal soldier boy, recruit, *not my thing really*, was still struggling into his uniform, staggering out to formation bleary-eyed, unshaved, his vision of the machine, so perfect last night, diminished into something like a rusty old farm implement. And no wonder. He never got off the farm himself. He had continued to ignore the advances, dismiss the dynamo hum, of technology, discard the principles of science and physics that had taken other men thousands of years to evolve in preference for a mixture of mysticism and faith, his approach completely unsophisticated, uninformed, a pilgrim in the wilderness, as primitive as traveling to the stars in an oxcart, governed by a simple ideology (attain super human strength) and methodology (lift more weight). He was like a medieval alchemist, yes, say it, mad scientist, attempting to transform lead into gold with his retorts and alembics when the rest of the world was transforming reality into virtual. What did he know about smart machines, AI, IT? What did he know about cutting edge training systems, applied technology, methodology, physiology? What did he know about anything? But instead of opening his eyes to the shiny world of technology and possibly even enlisting the aid of a friendly peer, maybe even a *girl* he met in the public library, cute, kind of shy, like him, and what if he and she, they—*fuhgeddeboudit*—someone, anyway, to help him find the path into this distant future everyone else had already arrived at years ago, *instead* of that, he continued in the old way, retreated into ancient methods, convinced himself he could accomplish even greater feats by brute strength alone, and yes, possibly even magic.

With no clear purpose in mind he began to scrounge in junkyards, garbage dumps, construction sites, carried home car axles, cogwheels, angle iron, pistons and cam shafts, drive trains, universal joints and transmissions. One night, exiting a salvage yard, an electric motor he'd filched in his backpack, a spotlight illuminated him, stopped him dead, like a deer in its tracks, Officer Paddy O'Dooley, gone from walking a beat to jockeying a squad car. Belly built on bagels with cream cheese and jelly-filled donuts, Officer O'Dooley grunted, groaned and scrunched his corpulent corpus out of his vehicle, squinted a gimlet eye at him, glanced at his backpack, What've ye got in there, son? Nothing, he replied. As Mister Schrödinger proved, until proven otherwise, a factual statement. But no student of quantum mechanics, Officer O'Dooley wanted solid matter. Nothing, ye say? The kind o' nothing that can get ye a ride down to the station, 'tis it? I meant, he corrected himself, eyeing a rusty mainspring lying at Officer O'Dooley's feet, it's only my dirty laundry. Officer O'Dooley's Cro-Magnon brow contracted into a hound dog wrinkled frown. Dirty laundry, ye say? his brain conjuring, among the evening pints of stout and shots of whiskey, leprechauns and shillelaghs, cartoon-like spinning over his head, the unpleasant image of soiled underwear, sweaty socks. Nothing this bobby wanted part of. Well, all right then, lad, move along and be off with ye. As soon as Officer O'Dooley had managed to squeeze himself back in his seat and drove his vehicle out of sight, the lad doubled back to pick up the coveted mainspring.

So he began, tightening down bolts, pounding rivets, soldering and welding, sweating joints, casting and forging new tools and implements as he needed them, extruding metals and alloys and milling couplings within the finest tolerance of sanity, his original barbell both the axle and fulcrum of this machine he was building. He installed hydraulic and pneumatic lines, ball bearings, belts, pulleys and chains, flickering dials and gauges to measure pressure, safety valves to let off steam. But alas, he was still no proper young scientist, impossible for him to be patient and thoughtful, to proceed with caution, testing hypothesis with experiment and observation. Pipefitter, high iron worker, oil rig roughneck, yes, maybe. By-the-book analytics professor, no way. He still plundered and rampaged, twisted and abused to his worst advantage everything he put his hands on, only vaguely followed his original vision, relied on intuition, impulses of the heart. Because he couldn't see it as a plan, a gathering of components that gradually fitted together piece by piece, pound by pound into a whole. Rather, he saw it all at once, an enormous thing he had to lift, raise over his head and hold there unwavering as if he were charged with holding up and supporting the celestial firmament for all of eternity. His already years of madness and obsession grown into a half-baked science, theology, calibrating existence to an exact weight and dimension according to the specifications of a dream and a design that had suddenly sprung up in his brain or existed there even before his birth, the germ, seed, inchoate, passed down through the ages in the blood, in the genes of ancient masters, madmen before him, finally arriving at his sleeping crib and surrounding, engulfing, inhabiting him like a succubus. Every time he came up with a new idea he had to rush back downstairs and test it immediately and the very next day have that vision of perfection shattered and surpassed by the next. Plunging ahead madly with each new theory and formula, wrecking everything he'd built up until now and rebuilding it, each new goal attained immediately abandoned in pursuit of the next and the next and the next. Trying to compel the iron to conform to an idea or image in his mind that he could never clearly define but continually mutated to reveal further possibilities of form and structure.

He scoured the public library, booksellers, odd little rare book shops, studied ancient treatises and tomes, periodicals, scientific publications in search of anything that even vaguely resembled his vision of the machine. Imagine his shock, surprise, when he came across the research of a stranger in a distant land who had already managed to lift so many more tons of iron, conquered another part of gravity and existence, gone so much farther beyond anything he had ever dreamed of, made all his previous successes failures, and then he felt discouraged again, he felt like quitting, giving up altogether. It sickened him to think he had wasted so much time and effort. And yet, he had an odd suspicion, counterintuitive, contrary to reason, an *inkling*, maybe it was better this way, that in order to succeed he must fail. But the thought was too novel, too startling, he couldn't grasp its meaning. *But how can I explain that to you? The idea of failure again. Not of learning through your mistakes, of overcoming and conquering, but failing utterly, miserably, irrevocably, to prove to yourself that you are precisely what you perceive yourself to be: nothing, a worthless little goat turd in a barren rocky wasteland in some forgotten corner of the world baked by the scorching sun in summer and frozen into hellishly cold stasis in winter, and by that standard, that degree, you must rise up from the utter oblivion and nothingness of goat turd-dom and overcome and succeed. But how can I communicate to you what can not be communicated, that which can only be learned by oneself through one's own years of struggle and travail, of trial and error and not just error but gross mistakes, back breaking and life threatening mistakes that can crush you into the dirt. Because no old wise man was born old and wise, master, wizard, guru, on the mountaintop of wisdom, he got there by climbing over the foothills, the cataracts and crevasses of all his errors, mistakes, abject failures, each one greater than the last.*

Out of this cauldron, chaos, out of this forge, mill, he built, constructed, watched emerge as if he were a spectator to his own creation, something like a giant mechanical crustacean, a mutant anthropomorphic exoskeleton he could actually climb into and make mimic his body movements. He started out slowly, bent fore and aft, squatted up and down and clattered his claws, when he felt comfortable he picked up the pace, pulling levers, pushing pedals, the machine beginning to hum and glow, and then faster and faster, his arms and legs pumping like pistons, pushing the machine as hard as it could go, redlining every gauge, warning bells ringing, sirens screaming, steam blowing out of failing joints, the whole thing rattling, shaking, about to explode, he didn't give a damn, throw caution to the wind. Faster! Faster! he laughed madly, screamed to himself. His mind was burning up, spinning inside like a gyroscope, top, dynamo, he was on fire, a piston pounding internal combustion explosion and radiance of heat and light. He was hurtling down a rural highway at night behind the wheel of a plum-colored 1950 Plymouth coupe, he was in a diamond-hulled spaceship hurtling across folds in the space-time continuum. He had finally managed to build the hot rod jalopy of his adolescent dream and fervor, and he was the motor, engine, dynamo that drove this machine, he was the madman driver of himself. His only limitations the limits established for him by the limitations of his own mind, by the limitations of other men's imaginations until they became his own. Human limitations. But he wasn't human, he was a machine, and machines functioned perfectly according to a preset pattern of expectations, machines did not falter, did not fear or feel pain, they did not hesitate, they did not make mistakes, the humans who operated them feared, faltered, hesitated, felt pain, made mistakes. Yes, delusional, on the brink of madness, those moments, occasions, drunk? on some kind of drug? or no, just that manic state, euphoric, when he really believed he possessed superhuman strength, that he could, would, perform superhuman feats, raise up the whole world over his head like Atlas bearing the burden of the planet Earth on his shoulders, like Archimedes with his lever long enough to move the world, when he understood, thought he understood, grasped in his hands, tasted in his mouth, the nectar, ambrosia, the ichor of those great kings, gods, demi-gods, David, Alexander, Genghis Khan, who really did conquer, possess and rule entire continents, the known world, what they felt, that inferno raging in their brains. The world is mine! All of it! And they were not insane. They laid claim to that title before the eyes of all men and all men acknowledged by their eyes, by their voices raised as one, King! Master! Ruler of the world! Alright, a little insane, let's admit it, you'd have to be, okay, *crazy*, to want that title. What else can you call it, *genius?*

VI
STUCK IN THE MUD

BECAUSE DESPITE ALL HIS PROTESTATIONS (to whom? himself? to nobody? The same thing, no difference?) that he was finally going somewhere, he was going nowhere, he drove and he drove and he got not another mile down the pike. He strapped himself into this clanking, banging contraption, steampunk machine, postmodern fusion of industrial and modern, okay, more industrial than modern, already a museum piece, long obsolete, he climbed into, cinched, fastened, tightened leather and Velcro belts and straps, and spun his wheel faster and faster like a rat in a cage *like a rat in a cage.* That further epiphany, this late in the game, how could he be so *fucking* stupid? It hadn't even occurred to him until now. He was, yes, hopelessly stuck in one spot, even more rooted than before, his machine too big, unwieldy, he couldn't climb up the damn stairs, couldn't climb out of this fucking dungeon basement. Yowsuh, young Marse, dat wiley rascal Br'er Rabbit done got tricked by dat der ol' tar baby. Sucker puncher sucker punched. Compounding this revelation, the dominoes falling, train cars piling up, the veil removed from his eyes, *delusion, all delusion*, his never-ending existential crisis swelling to encompass his entire, well, existence. For example, what was he doing in this hole in the ground, in this house that was not a home, living with, sponging off (co-dependent? symbiotic? *parasite?*) these people who were somehow his parents and not his parents? He was a *grown man*. Couldn't he take care of himself, go out on his own, find a job, start a family, build a home, make a mark in life? How had things gone so wrong? Was, as the notmother speculated, her eyes bright with the flames of her own flourishing madness, his return to the notfamily nest part of some twisted plot, even worse, a punishment from God? But why? For what? The notfather, perplexed at any suggestion of his having, shall we say, *fucked up* in the child-rearing department? After all, why should he, the notson, have any reason whatsoever for wanting to *torture* them, his perennial enemies, the notmother and the notfather? To *get even* with them even at his own expense for the years of *oppression* and *neglect?* But what was he saying? Surely he was being sarcastic? Playing the devil's advocate? How had he come to be so filled with vitriol and hate? And with those two miserable wretches the object of his contempt? They'd grown so old in the last couple of years. They'd lost what little fortune they'd ever had, they lived in filth, they were dressed in rags, they had nothing to eat, they chewed on the soles of their shoes until dinner time, then filled their bellies with dandelion greens boiled in rainwater, bitter rue sautéed in rancid rapeseed oil, the scanty meat of equally starving mice and rats and whatever creatures smaller and weaker than them they could catch (while his paleo diet, on the other hand, had improved greatly with his recuperation). They clearly despised each other, nagged, carped at and criticized each other, sometimes shouted at, shoved, *slapped* each other. All those years locked up together in that filthy cage like a pair of indiscriminately mated animals not necessarily even of the same species. How was it possible they never felt, at least never demonstrated love or the least sign of affection for each other? How could he himself have come into being without love? Or was that another of their god's horrible little oversights or, more likely, a joke, a jest? That their nonlove should produce, create, this monster, *him*, by the equally *monstrous* (the notmother) act of procreation and set it loose upon the world. And was he going to pass that notlove on to the next generation, given the unlikelihood of his finding a willing mate if he continued this way? But now what was he doing? Passing the buck? Denying his own responsibility, casting blame? Lying in his little boy bed whining and complaining? After all, the notparents didn't exactly force him down into that dungeon, okay, that stinking cellar, basement. They didn't whip him and beat him the way some parents did, used to, still do? They nurtured and fed him as best they could (um … ?), tried to give him parental guidance (uh … ?). Wasn't it up to him to take his life in his own hands? His life. There was that joke again. The life he had devoted, sacrificed to the iron, and for what? All that he had raised up, all that he had conquered and succeeded in lifting, nothing, all nothing. *Come, boy, help me lift up and raise all this nothing if you want to know how heavy nothing is. I know you're embarrassed. You think it's silly, somebody might be watching, but come, help me raise up the nothing of creation and the universe, help me raise up the black sky at night and the bright sun again in the morning, help me raise up the clouds in the sky and the rain falling to the earth, help me raise up all the oceans and seas, all the planets and the stars, all matter, all* stuff *and it's still all nothing.* Sitting on his wooden bench, staring into the white glare and orange glowing element of that bare bulb burning overhead, staring up at the dust-clotted cobwebs strung across the rafters, at the gleaming plasticine carcass of a wasp caught in a spider's gossamer threads, suspended there ever since the very first year, the very day, he undertook, set sail, launched himself on this odyssey. All those years of emptiness, loneliness, *madness.* Whether he was born with the germ of this madness inside him and he nurtured it with another's madness, that old wise man, wizard, real or imagined, or it was entirely foisted upon him by that other, transferred like a dromedarian hump from one overburdened back to another. But to say that's how his life began, already hobbled.

All those years of *sloth.* What else to call it? Wallowing in his obsession,   convinced   he   was   accomplishing   something important when he had accomplished nothing, no product, paycheck, nothing of value, marketable, not even won some small victory, triumph, a little trophy, cheap, a gilded figure of an athlete, paint chipping off. All over now. No more. He was going upstairs this minute and take his poor old parents in his powerful arms and ask—*beg*—their forgiveness for his years of ingratitude. He would let them know, assure them, that he was going to go out and get a job and support and care for them the rest of their lives. He'd hug, chest to chest, face to face, the notfather's scratchy beard stubble and dollar store cologne, he'd embrace the notmother's cold, stolid fortress whose formidable walls nevertheless bore traces of rosewater, he'd recognize and acknowledge at last the brothers and sisters as his own, *Moe! Larry! Mary! Jane!* (or, Leslie, Lionel, Lois and Luanne), he'd hold little Fluffy (or Socks or Sylvester) the cat in his lap, pet Bowser (or Buck or Snoopy) the dog on the head.

Thusly resolved, he creaked his way up the sagging wooden stairs, a strange uneasiness nagging at him with every step, not a noise, in fact, the absence of noise, an abundance of silence. He had been so immersed in his keening and lamentations and self flagellation that he hadn't even noticed until now that it had been quiet overhead for quite some time. He had heard no shuffling of the notmother's heavy slippered feet, no hard-soled clomping about of the notfather's oversized brogues, no trekking and forays from living room to kitchen, from bedroom to bathroom to hall closet of putative brothers and sisters. Indeed, he hadn't caught so much as a glimpse of anyone in weeks and no wonder, everyone in the notfamily had long ago established private and circuitous routes, essentially tunnels, through the maze of clutter and garbage piled up throughout the shambles of the house, not only to avoid meeting each other, but the unpleasant and really quite disturbing acknowledgement that they shared this misery with anyone else. With a growing trepidation weighing on his shoulders he pushed open the cellar door. A crow squawked and flapped out a broken kitchen window, a mouse scurried across the filthy linoleum floor, urged to flee, run for its life, by the ghosts of its ancestors skewered over roasting fires. A gaping hole in the ceiling where the plaster had rotted and fallen down revealed leaky plumbing, termite riddled wooden beams. Windows and doors were thrown open or missing, the wallpaper was peeling, there were holes in the walls, cockroaches, crickets, mice and rats hurried, scurried everywhere, but no notmother, no notfather, no speculative siblings, no pet cat, dog, canary in a gilt cage. He shouted, called out their notnames. He clambered up the rotting stairs to the second floor, ran from room to room, looked in the empty closets, got down on his hands and knees and peered under the bare bed frames. Nothing but dust balls and spider webs. He ran back downstairs, out the front door. The whole neighborhood seemed abandoned. Had there been an outbreak of disease, a mass evacuation? Had everyone died and been carted off to the bone pile or the bonfire? Had they only been waiting all this time for the opportunity to sneak off in the night to escape his return to madness? Was that itself madness, *paranoia?* He felt abandoned, betrayed. All his good intentions for naught without a recipient. A hot, wallowing wave of repugnance and self-disgust surged through his body. His life seemed even more worthless than ever. He gnashed his teeth, tore at his hair, beat his chest. He blamed it on the iron, on his own stupidity. If only he had paid attention to events around him. Groping, grasping, desperate for something to alleviate his misery, he flung open cabinets, drawers, at last found a bottle of holiday brandy stashed behind a vat of dried beans, unscrewed the cap and without bothering to test the nose, drank, got drunk. Time to go to work! he shouted to no one and clattered back down the stairs to the basement.

He woke the next morning with a pounding headache, pried open his gluey eyelids, peered about him, his brain still not making sense of what he saw, gleaming pieces of iron, springs, axles, levers, scattered everywhere, like the parts of some giant clockwork insect, legs and thorax, wings and feet, beady eyes and sproingy antennae. He clutched his head in his hands, groaned like a wounded beast. What had he done? His life's work destroyed. All the years, the suffering, the pain and sacrifice it had cost him to come this far, to create this machine, ruined in a single night, in his drunken rampage.

Now there truly was nothing anchoring him to the earth, no reason to stay in this ruined hovel, this nothome, neverhome, in this wasteland of his notlife. He gathered a few things in a pack, went up the stairs one last time, the weight and burden on his back and shoulders growing heavier with each step, even in ruins, the machine tugging, pulling at him like a giant magnet, at its core his precious iron bar. He placed his foot on the final tread, opened and closed the cellar door behind him, exited the house. *Leave*, he had to, must. He turned away, started walking, set out on the road in search of salvation.

Ah, but the irony of the iron again, when at last he sought freedom from the iron, the iron found him. Poor ignoramus, never paid attention to events around him, never heard the drums of war pounding over hill and dale, from the greatest sea to the least backwater. He thought nothing of it when a truck stopped and the driver said, Hop in! Sure, thanks, he said, climbing up on back and squeezing in among a bunch of other young men. Hey, guys, where you headin'? *What?* Oh Lordy, wee Geordie. Don't you know? You're in the army now. Army doctor didn't blink an eye at all the bruises and contusions, the stiff and fused joints, muscles, ligaments and tendons. Boy ain't limping, just struttin' his stuff. A soldier's life wasn't all bad. They gave him plenty of food to eat, a clean uniform, a new rifle, admittedly a pathetic little stick of iron and wood next to the great iron bar he had lifted, although yes, he understood perfectly well that the insignificant ounce of lead it projected outweighed all the iron he'd lifted in his life. An added benefit: camp followers, not just the usual mewling, whining, complaining wives and children, the provisioners, the medical quacks, the grifters, conmen, sellers of booze, drugs, but women, everywhere they went. He didn't question if it was right or wrong, love or lust. Just drink, get drunk, lie down with whatever body was available that night, wake the next morning, his head aching, his thoughts a gray fog, put on his uniform for morning formation and for the rest of the day let them do whatever they wanted with him, march and drill, *left right left*, fire his rifle at targets *bang bang bang*, throw hand grenades *Boom!* crawl on his belly in the mud, the drill sergeant, platoon sergeant, the company commander yelling at him, *Worm! Maggot!* After the happy home life with the notmother and notfather, after the tyranny of the iron, all the sergeants, captains, colonels and generals seemed like a bunch of boy scout counselors at summer camp. Besides, it was all a joke, right? A bad joke. He didn't really belong here. They knew that, he knew that, but nevertheless, just to humor us, sling that pack over your shoulder, pick up that rifle and bayonet and get on over that hill, boy. And so it went. Through muck and mire, over barbed wire, fallen logs and deep roaring ravines on two, three hours of sleep and a bellyful of gruel gulped out of a long wooden trough with the rest of the bellowing, grunting herd, everything around him a reminder of the iron in its military incarnation, tanks and planes, rifles, grenades, bombs, bullets, barbed wire, iron souls, wills, eyes, iron bayonets stuck in bodies, a fertile field of rotting corpses. Wait, what? He didn't even realize the training was over and the real stuff had begun until his buddies started falling down around him with their faces missing and their legs and arms blown off, raspberry jam oozing out of holes in their body and their guts hanging out of their stomachs like sausage links while red-hot chunks of iron, steel, lead and copper rained down from the heavens, shredding the air around him, and all he could do was huddle in the mud pie swamp of his foxhole and clutch his meager little iron rod to his chest and tremble and quake in his boots and mutter desperate, blaspheming prayers between his clenched teeth to God the father and benevolent old man upstairs if you just let me get through this I promise I'll never use your name in vain again or aspire to your throne, and if you don't, motherfucker, I will hate you forever, reject your compassion, forgiveness, deny your existence! Because of course it wasn't that simple, never that simple, just to offer your feeble trench prayer and be rewarded, answered, *saved*. He shivered and trembled, muttered, shouted all the religious mumbo jumbo that came to his mind until he could no longer deny even to himself his own cowardice and fear of death and somehow in this capitulation find courage, call it madness, further madness. He saw the machine guns, the advancing tanks mowing down his comrades, harvesting their lives like stalks of wheat, he saw the mindless slaughter and his own rage rose inside him, he wanted to kill, he wanted to wound, hurt, he wanted to inflict as much pain as possible, he wanted to do unto those as they had done unto others, he wanted an eye for an eye, a tooth for a tooth, he wanted to disembowel, murder, mutilate, he wanted revenge, retribution, he wanted what could never be had, never obtained, salvaged from the wreckage of humanity. He wanted justice, the return of civilization. And barring that he wanted chaos, utter annihilation. He stood up in the ragged gray smoke in the steaming gray muck in the acrid smell of combusting nitrates and burning flesh and scattered his leaden gray seeds at his enemy, at God and all of mankind, at everyone and everything that was to blame for this madness until the madness put a stop to him. A red-hot fist smashed into kidney and spine, shoulder blade and the back of his head, knocked him to the ground, laid flat, unconscious. How long? Minutes? Hours? Better if it had been eternity. He gasped awake into a shock and pain so great he couldn't breathe, couldn't move or cry out, only lie on the ground and moan the way he did in dreams when he was helpless to move away from or avoid, parry, fend off the imminent danger of some monstrous evil thing closing in on him, but it wasn't a dream, didn't end with the end of a dream, it kept happening over and over again, wave after wave of shock and pain exploded through his body, flashes of heat and light detonated in his brain. Time passed in tattered fragments of consciousness, smoky gray daylight, cold black night. He alternately trembled in a cold sweat, boiled in the hot swamp of

fever, sank back into unconsciousness when the pain and
exhaustion overwhelmed him. Somewhere in that agony
articulating to himself snatches of rational thought, why didn't
anyone come to help him, to take him in their arms and tell him
it was going to be all right the way they did in the movies? He
knew how it worked. Prick your finger on a thorn and the nice
nurse came and kissed it and made it better. But that was more
nonsense, you're going to have to stop this nonsense now, son,
your mother and I expect you to get a good job and support us
in our nonsense. His fever transubstantiated, became a fire on
the hearth and a glass of brandy, his chills a plunge in a cool
mountain lake after climbing all day in the hot sun. He lay in
the rotting cess of his own excrement and putrefaction. His
mouth tasted of blood and rust. He was aware in distant parts of
his body of the tiny hydraulic contractions of muscle and
tendon, of the shutting down of vascular and neural systems, of
the molecules of iron, whether the enemy's invasive iron or the
iron in his blood, banging into each other with slower and
slower velocity as the ice crept through his veins and he lay on
the frozen ground like a cold iron bar. Then he, or the *he* inside
a body, not necessarily his own, was struggling forward through
a dark, viscous medium, he could barely move his extremities,
in fact, he had no clear sense of his extremities, arms or legs,
hands or feet. A dense pall lay ahead, like the smog surrounding
an industrial city. Shapes and forms began to appear around
him, crumbling walls, blown open foundations, twisted and
smoldering girders and beams and pieces of reinforcing bar
sticking out of chunks of concrete. Somehow he knew this was
the place of his birth, but laid low in ruins. He fell to his knees,
weeping hot heavy tears of sorrow. Then he saw a group of
people coming toward him and he felt a profound outpouring of
love. These must be his old neighbors, members of the
community. True, he never had anything to do with them,
strangers, complete, but now, now he would embrace them with
love and camaraderie *friends, Romans, countrymen*. But
something was wrong. As they came closer he saw they were all

dressed in rotting rags, their flesh was rotting, they were in fact ghouls and they said to him, What are you doing here? Why have you returned? Go back to the land of the living where you belong. But he refused to listen, he pulled himself up from the ground, pushed past them, went searching through the ruins until he came upon a pile of rubble he recognized as the remains of his home, everything caved in, collapsed down into the basement. He stared into this pit as if he were staring into the desecrated grave of a loved one. He could see pieces of his machine rusting in fetid pools of water. His nostrils filled with the rancid smell of sewage, death and decay. He felt a deep internal pain, like the phantom pain of an amputated limb or worse, an amputated soul, and even worse still because he could see that tortured, truncated soul-limb lying in the mud right in front of him, feel it aching, pulling at him, as if he could reattach it, make it whole and functioning again. Like an automaton, a machine himself, he set to work, hauled off fallen timbers, broken furniture. Like an archaeologist he lovingly brushed away layer upon layer of accumulated silt and sediment, uncovered and extracted machine parts as if they were rare antiquities, caressed and wiped clean incongruent pieces of metal, ground away rust with a wire brush, oiled the steel bar, the cast-iron plates, metal wheels, cogs and gears with his bare hands, reattached and rebuilt the machine until it gleamed as before. And then he set to work again, pumped the great bellows of his madness and fury, stoked the forge again, clanking and banging and laughing to himself, grunting, sweating, steam pouring from his naked body, the cold wind howling, snow blowing around him. He wouldn't allow himself to be stopped this time. Never again stopped. He'd go on and on and …

He opened his eyes, blinked against the light. His rifle lay next to him. He gripped the cold metal barrel in his hands, managed to push himself up into a sitting position, then remained like that, his legs splayed in front of him like a child in a sand box. Finally, with a great effort, leaning his weight on his rifle, he pulled himself to his feet. Dark mounds lay as far as he could see in the vast whiteness, faceless, limbless, empty, the gutted larvae that had been his comrades in arms, friend and foe. That simple. The switch thrown, animate life eviscerated, terminated, transformed into the nothingness of death. All his life he had denied life, forsaken life, and now, when life lay everywhere forfeit, he wanted it back again, he wanted to live.

And somehow he did live, survived his wounds, found enough strength to stay on his feet, hobble along using his rifle as a crutch. At least he could move, he could bend his knees, lift his legs and throw them out in front of him like sodden logs. Sometimes sharp pains shot up his spine, slammed into the base of his skull. Sometimes his legs gave out under him and he fell to the frozen ground in a heap. And still he struggled on like a stray dog driven by the inarticulate hope of a lighted window, a warm fire to lie down by and something to eat. He sustained himself drinking snow melt that carried the taint of dead bodies, bone water, he ate whatever he scavenged from dead men's packs. He had no idea where he was going, which way led to freedom, to life, and yet he went forward with determination. When he was strong enough to walk without the rifle he threw it away *farewell*. He looked like a complete vagabond. His scratchy old uniform had fallen into rags. His combat boots were falling apart. The toes had sprung open, there were holes in the soles, the heels were worn down and the nails were driving themselves into his feet. And still his spirits continued to rise. The last of winter's frozen whiteness melted away, the first signs of spring appeared, green sprouted out of the earth, the sun shone, a warm breeze stirred the air. He trudged past stone and stucco walls, soot-blackened chimneys erupting out of startlingly green patches of weeds. He had picked up a branch for a staff and now he stretched out his stride, walking longer and faster each day as his body and mind healed and he felt the warm earth under his bare feet. When he was tired he lay down in the roots of a tree or in the moss along a stream or in an abandoned haymow and sank deep into sleep.

Spring passed and summer followed soon after, as it always does, except in the polar climes (but that's changing), and also when the long shadow of Krakatoa fell upon the earth (let's hope *that* doesn't happen again). For the first time in his life there was nothing to tie him down, no more anchors and chains to bind him to that dark pit, no more home or homeland, he was free to wander as he would, down dusty back roads shadowy and overhung with old maples and oaks, the silence broken only by birdsong, past dark, quiet farm ponds where red and blue and green dragonflies flitted like pieces of winged jewelry in the dusty yellow sunlight. He followed footpaths and goat tracks up into the mountains where wild brooks babbled over stones and the thin blue sky stretched to the horizon. And he saw all of it as if he were only now seeing it for the first time, as if none of it had existed before or it had somehow been held in reserve all those years he had buried himself beneath the earth, beneath the iron. He felt alive and awake, invested with a lightness of spirit and body he had never felt before. He burst out laughing and singing and didn't look around to see if anyone was staring at him or thought it was nonsense. It felt good to laugh, to shout and sing, it felt good to *feel*. He saw returning signs of society, civilization, people beginning to build and plant again, help wanted signs, apply within. He worked here and there as an itinerant laborer. Applying his great reserves of strength he broke boulders with pick and sledge, hauled slabs of stone, pushed wheelbarrows loaded with sand and gravel and cement, heaved iron girders and wooden beams across his shoulders and raised up homes and buildings. And he took pleasure in his work. It felt good to use his strength for something real that benefited other people. It made him feel vital and healthy and alive. Even the heft of a shovel or a pick or a sledgehammer, simply to feel his hands sliding up and down the polished wooden shaft, itself crafted by another man's hands. His fellow workers were good men, brothers in labor. Come, have a beer with us, they said to him after work. Soon they were all laughing and shouting, arms around each others' shoulders, *best friends*, when he spotted a woman across the room. She had laughing eyes, a wicked smile, inviting. He didn't hesitate, he went over to her table, introduced himself. He had wood shavings in his hair, sawdust and the sweat of labor in his clothes, his complexion was ruddy from working outside all day, he was as handsome and charming as a monster can possibly be. He offered to buy her a beer, never thought that she might prefer wine or a mixed drink. As she sipped from a mug of a strong and earthy tasting stout, he asked if she liked to hike in the forests, the mountains. Yes? Maybe this weekend? They climbed for hours up a steep canyon next to a splashing stream, came at last to a crystal clear pool, like a giant reflecting glass. Hot, sweating, they took off their clothes, waded naked into the cold water gasping for breath and swimming around in circles until they couldn't bear it anymore, climbed out of the water and hugged each other for warmth, then made love in a grassy patch of sunlight. Afterwards they ate lunch and drank wine— yes, she did prefer wine, red, dry, she provided it—and then they made love again and slept. Thus began an idyll, *the happiest time in his life*, making love, experiencing love, the discovery of discovering another person intimately, wholly, entirely. Too good to be true for our former ironman, right? Yep.

VII
DAYS OF WINE AND ROSES

WHILE HE LAUGHED AND PLAYED, drank beer and wine and made love, something nagged, tugged at, haunted him. No, you premed and theater students, not an unsuspected brain tumor (that explains everything!), or PTSD, or melancholic memories of the long lost notfamily, but the weight of nothing at all, the weight of absence, subtraction, of the void inside himself, a secret compartment where the iron still reside. He woke out of restless, sweat-drenched dreams, himself, naked, working in a red-hot forge, the heat on his body a physical force, sweat streaming from his open pores. He went through the day, climbing up and down ladders, hauling lumber, hammering and sawing, all that time carrying that weight and burden on his shoulders, in his thoughts, and didn't realize until somebody said something, spoke to, called him back to the here and now, S'up, *bro?* Where you at? or he caught himself reconstructing, in his mind, on the screen, virtual, his ruined machine buried in the wreckage of his notchildhood home. And he said, *lied*, to himself, Thank God, that's behind me.

In the evening he sat on the front porch and watched the sun sink below the horizon in an orange glow and the sky dissolve into ivory and cobalt and then the blackness of night pinpricked with stars, and he stared up into that candlelit abyss, the great hall of ancient and fallen gods, of titans, heroes, of conquerors and even conquered, but mighty warriors all, deserving of the name, recorded in history, the fame, and he would never, no epic, ballad, no memory or song, simply an empty pedestal, plinth, with no name, no birth and death dates chiseled, carved in marble, stone, lapidarian. So lost in his thoughts he didn't hear her, the woman, no names, remember? okay, Martha (or Maggie or May), come up behind him. What is it, my dear? Why do you sit here so late and stare into the night? Come to bed now, let's make love. She said in a soft, warm voice full of compassion. She said in a voice edged with impatience. She said with barely suppressed anger. With flashes of lightning in her eyes. She said what she wanted to and didn't say, not yet anyway, *I didn't sign on for this shit!*

These lapses into silence, this paralysis, immobility, when he seemed incapable of moving, taking action, when he didn't want to climb mountains, hike in the forest, swim in the lake, when he seemed rooted in the earth, tied, tethered, *anchored*, his transoceanic ship run aground, his world-circling hot air balloon deflated, collapsed into a mound of useless fabric. Where was the laughing man, gypsy, wanderer she fell in love with, carefree and wild? Or was that her own delusion, a fabrication of her desire, who knows, maybe, for reasons unknown even to herself, she had seen, sought, needed that stolidness and rootedness lurking inside him? Or was that his own justification, another lie, excuse, to himself, that she would, should fathom and understand this burden he carried? She saw him rotate his arm in its socket or roll his head on his shoulders and she asked if something was bothering him, if he was in pain. It's nothing, he said, a cramp or a crick, a minor ache he brought home with him from work, a small token, memento from the war, and never said it was some old treachery of the iron, not necessarily an injury, one of many, but the excision of the iron from his life, the void it left behind. When they made love and he winced, made a face, *excruciate*, he let her believe it was passion, the torment of pleasure. Or when they did go hiking in the mountains, the forest, and, climbing over a boulder or a fallen log, he felt an icy stab in his back, a shiver up and down his spine, he masked his pain with a look of determination, *Follow me, men (woman)!* He had to charge ahead, run up and down steep slopes, jump over splashing streams, make love in a sylvan glade, and pretend he didn't feel that phantom, ancestral pain in his body, didn't still glory *warrior* in his previous battles, won or lost, but *fought*, pretend he didn't ache over the iron's absence. Yes, portentous, something in the air, you can smell it, *change.*

Walking home from work one evening, a hazy autumnal sky, the trees in the park aflame with color, a cool breeze on his face, children's laughter chiming like bells, he heard another sound, metallic, in the periphery of his consciousness, followed the familiar *clang* and *bang* down an alley to an old garage, shingles missing from the roof, nails popping from weathered shiplap siding, and having gone that far he had to enter, go inside, and going inside, the distillation of aged petroleum smells, motor oil, gasoline, transmission and break fluid, penetrating his nostrils, mating with the profligate opiate receptors in his brain, he saw as if in a vision, dream, the great iron bar and the great cast-iron plates, and approaching, drawing closer, he had to bend down and touch, turn, squeeze the bar in his hands, he felt his muscles start to tighten and contract in ways familiar to themselves (inculcated, programmed, learned? Those wise, scholarly triceps and biceps?) even as a familiar little siren, not mermaid, *fish tale*, but alert, alarm, a klaxon, bell, trying to shout, to sound its warning, deep in his brain, *help!* Oh, but those long dormant muscles, treacherous, plotting, had their own design, they continued to tighten and contract and demand in that conspiracy against reason, against all the promises and resolutions he had made, *too late*, the molten iron starting to glow and spread through his body like volcanic magma moving underground at the same time the rough metal knurling bit into his flesh and the weight began to separate from the platform, from the surface of the earth, even as that terrified voice simultaneously of panic and reason struggled and even shouted to be heard, to insert itself into the fray, Gentlemen!

Please! That way lies madness! Do you hear me, gentlemen? *Stop!*

He released his grip, let the barbell crash back to the floor, seismic tremors dislodging, sending up plumes of cement dust from cracks in the concrete. His chest heaved, his breath came in gasps, he turned, staggered past, only now saw, the horrified faces, two? three? a young man, presumptive owner of the iron? a couple of teenage boys? and back outside into the fresh air, the warm sun and the cool breeze on his face, the birds singing, children laughing, screaming, *life*. What was he doing? What had he been thinking? He couldn't just rush back into it like that, couldn't expect his body and mind to endure that kind of punishment again. He had to know what he was doing, think about it first, be prepared, *всегда готовы*. O proud marmoset, thou art called Boy Scout, Young Pioneer.

But wait, breath caught, heartbeat returned to normal, more or less functionally sane again, what was he saying? Just like that, already decided, signed the contract in his mind, in the swoon of the moment, overwhelmed by his longing for, absence from the iron, long lost lover, phantom limb? A contract, that is, of betrayal, betrayal of his resolutions, his vows and promises to himself, betrayal of his new love for his old. And so you could say that at the same time he was healed he fell sick again. *But don't expect me to speak bleakly about gravity and the weight of iron, launch into diatribes, jeremiads, oh puh-lease, spare me your tears for* poor, poor *Cassandra. Remember, Spartan,* with *your shield or* on *it.*

Into the woods he walked, longtime refuge and retreat, arboreal chapel, cathedral, sat on a log fallen across a narrow stream, dipped his hand in the clear cold water trickling over the velvet green moss and shiny pebbles, bent back the blood red and purple hood of a pitcher plant to watch a small black beetle crawl out of its water-filled cup. He looked up at the interstitial patches of blue sky and white-hot cuticles of sunlight showing through the green stained-glass canopy of leaves and he asked himself and everything around him, nature, the world, *God*, just as possibly, a hamadryad peeping out from behind a wood fern, all these things that had spoken to him, called to him throughout his life, that he had finally acknowledged as essential to his life, *What should I do? This is the thing I know, the thing I love. I've denied it all these years but it's calling me back.* And everything around him said, or so he thought he heard, biased, naturally, *If you do this, and apparently you must, don't forget us.* The blood pounded in his temples, his chest heaved. *No, of course not, never, I won't.* Or so he said to himself, convinced himself, so easily trapped, netted once again, by his own sophistry. He raised his head, opened his arms wide as if he were about to begin an invocation. *This*, this was it exactly, what he had sought, desired, from the moment he first envisioned the machine in that brilliant flash, *pyrotechnic*, who knows how many—one-two-three-four-*five?*—years ago, to take all of this, nature and life and existence, and express it through the iron, make the iron the torch and the laurel he raised over his head for all to see in his moment of triumph. Ah, but that wonderful, glorious machine, he sighed to himself, his memory colored, *clouded*, by nostalgia, the passage of time, the crosscurrents of other events. He forgot, overlooked the failures, the limitations, remembered only success. If he had that machine now knowing what he knew now he could achieve so much more with so much less effort. And in the same breath realized what he was saying. If he had to start over, now, at his age, it'd take him forever. Meaning never. He was almost thirty years old. Still a young man, yes, in some ways younger than ever before, at the same time on the very cusp, the edge, brink, of the abyss, of being irrevocably too *old* to accomplish this task. And then he laughed, made the forest echo with his laughter. What was he thinking? Was that all it took to send him back to that madness, to bury him beneath those tons of worry and anxiety? Hadn't he learned anything in his time away from the iron? He must never let it get as bad as it had been before, and he must always think first of her, the woman, his lover, partner, *help*mate, Maria (or Mariah or Merope).

He resolved to tell her about his past with the iron, about the madness. But when he looked into her eyes and saw the spirit dwelling there, the desire, lust for life, freedom, fresh air and sunshine, the exact opposite, contrary, of everything to do with the iron, the speech he had worked up in his mind came out truncated, abridged. When he was younger he worked with iron, steel. You mean like a foundry or a mill in the valley? You cast molten iron into steel? Something like that. It did involve cast iron, molten iron, tempered steel, cast, made molten, tempered by his will, his *madness*, but *don't*, he didn't say that, he said, suddenly, breathlessly, rushing ahead, what I mean is, what I'm talking about is, the thrill you get, the sense of triumph, victory, *in the eyes of God.* But, *uh-oh,* now she was looking at him *oddly?* with skepticism? concern? and he realized, thought twice, brought that barreling locomotive, ninety miles an hour, brakeman's drunk, passed out, engineer's taking a nap in the coal bin, to a stop, tried to change the subject, muttered a lame excuse, that was in the past, it's all over now, I'd completely forgotten. What he really meant to say, what he was getting at, trying to explain, was that it was important to have an avocation, hobby, outside of work, something he *loved.* Okay, that was a little extreme again, *overboard*, now she looked perplexed. But before she could ask her question, the one she was going to ask, her brows furrowed, lips parted, the first word partially aspirated *Buuu* … he said, After all, it was just a pastime, he wasn't going to *kill* himself. Damn, why did he have to say that? Now her face, expression, her eyes, looked clouded, dark. Look, he said, playing the Lemming card, everybody's into the iron now, men, women, nonagenarian bonsai enthusiasts. Oh? Her eyes brightened, the sun coming out. Maybe I could try it? Ha! Did you hear that, ladies and gentlemen of the jury? *Maybe she could try it?* The scoundrel, rogue! Exactly the answer he hoped for. Buoyed by her curiosity, by his own boyish excitement, he began to describe and build, rebuild, his machine in front of her eyes, but the way he envisioned it now, the machine he hoped to build some time in the future. But I—*we*—can't do all that immediately, it'll take time, new technology, discoveries, cutting edge. For now we'll have to make do with somebody else's equipment. They enrolled in a fitness center, he showed her how to use the machines, lift free weights. Backpacker, mountain climber, river swimmer, she was strong, athletic, she learned fast, a natural, lifted the iron over her head, a barbell, twice, three times her weight, with *fierce determination* and *grace*, marvelous to watch, all eyes on her when she stepped onto the platform, approached the bar, the center of attention, other women, the men in the gym, guys hitting on her all the time, *in front of his eyes*, one in particular, the looks they exchanged, the words he overheard, *laughter*, jealous, he was, he criticized everything she did, criticized her for his own failures, he couldn't stop, hated himself for it, knew he was destroying their relationship, everything they had, they fought often, shouted, screamed at each other, what next, domestic violence? The *police*? Wait, stop, this isn't going in the right direction, not at all where we thought we were headed. Let's start over. Yes, sure, she was intrigued by this machine he described, by this *art* of his, but the iron never appealed to her the way it did him. She was spiritual, loved life, the outdoors, had no desire, intentions of locking herself in that cage, behind those iron bars. But sure, if that's your thing, knock yourself out.

He went in search of a gym, *fitness* center. He hadn't realized how popular the iron culture had become. Physical fitness fanatics, personal trainers, health nuts, gurus, prophets and priests of iron, rabbis and imams, even junkmen, scrap metal collectors called themselves masters of the iron craft, opened up gyms, clubs, spas and salons for the study and cultivation of the iron. Everything chrome-plated, mirrors on the walls, disco thumping, soft cushions everywhere, air conditioning, swimming pools, saunas and hot tubs, a large stone fireplace for the winter. A glass of chilled potato juice, sir? A rubdown, alcohol bath, blowjob? Hmm. Not what he would have expected from a sports club, gymnasium, a place designed, purposed for hard physical labor, *naked*. Men and women working together with the iron, bodies merging, melding in sweat and blood, in the bodily fluids transfused and exchanged through the intermediary of the iron. *Come on, baby, give it to me, yeah, that's so good, come on now, give it to me again, ooh yeah, faster, harder, yeah!* This one guy's bare-chested, straining, sweating profusely, muscles popping out, hard not to notice he's got some pretty nasty stretch marks on his pecs. You checking out Nancy the Amazon? guy next to him says. *Nancy?* Short story, she had her breasts removed to eliminate unnecessary weight, to make it easier to work with the iron. There's a whole crowd of enpuffalated bodybuilders, bulked up like balloon creatures, airship boys and girls, massive, muscles sprouting from muscles, *aliens*. Between lifts they consume huge quantities of protein drinks, they gulp herbal *supplements*, powders and chemicals extracted from the horns and testicles of monsters preserved in ice, from exotic tropical plants, rare species, *almost extinct*, they're all red in the face, they're seething and snorting like enraged bulls, steam's pouring out of their ears, they're gnashing their teeth, jaws clenched, eyes bright, blinking with insanity, indiscriminate rage, they wanta beat somebody up! they wanta *kill* somebody! Bah! He was disdainful of them all. They knew nothing about the true art of the iron, the years of dedication, the suffering, loneliness, pain.

Finally he applied for a job in a machine shop, industrial age, soot-blackened corrugated tin walls, heavy metal tools hanging from pegs, iron shavings scattered on the floor, pools of oil, grease smeared everywhere, a dust clotted stand-up fan blowing hot air around. The boss a crusty, lantern-jawed, broken nosed, squint-eyed, pot-bellied wreck with a massive chest, forearms like smoked hams, his qualifications for employment simple. Let me see you handle that piece of iron. He passed the test, yep. Every morning he woke in the early a.m., went out the door in his cloth cap, clean, starched chambray shirt, coveralls and work boots, black metal lunch pail in hand, tuna sandwiches on whole wheat, an apple, healthy, clean, jumped on the clanging streetcar trolley and rode across town to the machine shop, punched in the time clock at seven sharp. *Toooeeet!* The whistle blew, time to work, nine to five, eight to six, sometimes seven to seven, *equinoctial*. True, it wasn't much of a job. No future here, no ladder to climb, no promotions on the horizon, just work, work, work. At least it was iron in some form, he made the best of it, threw himself into the job with his usual zeal *obsession*. We see him in film clips, mostly black and white, sometimes grainy lurid color (an ancient security camera?), in his denim coveralls, sleeves of his blue chambray shirt rolled up above his elbows, he's got a huge pipe wrench sticking out of his back pocket, black grease and iron filings on his face, forearms, he's pulling huge metal levers, turning great iron valves, operating lathes and drill presses in a dervish flurry of arms and legs, he's a force of nature, can't stand still, gotta move, *work*, machines grinding away, milky white lubricant splashing everywhere, the clock on the wall ticking away the hours, minutes, seconds *tick tick tick tick*. Oddly, the heart, the essence, of the job's got something to do with lifting an iron bar very much like his old barbell. He thrives on, excels at his new occupation. The other men, journeymen all, knew nothing of finesse, specialization. They came in the morning, shouting, laughing, horsing around, didn't bother to go through the rituals, warm up, stretch the muscles, focus the mind. They jumped right in, loaded the bar, started bouncing up and down like monkeys on a string. One day one of them challenged him. You don't say much. Let's see what you can do. No choice now. He had to prove himself. The other guy went first, lifted the bar over his head, okay, now you. Ah, but not so fast, says he with Mighty Casey confidence. Add a hundred pounds. *Wait, what are you doing? That's crazy, no one asked you to. Too late.* Adrenaline pumping, that resurgence of madness, he was doing it, lifting the weight from the platform, the bar moving along its familiar trajectory, yeah, sure, little aches and pains registering their complaints in muscles and nerves but it's going up, it's locked over his head, hold it, hold it, hold it, *there*, he did it, he succeeded, whatever success that was, to lift that weight, to make it look relatively easy, to win the admiration, respect. *Yo, bro, you alright.* And based on that glory go on for the next six weeks, six months, in the raised estimation of his fellow workers, a bunch of dumb mill hunks, *woo-hoo*, and quietly nurse the injuries sustained in that moment of folly, don't let anybody know how much it hurt, the damage incurred. But, unforeseen, the consequences, now he was marked, the boss, the other men, watched, expected more of him, put him in the lead position, in the dog harness, horse trace, tied a bell around his neck in the goat pen, sheep fold, cow pasture. He led by his example, his voice when needed, Let's go! Let's do it! Gave it his all, every day a full day's labor.

And let's remember that while he was pushing himself like this on the job he still had his dream, to build his own machine, *a new generation! improved! a leap ahead!* But no, not like that, shiny gimmicks, bells and whistles, this time was going to be different, a mixture of the old machine and some visionary machine still in the future that incorporated everything, all the good and bad, all the flaws, failures, mistakes, all the bullshit and lies, all the world's great works and, yea, even its poverty and hunger, and raise it all up in its entirety for God, whatever god that may be, to see, and say unto this god, This! This is what you have given us or we have made of it but still with your approbation, your complicity, for without you, how? Although since when had that become a concern of his? When had he ever cared about the pain and suffering of other men, the crippled and diseased, the lunatic, crazy, insane. Yes, but why should he exclude himself from their ranks? His life, too, consumed by pain, madness, obsession, by the devastation of war, by the futility, fruitlessness, the useless *slaughter*, by PTSD, shell shock, by the *betrayal* of his own government. *Shh*. Yes, but they, the other madmen, the damaged, broken-winged, phantom-limbed, they at least had the pity of God, their god. He had nothing but the iron.

Every evening he rode the clanging banging trolley back home, worn out, exhausted, his face, hands, the creases in his hands blackened with machine oil, grease, his chambray shirt and denim coveralls streaked, soiled, his mind a blur, photographic images, the white-hot furnace in the oily blackness of the foundry, the molten iron, blue-gray steel, outside the trolley windows the continuum of seasons, the flaming hills of autumn bearing that bittersweet reminder of things passing, of things dying and coming to an end, the first snow of winter's cold white quietude, followed by the frozen siege, endless, gray, the fresh breath and green vestments of spring, the hot sultry days of summer. And mixed in with all that, infusing, investing, ever present, every hour, day, an inchoate vision of his machine, its inner clockwork construction, its external functions. Gnawing at and chewing on this vision throughout dinner while conversing, trying to converse with her, the woman, to listen, hear, focus on, what she was saying, something at work today, her job, *fucking prick grabbed my ass*, wait, what? at the same time trying to maintain in his mind that fire, that urgency for the work still to come later tonight, fueling that fire with hot black coffee, rivers of caffeine flowing in his veins, nerves jagged, wired, spots pinging before his eyes, to take all of that, the day at work, the glimpses of sunrise before work, of sunset after work, the fragments of conversation from a fragmenting relationship, to forge all that, transform that in his mind, in his hands, squeeze, mold, cast it into existence when he finally went down, Moses, into the basement, dungeon. (Ah yes, and didn't she wonder at his delight over the discovery of this large subterranean chamber in their new home, flashes *eee eee eee* of a secret torture chamber, burial ground, all along married to a serial killer and *she didn't even know it?*) Trying to remember where he left off last night, to pick up the momentum again, to keep focused on that vision in his head, drafting, diagramming machine parts, clumsily fitting together gears, axles, miniaturized electric motors, sensors, motherboards, all of it built around a simple iron bar, the essence of the machine the physical act, he worked on his technique, specialized exercises that broke down each lift into discrete segments, focused on specific muscle groups, power pulls, partial pulls, *shrugs*, repeated each movement again and again until it became a reflex, until he moved the bar as if it existed only in his mind and his thoughts alone were enough to lift it, using up all his energy reserves, draining the storage cells of his body and still demanding more, repeating to himself that ancient mantra, *the iron is not dead, I am not dead*, in the few hours remaining before he collapsed in bed, into sleep and dream or not sleep, not dream, lie awake tossing and turning, obsessed, obsessing, when was he ever going to finish, have enough time to finish? And finally sleep, knew he slept when he woke again four, five hours later, ate breakfast, something fast, easy, too sleepy, groggy, to make much, black coffee, whole grain toast, yogurt, protein supplement, take the trolley across town, stand again at the lathe, drill press, stamping machine, expend all his energy working on this machine that was not his machine, torturing the iron, trying to make it conform to some design and inspiration screaming inside him, promising himself that tonight he would finally make progress on his own machine, accomplish at least one of his goals, even as the hours passed and he felt that fire and enthusiasm ebb, drain from his body, his face contorted, twisting into horrible grimaces, expressing his inner turmoil, and didn't even realize until the whistle blew *toooeeet*! and the silence reawoke him, he took off his goggles, pulled out his earplugs, looked up and heard, saw all the other machines shut down, his alone grinding on, his workmates staring at him with horror and only then did he realize and stop.

And then after work, the guys, his work buddies, *friends*, he had friends again, wanted to stop for a drink, just one for the road, and sure, a cold brewskie sounded great, an icy mug of golden hopsy carbonation, to relax and bullshit with the guys and try to fit in for once in his life, because after all they weren't ignoramuses, big-mouthed louts, they were good guys, they just wanted to enjoy what free time they had away from the job, C'mon, bro, what's this dark cloud hangin' over you? But then it was never just one or two, but three, four, five, until he was just as drunk and stupid as the rest of them, shlurring hizh wordzh and trying to tell them about this thing he was doing. But what was he doing? Something about a machine, You mean like a hot rod? Low rider? Street machine? You're a motorhead, car enthusiast? No, not exactly, that wasn't it. All those brilliant theories, ideas he had conceived about the machine, diffused, lost in drunken nonsense. Finally go home, trashed, pass out with his face in the plate of cold stew the woman had prepared for him. Snore through a restless sleep. Drag himself out of bed at the alarm clock's strangled rooster crow *err err err*. Gulp a cup of hot black coffee and out the door already beat, worn out, the whole day passing in a gray fog in the grinding machine shop din and roar, knowing it'd be impossible for him to do anything that night either so, sure, why not stop for a drink with the guys and enjoy life, right, his best buds? *I love youzh guyzh.* And on and on until he couldn't go on, not like that, he'd never get anywhere, never finish the machine, he finally had to just say no (you were right, Nancy), sorry, not tonight, guys. Go on the wagon, get cleaned up, eat right, sleep tight, the man of iron will, discipline, no more happy hoursh, no more friends, buddies, maybe some other time, guys.

And go on like that week after month after year telling himself and telling himself until it became a litany, when things finally change, when I finish my machine, when I no longer have to work for a living, when I have the time, but the only time you have is a few hours at night, on the weekend, jammed in between all the other things you *have* to do, home maintenance, shopping, pay the bills, etc., etc., the only break from this routine when you injure yourself, when you get sick, when all you can do is lie in bed and moan. But what good's that? You're too sick to work on the job, too sick to work on your own machine, nobody's paying you for time off, and it's not really *that bad*, so you might as well get up and drag your sorry ass to work. And every day ask yourself, How did this happen? How did you, I, *he* come to be here? He wasn't even forty years old yet. He *was* forty, oh God, forty, how can I be forty years old? And still I carry this burden, and still I'm so far from my goal. That betrayal of age, of the self, his own body starting to work against him. He couldn't simply throw himself into it as he had in the old days and make quick gains. He took longer to warm up, to stretch out his muscles, his brain. Weights that had been toys in the past could be monstrously heavy depending on his mood, old wounds resurfaced, the rusted machinery, scar tissue, damage to cartilage, ligaments, tendons, every day another ache, pain, his shoulders, elbows, knees, back, until his entire body became a gladiatorial arena of pain. And still he denied, joked with the younger guys, yep, getting to be an old man, might have to retire soon, make room for you pups. Then he had to prove he still had it, lift enormous weights. Afterwards get drunk and shout in their faces, I tell ya, fellas, I'm stronger now than ever. D'ya see the way I threw that iron around? Lentils! That's the secret! Lentils'll give you the strength to get the job done! The whole time he's shouting you can see in his eyes, through the telescopic lens of his eyes staring off into space in search of some distant planet or star named victory, flickering, blue, like a sapphire, then fainter, white. And not until later that night, falling asleep in his soup, yes, lentils, or the next day at work, feel his body rebel, his neck and back stiff, aching. Fucked up again, didn't you, bro? As always, spartan, stoic, he couldn't let anyone see, had to hide the pain, sudden, stabbing, *ow!* when he bent down to pick up a dropped wrench, when he twisted, turned, rotated his trunk, torso, on its axis and *ye-ow!* felt a broken cog or rusted gear jamming, catching in his spine. That small victory on the platform another defeat, reminder of the impossibility of what he sought to do, the betrayal of the body, the confusion in his mind, parts of his machine scattered all over the basement floor, somehow he had to put them together *upon pain of death*, impossible, square pegs and round holes, mixed up jigsaw puzzle pieces, desperate, jamming, shoving them together, unsuccessfully, *help me!* Waking in the middle of the night from a dream, nightmare, his arms wrapped around himself, clutching at his chest, shivering, filled with terror of dying without accomplishing anything. And couldn't say to the woman, couldn't wake her, tell her, because then she'd say, What's wrong with you? Why don't you just give up on this nonsense, stop?

Oh yeah, we forgot about the woman. Left her on the sidelines. Did you think she'd just sit around and twiddle her thumbs, patient Penelope? Knit pink and blue baby booties for the children to come, maybe, starting to look like, never to come? Why are you doing this? Who are you doing this for? Nobody expects this much from you. You think this god you talk about is going to stick a gold star on your forehead? What about me? Do you think this is doing me any good? And now, now she said it, fed up, let it out, *I didn't sign on for this shit*! And then the tirade, everything held back, kept inside. You lied to me, made it seem like it was no big deal, a hobby. But it's crazy, *you're* crazy, the iron isn't all there is in the world. What happened to climbing mountains, hiking in the forest, swimming in the lake? You used to be wild, free. He laughed, sarcastic, practically operatic, *Ha!Ha!Ha!* He was never wild, never free, that was only a blip, a deviation from the norm, his norm. Her anger and resentment fed his anger and bitterness. He looked at her with coldness, hatred, I made terrible a mistake, she doesn't understand, never understood, she thought there was a purpose, an *end* to this process. Even as he said this, to himself, in his head, he heard the echo, the question, Wait, what? You're saying there's not? There is no purpose to this, no end? Meaning you really are sick, delusional? So what now? Counseling? Let's talk about this? Establish boundaries? Not bloody likely. He told her more lies, excuses. *Company loyalty.*

They *needed* him. *The economy, stupid.* Downturn, recession, depression, pink slips, layoffs, he couldn't afford to quit his job now. Besides—uh-oh, warning flags, an even bigger lie coming down the pike—he was *on to something*, close to a discovery, with the machine, I mean, *his*. Oh boy, forked tongue, pants on fire. Not even close. And, her eyes gimlet, wary, fox eyeing a piece of raw meat in the jaws of a steel trap, *she knew it*. Even to himself he lied, denied the hopelessness, impossibility of what he was trying to do, scoffed at the iron even as it crushed him into the ground. He quit trying to explain, didn't bother, to lie, fabricate, they talked less and less, finally not at all. Strangers in the same house under the same roof in the same bed (thanks Mom and Dad). One night he came home, the house was empty, he felt it immediately, sucking at him, his gut, the cold, dark vacuum of space. And then he understood, the vacuum was her absence.

What about the children? What children? I heard voices, children laughing, a baby crying. I don't know, he never mentioned anything about children to me, you must have imagined it. But it isn't true, I know there were children. She loved life, she wanted to create life, she wanted babies, she made him promise there'd be babies, a whole brood of babies. Was it possible *was it?* he was so lost in the iron that he didn't pay attention to, maybe didn't even know his own sons and daughters existed? And therefore didn't, couldn't, mourn when she took them with her, claimed custody in a vicious court case, law suit?

His reaction? Adult, mature, all for the best, after all? Sure. He drank, got drunk, disgustingly, sloppily, self-pityingly. It wasn't my fault, he blubbered. He was just a wee baby boy at heart, how could he be husband, father? He blamed, raged against the notfather for being absent, and when he was present always angry, aloof. He cursed, reviled the notmother for being hateful and contemptuous of everything he did, attempted to do. He blasphemed, took in vain, renounced any pretensions of faith, may even have been on the verge of making a pact with the devil, *Satan*, when he crashed, passed, escaped into sleep. In the morning he woke late, hung-over, went out the door unshaved, uncaffeinated, rode the trolley across town, woke again an hour later standing over a lathe, in a fog, used himself up, his energy, life, on the job. Rode the trolley home again at night, *clang, clang*, ate something out of a can *Rice-A-Roni*, out of a waxy white deli carton *no tickee no takee*, afterwards drank again, got drunk again, passed out on the couch, forgot about, gave up on his dream machine. Once again lived, survived, sort of, beneath the weight and burden of the iron, beneath the industrial pall of factories and mills vomiting clouds of cephalopodic black ink into the sky. He looked at the steel skeletons, at the ironwork, girders, at the tower cranes raising the metropolis ever higher, and he saw the insidious workings of rust and decay already eating at these great monuments of industry and labor even as it ate at him now. Having escaped, fled, from one old, worn-out and stagnant iteration of the past only to find that he had returned to yet another iteration of that past, fallen back into the trap of the iron, confused the iron with life and so sacrificed life, the life he had with her *to have and to hold*.

VIII
HUH-HUH-HUH

BUT MAYBE IT DIDN'T HAPPEN QUITE THAT WAY. Not quite. Maybe there was a change in course, he took a detour, another route, routed by life, fate, by, say it, *failure*. He resolved to begin again, shrug off the manacles and chains of despair, disillusionment, find the true path, rededicate himself. Let's suppose he put to practical use his years of calculating tonnages of iron, of engineering and re-engineering the design of the machine, drew up a plan, graphs and charts, marketing goals and sales targets, went to the bank, requested, applied for and was granted a small business loan, bought out the failing company, sent the former owner and boss, old Sam (or Roscoe or Ed), packing, into retirement, happy trails, don't let the door bang yer' butt on the way out, gradually let go the old hands with their old habits, *adiós, amigos, adiós, my friends, the road we have travelled has come to an end*, hired all new employees, *young people*, plenty of those, full of pep, all in debt, over their heads, college, yep, but, wait, what about a good job, decent pay? Oh, *come on*, who told you *that?* Sign here, boys and girls, on the dotted line. He intended to revive the dream, build his own machine. But no more mindless flailing about, no more misguided applications of ancient formulas, voodoo ergonomics, this time a new rationale, logic, his youthful vision transformed, the years of putting his shoulder to the wheel, back bent beneath the yoke, of blindly grasping for the stars, *groping,* distilled into a new approach. Not only must the perfect machine incorporate everything in the known world (that's certainly not an unreasonable expectation), but, taking the final leap into the flaming abyss, the white-hot cauldron of ideation, it, the machine, must be ever evolving, able to adapt to every challenge, change, mutation, external and internal, to its very core, its heart, brain, *soul*. The words, thoughts, of a man of the cloth, of the uniform, a priest or military man who has found faith again in justice, *God*, even then risking that he will be driven mad by the injustices of mankind and possibly even that very same god, but justice nevertheless, divine, inexorable. So you think.

And so, armed, girded, with this renewed vision, this new epiphany, the latest in a chain, links, of epiphanies, the forward leaning element in a column of falling dominoes, he set to work again, put his best minds to the task, young men and women, enthusiastic, full of energy, ambitious, *driven*, yes, sure, argue, disagree, debate, he encouraged it, but working together as a team, cohesive, to achieve his dream, committed to making not just a *product*, but a valuable commodity, durable, aesthetically pleasing, that people, consumers, wanted to *own*, took pride in. And it worked. Everybody wanted his machine. Sales were over the top. The business exploded, venture capitalists, IPOs. How did that happen? Who knows, the biographers will decide, figure it out. The once bashful, the shy and retiring, the isolated, alienated, withdrawn, cave dwelling ogre transformed into Prometheus, Lucifer, bringer of light. He appeared on stage, the big screen, to huzzahs, hurrahs, cheers and applause, the new breed of CEO, a lean warrior chief, gaunt even, (*is he sick?* some wondered, whispered aloud, a rumor), constantly driven, a force of nature, high energy, indomitable will, forging ahead, every six months he, his company, issuing a new version, each time a closer approximation, of his dream, vision, everybody had to have it, lined up outside the store the night before. He was a success, rich beyond his wildest dreams. He built a mansion, the design based on some childhood notion of castles, fortresses. Stone walls, iron gates, a great oaken door bound in brass. He threw lavish parties, gave to charities. *Supporter of the Arts*, *Man about Town*, *Philanthropist*. Yes, he was a great success, so why was he so unhappy? Wait, say again?

Yes, unhappy. Because it hadn't occurred to him when he began this enterprise, he hadn't fully realized. Because it wasn't just the business of the iron but the business of the business. The machine had to be converted into training manuals, parts manuals, user manuals, the machine had to be converted into dollars and cents, taxes, insurance, bills of lading, itemized lists, spread sheets, catalogues, blueprints and diagrams, patent and trademark applications, legal challenges, law suits, copyright infringement, board meetings, public scrutiny, *ugly gossip*, until there wasn't any iron anymore, just the business. People demanded his time for lectures and seminars, TV, radio and magazine interviews. *The man and the machine!* They searched all over the country, tracked down the little hundred ten pound set of weights from his first adolescent foray with the iron, recovered it from the basement of a fraternity house notorious for its debauchery (nothing new, bestiality, autocoprophagia, oh, and lots of homoerotic hanky panky spanky—I was so drunk, etc.), as well as extreme hazing of its pledges (branding irons, sleep deprivation, lethal intoxication). Sentimental, perhaps a wee bit drunk (bubbly flowing like the Mississippi), he wept when he saw the rusted little black iron plates and flimsy bar. Laughing, pointing at the paunch he'd acquired as a handicap—don't get to the gym much these days, *ha ha*—he bent down, wrapped his fingers around the rough knurling, began to pull. But, *oof,* the bar felt alien, surprisingly heavy, and, *ouch*, that kink in his back caught him off guard, scared him. Grunting, groaning, red in the face, he managed to lift the weight over his head to polite cheers, a smattering of applause, the woman, his wife, the love of his life, rolling her eyes, Oh, Harry (or Leonard or Dirk), You're making a fool of yourself, you'll *break* something.

Wait, what, his *wife?* Maybe they reconciled, he agreed to see a counselor, or else he remarried, a trophy wife, the first in a string of many, gold diggers, bimbos, baby makers. He hardly ever saw the children. The children? Yes, I'm certain now there were children. Not that he concerned himself with child nurturing, messy diapers, a.m. feedings, the terrible twos, tantrums, toilet training—whoo, what a stink! Sorry, not for me, boys! Nobody at work, the men and women in the trenches, his top execs, even knew he had children, he never talked about them, didn't display their photos on his desk (of course there were rumors, speculation, whispered, *shh*, after all, he's a *genius!*). He might look in on them sleeping in their beds when he came home at night, maybe spend some time with them on Sunday afternoon, a few minutes anyway, try to instill some sense of manliness, duty, after all they were almost men now, ten-twelve years old. What? Five and six? Nevertheless, they must understand, indeed, it was paramount they grasp what lay ahead, the future, their duty, they would (of course) follow in their father's footsteps, take over the business, he insisted on it. Goddamn it, I didn't raise you little bastards to be failures. And stop your whining. You know Daddy doesn't love you when you whine like that. They're sullen, red-faced, teary-eyed, this isn't at all what they expected out of life. His poor unhappy children. They hate him, his guts, swear that as soon as they're old enough they're *getting the fuck out of here* and they'll never have anything to do with this son-of-a-bitch or his goddamn machine ever again. Okay, that was later, when they really were men, almost, fifteen, sixteen. In the end he shrugged his shoulders, threw up his hands, it was useless, pointless, kids these days, they knew nothing, dunderheads, dolts. No wonder he was always tense, ready to explode, Will you kids please shut the fuck up! No wonder she left him, took the children with her, attorneys, court orders, the horribly messy divorce, alimony, child support, who the fuck wants children anyway? They just get in your way, they demand your time and energy, your *life*, and then they grow up and go away.

In the prison of his anger and resentment he pondered how this had happened, how had he once again lost sight of his original vision? Which was what? The calibration of the universe? The unveiling of God? The weighing and quantifying of all matter and existence? Why did it sound childish, simplistic when he said it like that? Why not noble and true and the only thing worth pursuing? And why was that exactly what he was not doing? In fact, the exact opposite. The company engaged in useless competition, marketing wars, every six months a different color, a few more gimmicks, all this money spent on sales promotions, advertising, to convince buyers they didn't have to do any work themselves, didn't have to think, use their minds, their bodies, that somehow the machine would do everything for them, eat, shit, piss, fuck, while they sat back, spectators to, observers of their own dissipation, demise. The machine seemed to have developed a mind of its own, started putting out various un-programmed byproducts, spewed robotic spawn, physically desirable AI home appliances (French maid models available), talking, *conversive*, vacuum cleaners and hair dryers. Bi- and even trilingual waffle irons, food blenders and coffee roasters tumbled out of the machine like orphaned puppiebots, *Hi Mom, what are we having for dinner? Ho fame! Ich bin hungrig!* On top of that, wary, suspicious—you gotta be in this business—he saw, in his peripheral vision, the corner of his eye, his young employees, these *kids*, looking at him with varying degrees of, yes, affection, but also condescension, envy, *resentment*. Yeah, sure, in the beginning he encouraged dissent, radical thinking, now he was afraid of it, *them*, the young lions. Why doesn't the old fart get out of the way, let us see what we can do? Eliciting his own condescension and resentment in turn. If these punks knew how hard he had worked, his fingers to the bone, back breaking, the struggle to get this far, *when I was your age*. Increasingly erratic, his behavior (maybe there *was* something wrong, a brain tumor? *okay, we'll work that into the fourth chapter*). On a whim he ordered his employees to drop whatever they were doing, abandon months of research to pursue some new ~~chimera~~ avenue. He kept irregular hours, left his office in the middle of the day, returned to the factory late at night (security reported a *ghostly figure* hovering about), unlocked the back bay, went inside. The glare of a single light bulb on the ceiling revealed the company's first machine, the prototype, he climbed in, got it humming, not like when he was a carefree young man pedal to the metal and full steam ahead, but cautious, always looking at his watch, checking the dials and gauges, his vital signs, trying not to overdo it, trying not to give himself a heart attack, stroke, trying to find inside himself some new inspiration, the key that unlocked the door to the final, complete, the quintessential machine. All for naught, hopeless, a pipe dream. He turned into the next (best?) thing, demi-god, despot, *tyrant*, cast about blame for his own failure, demanded increased production from his already exhausted and dispirited workforce, impossible deadlines, he berated, ranted and raved, threatened to fire employees on the spot for failure, insubordination, *off with his head!* Top execs fled flapping and squawking like chickens from the coop, defected to the competition, resumes and proprietary intellectual property in hand. Just as well, he snarled. Bunch of useless yes-men. Cowards all. Stupid to boot. Not an original thought among the lot. *Losers.* Not surprising, morale took a dive. HR reported excessive turnover, hiring hectic, a revolving door. Naturally, the market took notice. *Under his watch*, headlines said. Shareholders, uneasy, were certainly watching. Accounting declared the company's potential losses catastrophic *if the trend isn't reversed.*

IX
UHHHH!

HE WOKE ONE MORNING, checked his messages, ten thousand inquisitors demanding answers. Time to rethink the situation, don't you think? Take stock, better yet, sell off stock, the whole damn company, kit and caboodle, get while the getting's good, while the brand's still hot, sort of. That's what you pay attorneys and accountants for, right? To smooth the wrinkles, grease the wheels, work out the details, fine print, guarantee maximum profit from a becalmed, listing, on the verge of *rumors abound* sinking ship.

Money in his pocket, now what? Take that vacation he'd been promising himself for the past ten-fifteen years? Shake the dust off his feet and hit the road? A change of scenery perhaps? At least before the creditors catch on or up? He felt an unusual restlessness, a primordial urge, nomadic, to tear up his roots, move, travel afar, see distant cities, marvelous sights. Yes, but. He couldn't entirely leave the iron behind, impossible, gotta have that fix, get his kicks, the attachment he felt, *welded*, dumbbells, kettle bells, barbells, the equipment, some ancient, *centuries*, he'd accumulated in his home gymnasium. He needed an appropriate vehicle, quirky, unique, that reflected his new state of mind, gypsy, wanderer, carefree. In a weathered old barn out on the lonesome prairie of the internet he found an antique circus wagon decorated with carved wooden angels, strongmen, elephants and lions, a *Doot-doot-Dootally-doot*

calliope that suggested barking seals and honking clowns, iron
bars that suggested wild beasts. With a whole lotta love and
elbow grease, he restored this ancient conveyance, gave it a
fresh coat of paint, bright red, green and gold, bought a team of
draft horses. He followed the back roads, country lanes, set up
camp on the outskirts of towns, villages, explored the terrain,
took in the sights, at some point in the day or even night
unloaded his weights, began to perform various exercises, his
quotidian routine, fix, elixir, the rush of endorphins, out in the
open like that, the fresh air. People saw his circus wagon, came
out of curiosity, stayed to watch him lift, *that old feller's purty
durn strong*. And he loved it. He got up on the platform to
satisfy that fire still burning inside. He was a total ham, it came
naturally, his years as a CEO ... *Laaaadies and gentlemennnn!*
At the beginning of each show he put out a bucket, the crowd
filled it with ducats, the money piled up. His circus grew. He
bought more circus wagons, hired out of work performers,
freaks. The Fabulous Balloon Boys! For the day's show they
inserted bicycle pumps into their veins, pumped themselves up
like balloons, bulging Aeolian cheeks, biceps like inflatable
swimming pools, had to be careful letting the air out after their
performance, too fast and they shot off into the sky making
rubbery flubbery squealing sounds. See the Amazing Amazon!
Nancy, a bit long in the tooth herself, but still quite
intimidating, those biceps, those *scars*. *Clawed by lions*,
someone said someone said (sic). He staged theater with the
Valhalla Vamps, in horned helms, chainmail, leather, *wings*,
they bore aloft the fallen warrior, he was that warrior, in his
cheesy Viking costume. He bought—okay that doesn't sound
right, kind of like slavery—he *hired* a gorilla, an aging highland
silverback, to perform feats of strength. He and the gorilla, both
in classic single strap spotted leopard strongman costumes,
wrestled around, took turns lifting each other overhead
Followed by a big ear-flap African elephant, originally virtual-
hologrammic (although oddly the turds weren't, large, brown,
like leather drums, tom toms, or cylindrical coconuts embedded

with yellow straw), but who or which quickly reified into the classic package of sagging pachydermic wrinkles, tusks and sinuous trunk, with which the elephant, eyes narrowed in concentration, and he, the once hermetic ironman now consummate showman, engaged in strenuous arm-wrestling matches, much to the audience's delight. (Both, by the way, the gorilla and the elephant, were paid the going union rates, with health benefits and sick leave, more than you can say, right?)

Time passed, fled, more accurately, time sat on the sidelines while objects, stars in the sky, lives on earth, human, cognitive, observers, flashed by, hurtled, *it's all gone too fast, my boy, grab onto what you can.* Like a late night talk show host, stand up comedian, aging, growing older, confidence waning, he furtively surveyed the crowd while he performed, yes, judging the audience's reaction, but also fixing now and then on a young man, occasionally a boy. No, you badge wearing members of the morality police, not an old pederast, letch, searching for his next boy toy, prey. But, yes, searching, for someone special, this notion that had come to his mind recently, an *apprentice,* to learn the craft from him and carry on—a new concept, reality dawning, unavoidable—*after he was gone,* to prevent all those years of struggle, *mein,* from being lost, preserved somehow in the body of another, younger. Plenty of young men showed promise, none of them worked out, rank amateurs, journeymen, wannabes, imposters, dilettantes, he saw immediately, the way they approached, handled the iron, they didn't have the gift, the determination, will, *madness* to push beyond all possibility and endurance and achieve that which even he knew was impossible to achieve having not achieved it himself. Yes, one like that, himself, obsessed, *deluded.*

Let's suppose there was such a one, a boy, orphaned, cast into the street by catastrophe, war, pestilence, plague, by hurricanes, tornadoes, by unloving parents, unforgiving institutions, who stood around watching, waiting, after everyone else had left, gone home, *home,* impossible not to notice, to ignore him, to finally say, What do you want, boy? What are you hanging around for? And when no answer came, to state the obvious in an interrogative, Are you hungry? Do you want something to eat? And after that, watching the boy gobble his potato and piece of meat with his bare grubby paws like a savage, Where do you live? Head down, no answer. Well, then, sleep? Still no answer. Long pause. Alright, *goddamn it*, you can lie down on the floor tonight but tomorrow you're on your way, hear? Yes, he took pity on, felt compassion for, this poor unclaimed child of the streets, although the truth is that he was as alone and unclaimed as the boy, himself an orphan of sorts, maybe that's why. And how long before that became a permanent situation, something to eat, a place to sleep, in exchange, maybe, for chores, a broomstick he threw at his feet, a shovel to clean up piles of elephant turds? And from that to training him, how not train him? The boy always hanging around, watching, *like a fox*, eyes quick, shifty, fixated on the iron, that hunger, desire, already evident, *madness*, a fast learner, quickly surpassed his own efforts at that age. Of course he was pleased, too easily, his vanity, he didn't realize he had brought a *viper* into his tent, a serpent, snake, *the old fool*.

His vanity. Every day he looked at himself in the mirror, examined his face, features for signs of aging, decay, examined his tongue for signs of a virus, cancer, saw the hoar frost spreading through his hair, the gray clouds creeping across his eyes, the vein throbbing at his temple when he was tired, he stared at his hands, fingers, opening and closing them, pondering their value and function and the degree to which they had lost such. Every day woke with its companion aches and pains, the nagging reminders of his mortality. His back stiff as frozen laundry, or he couldn't turn his head on his neck, or he felt a sudden searing pain across his shoulder blade when he raised his arm, or a joint that wouldn't lock or unlock. Every day another tic or cramp or ache subject to changes in the weather, another flaw to add to the catalogue of injuries accumulated and acquired over the years. As long as he could

still perform, *work*, above all else he must work, like an old
farmer, old bricklayer, mason, old railroad gandydancer who
goes on working the rails and laying brick and baling hay no
matter what state of wreckage his body is in. He had a recurring
dream, his face transformed into an iron mask spotted with
blood red flecks of rust, pale, lichen green patches of verdigris,
his limbs, his arms, legs, cast in bronze, splayed, da Vinci's
jumping jack man in stasis, clockwork gears frozen in place,
because in the dream he himself was the machine and he knew
exactly what it felt like to be a machine when all the lubricants
had leaked out, evaporated, and the cogs and gears ground to a
halt with metal shearing, shrieking, *wake up! wake up!* but he
couldn't, wouldn't wake up or move ever again, everything, all
his organs, his heart and lungs, liver and kidneys quivering as
the last warmth drained and trickled out of them and the crystals
of ice began to form in his blood, to creep through his veins, his
entire body gradually freezing into a cold dead mass, like lava,
molten iron, cooling, hardening, until everything, not only his
breathing and heartbeat and the flow of blood, but his thoughts,
his ability to perceive and understand, slowed down to an
infinitesimal point and, contrary to theoretical mathematics,
equally credible mythology (paradoxically, *Zeno*), i.e., the end
never reached, finally came to a full stop, *punkt*, and
disappeared completely, the corporeal self blanched, etiolated,
reduced at last to moon dust by the passage of time, of light
through space. But those are the thoughts of an old man,
ancient, fallen into ruin, and he wasn't ready to, couldn't give it
up, not yet, the crowds, the glory, that's all that mattered now.

There, you see, he finally admitted it, to himself, to the
boy, the *me* to be, next in line, his would be *maybe* apprentice,
inadvertently, always following, shadowing him, listening for
words, magic formulas, sometimes the truth, muttered aloud,
unintentionally. Yes, *hypocrite*, he knew it. He'd forgotten all
about his God, about calibrating the universe. He'd get up on
stage in that ridiculous costume, leopard skin singlet, purple silk
boxing shorts, black tights, red leather wrestling boots laced up

the ankle, nearly bald, that fake horsehair mustache glued under his nose, his body wired, held together with belts and buckles, braces and straps, his stringy arms and bandy legs covered with bumps, scars. He'd act hale and hearty, robust, thrust out his chest, flex his biceps. Inside he felt slow, stiff, *old*, like a rusty crane, derrick, *steam shovel*, reviving, resurrecting itself from years of oxidized slumber in an abandoned strip mine or stone quarry, cranking up its engine, blowing out black clouds of diesel exhaust, creaking and groaning as it prepared to once again lift tons of iron. He went through all kinds of rituals, lit incense, flaming torches, muttered incantations, invoked esoteric mind over matter techniques he learned from Master Boris Bedbugovich in a secret training camp in Siberia, pure hocus pocus, gibberish, all legerdemain, smoke and mirrors, distracting the audience, leading them on as he pumped himself up for the day's performance. Telling himself, I'm not afraid, I'm just as strong as I ever was. Repeating old formulas. It's just a question of hitting it right, the right time of day, the right hour, the right state of mind, the perfect alignment of all the celestial bodies in the heavens, the sun and the moon, the stars and the planets, with elbow, shoulder, hip and knee joints, with back aches, arthritis, rheumatism, every time he approached the iron fearful, telling himself not to think about, consider, his spine shattering, bones splintering, joints popping like plastic wrap, his body crushed into the ground like tractor-trailer flattened road kill. But, no, he couldn't show any of that, reveal that, the young men demanded with their eyes, wanted to see him resurrect that strength, wanted to see and believe an old man could do that because maybe that meant they too could do that, have a long life ahead, find their own small share of fame, immortality. The physical reality of what he was proposing to do *impossible* didn't even occur to them until he approached the bar and they realized, *OMG*, that old man actually thinks he's going to lift that enormous weight. And yet, even as they watched, before their very eyes, he seemed to emerge out of that wreckage of age, his flesh hardening, transforming itself into iron, his mind at work, demanding of his body that it match his will, his eyes fixed on the bar as he slowly bent down, wrapped his fingers around the rough knurling like gnarled roots, lowered himself into the pulling position, yes, a rusty old derrick, almost in the same moment the weight somehow, almost unbelievably, separating from the platform, beginning to rise, climb toward its zenith as he rose, stood erect, held the bar over his head, victory. Yes, indeed, unbelievably, *impossible*. And no wonder. The audience didn't, couldn't know, all a fraud, behind the scenes, the manipulations, illusions, the cogs and gears, levers and pulleys, how it all worked, fooled the spectators, even the weights, fake, made of Styrofoam, papier-mâché, painted black to look like cast iron. He fixed the crowd, one eye cocked, a fierce pirate parrot stare, a challenge to any and all who challenged his act. He invited hecklers, unbelievers to come up on stage and try their hand, and good luck, suckers, they were going to need it. Big galoots, truly giants, freaks of nature, brobdingnagian, capable of lifting cars off the ground, couldn't budge the weight an inch. He had the ape and the elephant give it a shot. Nor could they, mighty beasts both, move the great weight. And then the audience was all the more astonished and again they said, *OMG, that old man?* It must be magic. Yeah, the magic of electromagnets. He stepped on a button and, *shazam*. The pachyderm and the simian, both in on the deceit, are rolling their eyes at each other like, oh brother!

But he wasn't just deluding his dwindling audience, he was deluding himself, he didn't realize how bad it had gotten, he was nothing but a clown now. Everybody was laughing at him, mocking him. His costume was sagging in back, his dirty underwear showed. A large chunk of Styrofoam had broken off one of the fake weights and he hadn't even noticed. And still he actually believed he could lift those weights. Ha, imagine that old rummy lifting anything! The only lifting he did now was with a glass. Oh yes, and then he could lift something all right. He and the gorilla, Ned (or Sid or Dick), and Archibald (or Alfred or Alexander), the elephant, all palsy walsy now, best buds, played poker for peanuts (yes, the legumes, roasted and salted), got drunk, *toasted*, together, he's usually holding a losing hand, pretty much symbolizes the current state of affairs, his face swollen and burnished in the firelight, his mad bulging eyes, drunk, laughing and shouting, I'm telling you, boys, I see a bright future ahead. Sid (or Dick or Ned) and Alfred (or Alexander or Archibald) are giving each other knowing glances, like, yeah, right, we've heard this before. Then his mood changed. He'd pound on the table, demand that *I*, his minion, shadow, so-called apprentice, bring him another drink—*I said a bottle, not a fucking glass, you imbecile!* Well, time to hit the hay, the ape and the elephant say and head for the door. You see, at some point it always came to that, he erupted into that rage, betrayed himself, because he wasn't such an ironman after all, invulnerable to the slings and arrows. But I had no choice, I had to listen to him, his rants, slurred, rambling, regurgitating past triumphs, victories, all fabrications, lies, I'm sure. Not that he cared if I believed him, it wasn't for me, the exaggerations, braggadocio, it was a pep talk for himself, just like any other over-the-hill loser, pug, hanging off a bar stool, telling his drunken bullshit to any younger guy who'd listen, *I* did this and *I* did that. Because after all, it was his own story he was telling, always his own story, *he*, the hero of myth, legend, *his*. Later at night I'd find him passed out on the floor of his circus wagon in a pair of saggy long johns, a large wet spot in his crotch from peeing himself. Sometimes, less frequently, I'd find him in bed with a woman, some ugly old prostitute or sideshow carney act, a lot of good it did either of them, he needed a crane to lift that limp old piece of meat between his legs. He'd see me peering in from behind the curtain and sputter some drunken nonsense, an attempt at an apology or excuse, or curse at me to preserve what little pride he had left *get outa here you damn shnoop*. The truth is I didn't care. At all. What? Jealous? *Me?* He was old enough to be my grandfather. What did it matter to me what he did or with whom? More power to him. *Dickhead.*

But wait. Whose impudent voice was that? The faithful

apprentice? How *dare* he? But wait again, that voice changed, the voice's speaker, the apprentice, yes, but metamorphosed, transmogrified, the same and not the same, not a he but a she, *why not a she?* Who knows how. Magic. A spell. (So, like, it *is* a fairytale? Like that old guy Tiresias? Oh, that's a myth? So what's the dif?) Or modern science, hormones, surgery, *wonderful what they can do these days*, one way or the other, not gamin but gamine, or maybe trans, nevertheless, a girl, barely even a young woman, a wild and laughing sprite. And all that time the old fool fooled, he didn't know, see, or maybe he did, just didn't want to admit, yes, lied to hide, his hurt pride, painful even now, the memory, how the apprentice first appeared, came to him, by what manner, means, not an orphan, beggar boy, willingly indenturing himself to this tyrant, bowing beneath the abusive language, the beating fists. No, he first heard her—*her*—voice crying out from the crowd, laughing at, mocking him, You old fool! You can't even lift a block of Styrofoam, I'll bet you can't lift your sorry little dick either. He pulled the curtain, hid in shame. Dick (or Ned or Sid) tried to console him, *I didn't particularly like her reference to the male sex organ either* (pronounced with a British *I*-thuh). When he went out later at night she was still there. Whata you want? he growled. *You*, she said. Huh? How dare the little biiiii … *brat*, mocking him again, right to his face. He locked himself inside his wagon, got drunk, later came out to take a piss and passed out on the ground. It was a cold night, blue norther just blew in from the further north. The ape and the elephant found him nearly frozen to death, put him to bed, piled covers on him, but he could not get warm, and, lo, she came close out of concern for him and they said *let her lie with him that he may be warm*, and so she lay with him (it's alright, ma, she's at least fourteen, totally legal in several states *with parental consent*). The next morning she (Betty Ann? Peggy Sue? *Delilah?*) made bacon and eggs and banana walnut pancakes for everyone, a mysterious Mona Lisa smile on her face. Ned (or S. or D.) and Archibald (or A. or A.) looked at each other sideways, scratched their heads (yes, with his trunk). *His* smile suggested befuddlement rather than delicious memories of an erotic dalliance, indeed, traitorous memory, he remembered nothing at all of last night.

And that was that. She stayed on, no longer apprentice but boss, leader, captain of the ship, the diminishing fleet of carnival wagons, acted as his protector, his buffer against the audience's laughter and derision when he got on stage, put on his ridiculous vaudeville act. It took someone as tough as her, *nails*, with that quick tongue, to emasculate, slash off a male heckler's vanity, manhood. *Too bad your brain isn't as big as your dick, asshole.* Waggling her little finger in the air for emphasis. The asshole's face is flaming, *red as a beet*, he wants to kick somebody's ass but what's he gonna do, she's a *girl*. Yeah, a girl, and she'd probably kick *his* ass. Besides, she knew what they really came to see, what really brought in the do-re-mi, and she gave it them, wowed the crowd with her provocative dance, shaking her adolescent butt (padding? implants?) all over the place, flashing her tits (silicone? hormones?) like it was an accident, wardrobe malfunction, while he, the old fool, was shoved aside like a discarded pile of wreckage. Like we said, serpent, snake, *viper*.

Cooooooshmarrrr. He'd groan awake from yet another drunken nightmare, his dreams feverish, inflamed, *Igneus fatuous*, foxfire, swamp gas, his voice thick with catarrh, feel the hot brine overlapping the seawalls of his eyelids, tears for what may or may not have been. False memory, dream, hallucination, the face in front of him fading in and out, pale, liminal, nymph and pan, gamine and gamin. On the other side of that face a personality separate from his own, *discrete*, inspecting, examining him for signs of life, death, some transitory state in between. The old fool would stare at me, bleary eyed, his face, expression, befuddled, seeing something in nothing, sometimes weeping, sobbing, *I don't know what's happening, I don't know what to do, I can't go on, I must go on.* At times his despair caused me despair, because I could not help him, I could only watch, spectator to this tragicomedy, ongoing train wreck. Why don't you just stop? I finally said. Why not take a vacation from your vacation? Out of the mouth of babes, right? That untimely wisdom, inarticulate knowledge of lunar, mensal and circadian cycles and rhythms? But no, he, the old man, *Master*, didn't, couldn't stop, only stopped his ears against this blasphemy. *Stop?* he cried as if I were the madman. *Vacation?* You wretched whelp, I knew from the beginning you weren't right for the iron! Resurrected by his anger, he stood there huffing and puffing, face red with fury, indignation, repeating, *Stop? Stop?* and staring at me as if I really were the crazy one. The audacity! To tell him, a grown man, wise, older, practically a wizard, how he should act, conduct his business. And then he'd laugh, not at me, I realized even then, but at himself, at God and the universe, not a happy laugh, not the laugh of a wise old man cracking his ribs with laughter at his own folly and stupid mistakes, but the bitter, self-deprecating laughter of one who knows only too well that he has failed, that now it really is too late.

The signs were there all along, in the stars in the sky, in the ruts in the road. The carney was falling into ruin, down to one wagon, paint peeling, wooden wheels cracked, rims bent, broken spokes, the worn out old draft horses long ago made the passage to the glue factory. Archibald (the budget no longer allows for alternative names—Ed.) struggled to pull the carney through intense heat, dust storms, thunderstorms, ice storms, blizzards. We'd all get out and help push, me, the old fool, and Ned (ditto—Ed.), everybody shivering under blankets, heavy coats, blinded by the driving snow, the old fool muttering like Lear. Finally he couldn't delude himself anymore. One morning he called everybody together, it was the first time we'd seen him sober in months. He said he was going back home, he was giving it all up. He gave me the papers to the carney, titles, deeds and liabilities, I know you've been itching to try your hand at it, young man, or, um, lady, or, er … *never mind*. And what was I going to say, thanks for nothing, pops. Ah, but the old fool, okay, yes, maybe, *master*, had one surprise left. There was some money he'd been keeping back, he'd invested well (c'mon, it *is* a fairytale). He paid Archibald and Ned an extra two months wages—they'd decided to try their luck in Vegas—gave me enough to stake a new claim in modern metallurgy. Then we all said our goodbyes, everybody choked up, sniffling like a bunch of old ladies at a funeral, I admit I was too, crying. In spite of everything, I, yes, loved the old fool.

And what did he think, the old fool? Not the one, after all, that he was searching for? Just a boy, or girl, or—aw heck, you know what I mean—earnest, honest, hopeful, but not the true one, the apprentice? And now what? Go back home, defeated finally, by the iron, by life, dejected, a, say it, useless old wreck? To die?

X
TEN!

OR WAS THAT, TOO, ALL A LIE? Another story, version, diversion, *fairytale?* He never left home, never went anywhere, collapsed like an ancient edifice in his own ruin and disrepair, the house and the garden sinking into similar ruin and disrepair around him, the wooden roof beams rotted, paint peeling, the courtyard, grounds and vegetable garden grown over with weeds? Too old, weak, enfeebled to do anything but drink and talk to himself and rot. And so he would have done if something hadn't happened to halt, even reverse that decline, to rescue him from his own folly, the arrival on his doorstep of a bundle, a basket, filled with life, the promise, hope, slim, of life. A child. An infant, newborn, completely helpless, no more than a couple of hours, a day at most on this earth, its eyes still glued, sealed against the light and the atrocities of the world the light revealed, its mind and body completely unformed, unstamped, waiting for that old, weathered, but still strong hand to reach down for it, to discover the note and the words, to read the plea. To take inside that bundle of life and marvel over it, maybe, more likely regard it with displeasure, even revulsion, this disgusting little creature, probably lying in its own filth, and now someone, most likely you, old man, will have to bathe the filthy thing and wrap it in something clean. Later, that done, drink in hand (washed and rewashed, *disgusting*), look down at, examine more closely, maybe more benevolently (second glass), that ugly wrinkled little old man's face, see inside of it, yes, hope for the future, for all the things it could become, maybe even, who knows, a devotee of the iron. But was he really so desperate, to have thought this already, to think, believe, that maybe this was the sign, the one he sought all these years, the true apprentice to his craft, the disciple? Was it even possible, stretching belief into fantasy, this child was somehow the product of his own loins, or more accurately the woman who gave birth to it? And who would that be? One of the aging prostitutes he frequented? Or, both more and less likely, that lovely young creature who came to him? Surely she was only a product of his imagination *virtual*, not possibly real. But if she were? (It is *his* story after all.) Why? To give him reason to live again? Was anyone capable of such an act of love? Or was it not love *notlove*, but vengeance, to saddle him with that burden, here, I bore the damn thing, you raise it? Or simply necessity. To give up, deny, to repudiate her own flesh and blood as an unnecessary obstacle to her own chance for survival in that great wild world? Or, who knows, perhaps a different story altogether, a widower, bereaved of his beloved helpmate, wife, by his own son at childbirth, who left this precious treasure, possibly also beloved but just as possibly hated, reviled, at the first door he came to, hoping that within there was one well off enough and kind enough to take this child and possibly love it? All idle speculation, gossip, we've heard it before, that old hag Hadoula who hangs out of her kitchen window sending rumors flying like flocks of starlings. And after all, it was a boy child— whether by design or accident another question, unanswerable. Although what difference did it make to an old man whether it was a boy or a girl child, other than the unfamiliar maturation process of a female, the thought of that little round butt growing rounder and wider, of breasts burgeoning, pubic hair sprouting, the possibilities, the *temptation*. Did you feel it move, old man? Not quite dead yet, are we? Ah yes, but a boy child, a boy child was easier to trap into the iron, with all the pressures already established for a boy to conform, even when he thought he was rebelling against, rejecting the old order and the way of the iron he was only succumbing to it and embracing it even more wholeheartedly. But that would come later, much later. As he was reminded when the little bugger suddenly opened that hole in its blotchy little face and started to screech. Why *him?* Why was he the one to take care of this brat? He who knew nothing of that task, childrearing, or had last practiced it so long ago he'd forgotten? He found a wet-nurse in the village, learned the art of parenting by trial and error. Lucky for you, boy, I didn't pull your little peepee off, or stick a safety pin in it so it festered and drooled with something other than human seed for all the good it'll do you if you follow the path of the iron. But why that conditional, suppositional *if?* There was no question that he, the boy, would follow the iron, no question at all.

If you expect to hear that he fell in love with this child, marveled at the miracle of burgeoning life, at this unique entity discovering its own existence in an infinite universe, well, sorta. For its first two years on the planet earth the child was fairly immobile, crawling around the house on goo gooing hands and knees or pulling itself up on unsteady feet and stumbling from chair to table and back again, he creeping after it on arthritic joints, more or less the child's equal in his infirmity. A kind of therapy, really, physical, mental. He had to bend and stretch to lift this brat onto the table to change its diapers, to wash it in the basin and feed it spoonfuls of gruel when it was old enough for solid food, and, yes, occasionally give it a hug for comfort, human contact, this warm little body pressed against his, needing nourishment he couldn't give, no breasts, shrunken dugs anyway, okay, confess, he felt, yearned for it himself, this touch. Concurrently, enough perhaps to suggest causality, he felt a spark in his brain, disturbingly familiar, a small flame emitting the least heat of inspiration, a faint gleam in his cloudy eyes, a liminal glimpse of the machine in its final incarnation, perfect. A vision he nurtured, cautiously, uncertain—was it only a chimera, taunting him, tormenting him in his old age?—as he nurtured the child, infant, this dollop of increasingly sentient flesh.

Not unusual then that, this nurturing business a restorative of sorts, he began to make repairs on the house, tend to the garden, slowly at first, as much as his arthritis, lumbago allowed, weeding and hoeing, hammering and sawing, adding another brick to the wall, another stone to the path, another yew tree or ash, his hands working, giving order in accordance with the order and logic his mind gave to this new vision of the machine. *Because you can never relinquish entirely the dreams of your youth, your desires. Even when you are too old, enfeebled to do anything about them, you forget and say, when I do this, when I do that, or tomorrow I will do something else. You think there will always be a this and a that and a tomorrow.* Sometimes speaking his thoughts aloud, expounding, testing his theories against the air, the sky, against the child tottering along at his heels, a wild little thing, long tangled hair, bare feet, whipping a stick about, decapitating flowers, thrashing beetles, sometimes listening, sometimes not when he, this odd old man, ancient, pointed out things, naming them, the plants, insects, stones, those occasions when their minds merged, old and young, focused on the same object, inadvertently, unbeknownst to each other, pursued the same train of thought, one from the lofty intellect, wisdom, okay, maybe a bit alzheimerish, not all there, but fundamentally sound, sort of, the other from a juvenile perspective, still credulous, a child, the boy's eyes big, attentive, when this old man recalled his great feats, accomplishments, transforming them into something bigger, larger, *magical, heroic*, and how would, could he, the boy know any better, whether it was true or a fabrication of an old man's mind? Why *not* believe he was an all-powerful wizard, god, standing on Olympus, casting down his thunderbolts? That he alone could lift that great weight, the entire world, make it as weightless as his words were heavy? *I am iron,* he growled in a voice out of the forge, out of the bottle of fire he sometimes resorted to on a cold night, and the boy believed him out of fear, out of the possibility that it might be true, because even in his rusted wreckage, he, the old man, looked as if he could actually tear the iron girders out of a bridge with his bare hands, when the truth was he could barely even lift up the broomstick he threw at the boy's feet, here, do something more useful than stare at me like a little fool.

The broomstick that became the companion of his, the boy's, youth, humble symbol of industry, cleanliness, assigned to him by the old man's tyranny, by some design known only to him, *now we will discover if you have the iron in you.* Ordering him in the middle of his growing list of chores to pick up the broomstick and lift it over his head again and again until this insignificant weight forced him down on his knees, and the old man, a revival preacher exorcising demons from a wayward believer, admonished him, Now raise up your eyes to heaven and to God and repeat what it is that you are trying to accomplish, what it is you are trying to recreate, raise up the forests and the trees and the gardens, *yes*, raise up the day and the night and the stars in the sky and all of heaven and the universe, *yes*, raise up the sun and the moon and the clouds and the rain and all of the waters of the earth, *yes*, lift up all the living creatures of the earth, all the vaults of gold, all the veins of coal, *yes*, and then the punch line, mocking, insulting, catching him off guard, Now don't you feel silly, boy, down on your knees and saying those crazy things *yes, we've heard this before.*

And then, when he, the boy, the future and soon to be *I*, was older, when he had grown stronger from the chores the old man delegated to him, adding another wrinkle to this peculiar tutelage, leading the boy before the bar loaded with those great cast-iron wheels oiled and gleaming like a dragon's hoard so that the boy gazed at it in awe and yearned to touch it, all the more so when the old man said, not yet, not today. Or when he stopped his work in the garden to demonstrate with his hands a certain technique in working with the iron, or later at night over the dinner table gesticulating with a piece of potato on the end of his fork to indicate the trajectory of the bar in motion, or later still with the bottle in front of him and a drink in his hand recreating the iron before the boy's eyes with his words so that the metal softened, gleamed with the allure of a young woman's eyes and her soft voice whispering come inside to a boy, on the verge of becoming a young man, who, nevertheless, could not yet comprehend the deception, that he was being deceived, led into that world of struggle and pain. Because then, after all that, the old man denied the iron, repudiated it completely, a waste of time, bad habit, dangerous even, an *obsession*, the iron is a harsh mistress, boy, unyielding, giving nothing in return, on the contrary, taking. Trust me, boy. Best you find something else in life, these electronic games you kids play.

But how was I to believe him now when he had so filled me with the iron that even if he had told me this ambrosia I thirsted after was really arsenic I would still drink it? Because that was his method, he constantly affirmed as he denied. But maybe this isn't where your interests lie. Maybe you've already chosen another path or another path has chosen you. Go on then, leave, you'll be happier in that anonymous mass of flesh. Forget the iron. Find life. Until at last I grew impatient, my interest faded, I doubted aloud the iron as my calling. And *clannngg*, the trap sprang shut again. The old man said, Ah, but who knows, maybe you will succeed, maybe you are the one, tomorrow we will begin to train. Leading me on with his promises, filling my mind with the iron until there was nothing else but the iron. No words to say I'm hungry, I'm thirsty, I want something to eat, to drink, I want to *fuck*, none of that like any other normal boy discovering himself, what that thing aching between his legs was really for, only the iron. Say it, boy, *the iron is not dead, I am not dead.* Repeating this mantra, this prayer, invocation, even in my sleep, in my dreams, in a voice that I finally recognized as my own merged with his, the old man's. Did he realize what he was condemning me to, the ironclad habitation of his dreams, his vision? Questioning and challenging me, inculcating in my brain the theory of the iron and the glory of the iron, of all the ancient masters, the heroes, gods, shaping, directing me through his interrogations, the strange catechism of this strange religion, Socratic, syllogistic, the logic of cause and effect, sometimes specious at best, sophistry, so that I would begin my existence with those prejudices, that faith, ideology, firmly embedded. And how long beneath that weight before I even began to recognize it for what it was, *his* weight, burden, struggle, his *delirium* become mine. Because someone must continue the search for the final weight and measure and hold it up to God, to whoever or whatever is running this show, hold it up and say, Is this good enough? Can I take a break now? Rest? (Fat chance, huh, Sissyfuss?) Someone else who could be deceived and made to believe the iron is not dead, that it is eternal when nothing is eternal, to deny the decay of flesh, of iron into infinitesimally minute and disparate particles of nothingness that can never be brought together again. Someone who did not know yet that this disintegration had to be arrested and fought against every day, and still end in futility, that even this great weight made of hard cold iron and steel would disappear in the same way that he himself, this someone, would disappear into nothing, his entire life only a preparation and training for death. And still, despite that certain knowledge, tell yourself the iron is not dead, that you are not dead. Tell yourself there is a purpose, noble, heroic. Convince yourself that you are not alone in your endeavor, that inside the molecules of iron there is a force, a reason that wants you to succeed.

Although what he meant by success. To end up only a little better off than him, a little less broken, a little less ruined. Perhaps even to accomplish more than him, to achieve my own dreams, whatever dreams those were, augmented and bastardized by his dreams, his visions. So much more weight, so many more pounds to carry on my back, so much more of the universe, a bigger chunk of existence. And don't ask to what end, for what purpose this burden, this *penance?* Refuse to hear that heresy? Simply carry on and obey? If I had really wanted to succeed I should have done everything exactly the opposite of what he told me. I should have struggled for failure from the very first, sought ruin. In the end it would have been the same thing, only less painful. Better yet, I should have thrown off the whole thing altogether, declared and proclaimed my freedom and independence from gravity, from his tyranny, the dictates of that aging fool, from the gray leaden veil of death he erected over life. As if any of that were possible, as if you could ever unyoke yourself from and unshoulder that burden. But maybe that's my resentment speaking. Of course I made my own mistakes, I can't blame him for everything. Not entirely. Because after all he didn't know either, no more than I or any other man. In the end he was less than I wanted, needed him to be, not the elderly wise man, wizard, Zen master, the almost god who could answer all my questions and assure me everything was right in the world. He was just another old fool staring up bewildered and confused out of the hole he'd dug for himself in the ground. You think to yourself, you always think, not me! I'm not like that, I'll never let it happen that way. But it's always the same. There are thousands of ways to do it and in the end there's still only one, and that is still always the wrong one, it still leads only to failure. But who am I to say? I only wanted to finish telling you my tale and then you can go off to bed and sleep and dream of happy things.

The truth is, I don't know if I've come any farther, if it's any different for me than it was for him. What? Yes, alright, different and the same. You see, you're already beginning to catch on. But don't despair, little road apple. You seem like a wise young lad. I'm certain you can figure it out with some work and the passing of time. For even if the iron grinds your knees and elbows into bone meal and crushes you into the earth, be thankful it has chosen you and not someone else. Because it is nevertheless an honorable burden, the weight and the gift of God. Bear your suffering and carry on. I think maybe you were made for the iron, maybe the iron has chosen you. Maybe you will succeed.

Νίκη

ABOUT THE AUTHOR

REYoung was born in Pittsburgh, Pennsylvania and currently resides in a limestone cave deep beneath the city of Austin, Texas. He is the author of the novels *Unbabbling* (Dalkey Archive Press, 1997), *Margarito and the Snowman* (Dalkey Archive Press, 2016) and *Inflation* (TageTage Press, 2019).

UNBABBLING

A NOVEL

In the tour de force called America, one of the tired, the poor, the huddled masses struggles upward to the penthouse of God, discovering too late he's taken the elevator marked down. Resurrected from the rubble of dreams as a messiah and accidental revolutionary, his cry for freedom echoes like a broken record as they lower him into the ground. Like a hopelessly lost coal miner, he digs on, deflating the gloom with slapstick, pensive as a clown, gathering strength for the next round.

MARGARITO AND THE SNOWMAN

R F Young

Margarito and the Snowman

A NOVEL

A nation buried in snow and ice in an obligatory 365 days a year Christmas celebration, a tribe of Mayan warriors in comedy troupe disguise, an existentially challenged hero known as the Snowman on a quest that takes him south of the border down ol' Mexico way, and a B-grade movie director named Boone Weller with his own agenda. Is it a book? A movie? Told in a shoot from the hip Texas style, *Margarito and the Snowman* is loose, rangy, battered with an attitude and bound to offend everybody.

INFLATION

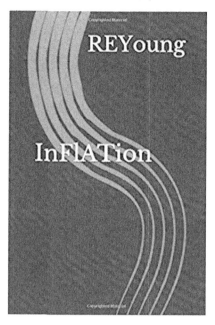

A NOVEL

Martin "Marty" Grasso (think Mardi Gras) wakes to find the world turned into a Dantesque "carnival of bloat." Excess consumption is patriotic, high fat and cholesterol diets are good, exercise is frowned upon, the price of fuel ticks upward by the second, and giant virtual billboards, or VRBLs, bombard citizens with advertisements for consumer products. As a mysterious vortex sucks up rapidly dwindling energy reserves and civilization faces famine, chaos and collapse, the impending catastrophe is blamed on a subversive element known as the sappers. Marty's quest for the truth intersects virtual worlds, utopian societies and ever-morphing nightmares—in a wild vaudeville cyber-punk noir romp that crosses into the twilight zone of "sic"-fi where nothing is ever what it seems.

Printed in Great Britain
by Amazon

46401956R00128